BEHIND THE
CANVAS

STEFANIE STRATTON

PAGE PUBLISHING, INC.
New York, NY

First originally published by Page Publishing, Inc. 2019

ISBN 978-1-64584-293-4 (Paperback)
ISBN 978-1-64584-294-1 (Digital)

Printed in the United States of America

Contents

Prologue

IT'S ALL LUKE'S FAULT. THOSE are my first thoughts as my eyes painfully peek open. The throbbing of my skull is like a steady drum in a band of only drummers, and my mouth feels like I swallowed a bag of cotton balls while the stench of whiskey pours out of my pores. It's all Luke's fault.

Luckily, Jessica is already out of the bed and I'm safe from the yapping. She's like a rabid Pomeranian when she's pissed. I know the questions are coming, hitting me like rapid gunfire, but at least they aren't directed at me the second I open my eyes.

I lay on the comfort of my mattress, eyes barely open, wishing I never took my brother's call. I was exactly where I needed to be. Waiting.

Without delaying the inevitable, I crawl into my uniform and head downstairs. With each descending step, I feel lighter on my toes. The smells that hit my nose carry me quicker into the kitchen. It's like a hangover's wet dream. Now I know the ol' lady got lucky last night in my inebriated state.

Normally, after a night out with Luke, I get a lecture that starts when my eyes open and lasts usually until my head hits the pillow at the end of the day. It's not the yelling that really bothers me, I tune that out. It's the little jabs, the passive-aggressive remarks that constantly poke at a person, like an annoying younger sibling, until you want to snap.

Instantly, my eyes are drawn to the plate—three eggs over easy, hash browns, sausage, and toast. My stomach is grateful while my head could use about four bottles of Tylenol so the food stays down.

I'm almost finished when she prances into the kitchen. I brace myself for her lecture while my fingers dig into the marble countertop.

"Morning." Her tone is chipper, borderline bubbly, and she's not yelling. Why isn't she yelling? I wish she'd just bark at me and get it over with.

"Today is going to be really humid. Drink a lot of water. You don't want to pass out; especially after a night out with your brother," she says in a pleasant, loving tone. Everything she says and does makes me think I'm going to pay for this one way or another.

"Thanks, babe." I watch as she skips around the island as if everything is okay. If I didn't feel my brain pulsating, I'd think I was dreaming right now.

I put my plate in the sink, staring at her firm ass while she pulls ingredients from the cabinets. Her blonde hair is pulled into a high ponytail, and her forehead still glistens with beads of sweat from her morning jog.

Looking at my wife like this reminds me of my very first time. We were both so young, although she was a lot younger than me; her light-brown hair was in a high ponytail and there was sweat all over her hairline, too. That day was so long ago, but every now and again, I think about her and the special moment we had.

"I know you don't want to talk about it, but last night…"

And so it begins. Before she can even start, I try to smother her flames of fury with the ol' blame game. "I'm sorry, but you know how Luke is. Once he gets started, it's hard to pull him away." I ramble on about some chick that broke his heart. It's not too far off for my brother. He's always drinking because of a girl—whether it's to get over one, get away from one, or get on top of one. If a glass is in his hand, it's usually because of a female.

"I'm talking about driving home that plastered. I don't even want to think about what could have happened." Her even-toned voice is almost worse than her angry one. She grabs a fistful of my shirt and throws herself into my arms. I know what she wants, and I give it to her. A kiss. It's the least I can do for not reaming me a new asshole and the amazing breakfast spread. "You know I hate it when you drink like that, but I had fun last night."

My mind races trying to figure out how I got home and what happened when I got in bed. Nothing surfaces, but I lie. "You liked that, huh?"

"Mmmhmm," she hums, smiling wide.

Her eyes still burn with lust, she must've really enjoyed herself. Too bad I didn't. All I think about is what I didn't get to do last night. I can feel it tearing at my insides, that needing I get. It's a craving I can't ignore, and unfortunately, my wife can't satisfy it.

I kiss her goodbye and head to the worst place you can be with a hangover—work.

****

The day is as brutal as the heat, filled with multiple shipments that need unloading. My brother isn't fairing too well either. I catch Dad watching us with disapproving eyes, checking off who knows what on the paper attached to his clipboard.

"Late night, boys?"

"You could say that," Luke answers.

Dad looks at us, eyes weathered with years of simple disappointments. I know what he's thinking—*Your grandfather and I worked too hard for the two of you to drink this place into the ground.* He's said it before and I'm sure he'll say it a thousand times over before he dies.

I straighten my spine as much as I can, urging myself to move quicker. He watches his two disappointments for a few moments longer before retreating to his air-conditioned office.

Luke lights up a cigarette as Dad disappears behind the door. "Last night was crazy. I don't even remember getting home. You up for round 2?" I shoot him a look. There's no way he's dragging me out again, and he sees my reluctance. "You are so fucking whipped. What were you doing before I called anyways? I know you weren't home."

The sun burns my skin as I lug more and more boxes off the truck, putting them on an empty cart. For every three boxes I haul, my brother only manages one. "I was out." I take a long sip of water and dump some over my head, letting it cool me off.

"It's back?"

"It could've been taken care of, but your fucking call ruined it." I can feel my blood getting hotter, thinking about my missed opportunity.

"Don't blame me for your fuckup, asshole. Put your phone on silent next time." He wasn't wrong. It was my own screw-up, but I won't admit that to him. "So, while you're out 'feeding' or whatever you call it, I can take care of the missus since you're ignoring her needs."

The box drops to the ground, and I rush my brother, slamming him against the building. His face is only inches from mine. The height I had on him growing up has disappeared, but I'm stronger. When you do what I do, you need to be fit, strong, and quick, not only on your feet, but quick thinking, too. He's not out of shape, but it's obvious his drinking has taken a toll on him.

"Go near her and I'll kill you."

"You're such a fucking hypocrite."

"And you're a fucking drunk." I release my grip on his shirt and back away, letting the fury motivate me to work harder. "I don't even know why I let you bother me."

"I may be a drunk, but that's still not as bad as you," he goads, with a fake non-judgmental tone.

The fifty boxes still left on the truck taunt me as I watch Luke walk away. "You're just gonna leave me to do this by myself?"

"Don't get your panties in a bunch. I'm just getting some water."

Our little altercation is already a distant memory for him. That's one good thing about our relationship. We can get into the worst fights but, five minutes later, act as if nothing ever happened.

I let my plans for tonight motivate me to get through the rest of the day, looking forward to restarting the process. After everyone is gone, I grab my keys and head to a new spot, pulling into a parking lot of a dive bar. I'm seconds away from settling into my seat until I see him.

He walks with a slight bounce to his step as if some dance beat is stuck in his head.

"What the fuck are you doing here?" I whine.

"I followed you."

"Yeah, I figured that part out, dickhead, but why?"

"Because you would have never *let* me come." He stares at me for a moment, waiting for me to argue his point, but I don't. I would have never *let* anyone come. This is my thing. "So, this is how you start? I'm just trying to understand the process."

"Understand the process? I don't want you here." The words come out like a childish cry, full of frustration and annoyance.

Luke ignores me completely. "So what do we do now?"

I let out an exasperated sigh, coming to terms with his presence. "We wait."

"For what?"

We sit in the car in silence. I refuse to explain anything, especially because it's not something I can explain. I just have to feel it. If I don't feel it, I keep waiting. People come and go, and then it hits me—the humming feeling—summoning me like a beacon. I quickly start the ignition.

"What's happening? Where are we…?" he starts to ask, but he sees the focus in my eyes, and stops.

My heart races with excitement, but I'm careful to keep the expressions hidden from my face as I drive down the darkened street, slowly trailing behind the car in front of us.

I'm the first one to break the silence that sits between us like a welcomed passenger. "Let the process begin."

Elana

His smell is heavy and overpowering.

"Get off me!" I yell as the tears stream down my temples. His strong hands pin me down.

"I'm going to show you a good time."

I gather enough strength in my frail arms to break free, and I push him off. Frantically, I jump off the bed, but he tackles me to the floor, pushing my cheek against the dirty sage-colored carpet. He presses his wet lips all over my face, and that God-awful odor infiltrates my nose, paralyzing my senses. Just as I think I can pinpoint the origin of the scent, the idea disappears quickly.

I feel the pounding of his cold heart against my back, beating as fast as mine as his arousal presses against my leg.

His hot breath is near my ear, blowing loose hairs onto my face when he says, "Don't fight it, baby."

His zipper slides down as my heart races with fear.

I jolt upright in bed, gasping for breath. My eyes have shed enough tears to fill the Grand Canyon, and my sheets are soaked through. It's just a nightmare, I say to myself, but it's the nightmare I have almost every night since I was thirteen. The dream itself may vary, but it always feels the same.

Falling asleep has become my fear. No dream-catcher is ever big enough, and there's not enough water on Earth that could provide the soothing ocean sounds I'd need to keep the images at bay. The only thing that has ever worked is my best friend, Evan.

Evan was your typical brat, pushing me on the playground at school and pulling my pigtails. Then, one day, Tony, the "cool" guy that picked on kids five years younger than him, pushed Evan into a large puddle of mud. All you could see of Evan's face were the whites of his eyes and his teeth against the dark, thick muck. I shouldn't have felt sorry for him, but something inside me did. I walked right over to Tony, kicked him in the shin and told him, "Leave Evan alone or else." Then I got pushed in the mud, too, and Evan and I have been inseparable ever since.

I stumble out of bed, still in a daze from the nightmare, when it hits me—that scent. I turn on the lights and look around my apartment, but nothing is out of place. The smell is gone. It was like I brought it out of the dream, but once the light was switched on, the darkness of that trauma vanished.

"You're imagining things, Elana," I say out loud, trying to comfort myself.

I jump in the shower, trying to wash any remnants of the nightmare away, replacing them with thoughts of happy hour and seeing my best friend. It's been months since Evan's visited with his hectic schedule.

Even though happy hour is chanting my name, I have to get through work first. I begrudgingly sift through my work clothes. Once I see the white lace top, I know exactly which navy pencil skirt to pair it with. I slide my heels into the perfect pair of blood-red suede pumps. Today, I don't particularly mind getting gussied up. I'll never mind getting dressed up as long as Evan is involved.

I spend a little extra time primping and styling my hair, letting the loose waves cascade down my back. I've never been one for too much makeup, and today wasn't going to be much different—just a classic winged liner, a little mascara, maybe a little blush, and lips to match the color of my heels. There's something sexy about a woman with a bold, red lip.

As I head into the kitchen to pour my ever-necessary cup of coffee, Kiki paces back and forth, rubbing her body along my legs, purring and groaning until I put down her food. As I sip my caffeine fuel, she inhales her meal, stopping only when I head to the door.

"Stay out of trouble today." I bend down and pet her again, feeling the vibration of her purr under my palm before heading off to work.

****

Pulling into my parking spot at Angel & Oly Apparel, I already know what kind of day awaits me. Not only will it feel like an eternity, and that's just until lunchtime, but it'll be like watching the last thirty seconds of a microwave when you're ravenous. Nothing will go as planned because I have somewhere to be after work, but I can't think of a single bookkeeping emergency that could keep me from my happy hour.

Most of the work is mundane and repetitive, but it's my overly demanding boss, Donald Glassman, that makes working here worse than cleaning port-a-potties. The pay is terrific, excessive almost, but sometimes, the stress of having to work with him isn't worth the money or the harassment.

He's a master at being condescending and the degree is hanging on his office wall. Almost worse than that is his refusal to wear undershirts. He'll stand right in front of my desk, belly protruding over his pants, as always, without fail. The button that falls right above his belt is always undone, exposing his hairy belly, and it's right at eye level. And every so often, when he stands behind me, his gut skims passed the back of my head.

As I walk to my desk, I can tell Mr. Glassman is going to be especially dick-ish today just by looking at his upper lip. I don't know who pissed him off this morning, but now I'm the one who'll pay for it. His tone is demeaning, and his patience appears to be as thin as his hairline. He doesn't disappoint.

Before I turn on my monitor, he's already asking me to fetch things out of the printer, knowing his legs aren't broken. The place where his hair used to be is shinier than normal, but I'm not sure if it's because he's particularly sweaty or oily today. Whichever it is, it's still gross.

He barks another order and I nod, an automatic response I've programmed for myself, accepting my useless project for the day. The only upside is knowing it's an all-day task and he won't interrupt too much. I will be on my own, running around the office, completing packets to his liking, all without having to deal with him every two minutes. He'll be forced to keep his petty demands to himself, and he might have to pour his own coffee for once.

I'm fully encompassed with my work—spreadsheets, investment statements, journal entry listings, ledgers of all sorts—some of which I don't fully understand. Nevertheless, it's what he requested. I'm minding my own business, doing my job until I feel it, that weird sixth sense that you can't explain. Eyes are on me, and not just any ol' pair. *His eyes.* I glance up slowly. He's burning a hole in the top of my head with a small, unnerving grin. His forehead and upper lip glisten with sweat, and his armpits have seen dryer days.

"How's that coming along?"

I look down at my various organized piles, and in all honesty, I could be done in about an hour if I really tried, but I fully intend on milking this to the end. "It'll be done before the end of the day."

"What's with the outfit? Do you have a date or something? Dressing like a sexy secretary isn't your normal attire," he comments. His tone, but mainly the way he said the word "sexy," makes every part of my skin crawl, itch even. A bath in a vat of boiling acid seems to be the only logical cure for how I'm feeling.

I shudder at my desk, but he doesn't notice or seem to care. He just stands there waiting for my answer. "My best friend is in town, so a bunch of us are getting together."

He leans casually on the filing cabinet by his office door, licking his lips. "He must be special for you to dress up for him like that. The red shoes and lipstick are a sexy touch." Another shudder rolls over my surface.

His mood from this morning is gone, but now he's on the other end of the spectrum—totally creepy and very much inappropriate. Besides the fact that he's in violation of chapter 12 of the company handbook, his sweat, coupled with his cheap cologne, assaults my nostrils. If I'm not mistaken, hygiene and appropriate use of scents are covered in chapter 4.

"He's just a friend," I try to reiterate, but by the looks of it, he's not buying what I'm trying to sell.

He purses his lips in disbelief. "Of course, Elana." My name lingers on his lips a little too long with another suggestive tone.

I knew I put a little extra time into my look today, but I didn't think it was a date outfit. Then again, I don't really date, so who knows what people wear on dates these days.

Mr. Glassman must see my internal struggle as if he knows I'm reevaluating something. He looks at me with a bit of disdain, but the expression quickly disappears. "If you need any help with that," he says, pointing to my piles, "let me know." He retreats to his office, taking his lingering odor with him.

Now all I can think about is my outfit and how I really did go overboard. I could have easily worn pants, but I know why I picked this body-hugging skirt. I'm such an idiot.

I get back to work, and by the time the final minutes tick away, I put the last staple in the paper. I can taste my freedom as I bring my organized packet to Mr. Glassman, but right before I'm one step out of his office, he calls me back in.

"Elana, I need you to run me 250 copies of this packet for my meeting tonight." He barely looks up from his desk, too much of a pansy to look me in the eye, but I can tell he's getting pleasure out of this. "I know you have plans, but it shouldn't take you *that* long." He jots something down on a piece of paper, looks like the swooping motions of some doodles before looking up at me.

That automatic nod isn't so automatic now. I head back to my desk with the packet clutched tightly in my hand, and briefly contemplate telling him to go fuck himself before realizing that I'm an adult and need the money for rent, food, bills, and booze. My coworkers look at me with pure empathy, even as they head out of the door to save themselves.

I kick my shoes off so I can maneuver around the office quicker. Lugging boxes of paper in heels can get a little tricky. Mr. Glassman sees me struggling, but he does nothing to help. His game of Bingo

Blitz must be cutthroat. Lord knows you can't pause it. I shuffle around the copier as it spits out each paper, checking my watch. I still might have a little bit of time to run home and change. Only 120 more copies to go.

As the machine shoots out the remaining pages, I box them up and stack them right in his doorway while he takes his fourth bathroom break. He'll need to climb over them if he wants to get back into his office. I grab my things, hoping to escape before he comes back and happens to need something else.

I push the elevator button a million times a minute, knowing full well it doesn't speed up the arrival process any quicker.

"Thank you for staying and finishing up," he says, exiting the bathroom with a paper towel in hand, wiping his upper lip. "I should have told you earlier that I needed those made but you know"—he grins slyly—"I forgot." I force a grin and continue jabbing the elevator button. "Have fun tonight with your *friend*. I'm sure he'll enjoy seeing you."

It wasn't the words themselves that were bad. It was the cadence of his voice that made them wrong. God, I hate working for him. The ding signals its arrival, and I jump inside before the doors fully open, then quickly press the button for them to close. I sink against the smoked-out glass, already feeling the freedom that awaits me outside.

My phone vibrates in my bag, and I see who it is. I know what the complaint is going to be.

"Kat, I got stuck at—"

"Elana Parks, where the hell are you? Everyone is already here," she scolds coldly.

"Dickhead Donald kept me late. He did it on purpose, too. I just have to run home and change. I'll be there in a little bit."

"Run home? Absolutely not. Get your ass here now." She hangs up without another word.

Having Kat on your bad side, happy hour or not, is never a smart idea, so I do what I'm told. I get in my car, looking like a sexy secretary, and head over to our spot.

Happy Hour

I WANT FOR NOTHING MORE than the company of my friends, lots of drinks, laughs, a few more drinks, reminiscing, and a healthy dose of drinks mixed with a few more drinks.

Lizzy's Tavern is the ultimate go-to spot for cheap buckets of beer and great happy hour food, serving us regularly for the past five years. It doesn't hurt that we all graduated with the co-owner, Elizabeth Franks. We even have a designated table every Friday night, and no one dares try to take it.

The one time a group of guys tried to snag our table, Kat, the feisty beast she is, ripped them a new one. By the time she was done, they were buying us round after round, either in fear of her wrath or because they truly felt sorry. I'm guessing the former.

Before I enter, it hits me again. It feels like forever since I've seen Evan.

The wave in my hair hasn't completely fallen, and even after the stressful day, my makeup looks surprisingly good. I hold the tube of red lipstick to my lips when I hear Donald's voice in my head. I reach into my mammoth-sized purse and pull out a tube of Chapstick instead, as my lips are still subtly stained.

In a sea of people, I can spot him immediately. All of my senses are drawn to him as if he were my center of gravity. My calming force. Seeing Evan always makes me feel at ease and whole, as if the other part of my heart has been fused back together.

Even though he's an actor now, stardom hasn't gotten to his head yet. He's the same Evan I know, and if his head started to swell,

I'd be more than happy to bring it down a size. He's the one person I don't have a problem being myself around.

Our duo started well beyond high school years, but it wasn't until then that the lines became blurry for me. It was his fault, really. Puberty did him well, and he became the kind of gorgeous that made you want to drool.

What wasn't there to salivate over when it came to Evan? He was the definition of perfection, from his light-brown hair to his blue-green eyes, reminding me of every picture I've seen of Caribbean waters. Not only was his physique sculpted perfectly, his kind heart had me swooning.

He was nice to everyone, and I rode on his coattails. The catty chicks in school never understood why he stayed friends with me through the years, telling him I wasn't good enough for his attention, but we shared something special, something deeper, something he never had with anyone else. We had an unbreakable bond.

As I make my way closer to him, all the day's stress slowly peels away, layer by layer. His thin beige shirt, disheveled jeans, and a pair of black Converse sneakers aren't exactly something you would expect to see on someone voted in the top ten Best Dressed Young Actors list, but he wears it well.

He's a bit more muscular than he was in school, but not too big, and his hair is cut closer on the sides with a purposeful mess on top, how I've always liked it. Seeing him standing by our table, although it's just his back, makes me realize how much I've really missed him. My insides do flips.

I look down to make sure my shirt is still tucked in my skirt. Then I hear it.

"Eleven is in the house!" Lizzy shouts, ringing the bell by the bar. I'm sure no one has any clue what the hell that's supposed to mean.

Whenever we hung out, Evan and I were labeled "Eleven", combining our two names into one since we were always together. One day, Kat looked up the number eleven and found it to be a master number in numerology. A number that represents inspiration and light, joy and friendship. And it wasn't too far off—our mission, when together, was to help others see the bright side of life.

"Finally!" he shouts, spinning around.

His voice makes my heart skip a beat and my legs go weak. It's soothing and familiar but sends a flutter to my stomach. Then the embarrassment settles in because everyone is looking in my direction. My cheeks burn red, but my face begins to brighten almost instantly. I ignore the glares in my direction as I focus my eyes on the one person who can make me feel anxious and whole, all in one breath.

"Hey, Ev. How ya been?" I throw my arms around his neck, pulling him close. His scent is my heaven, and I inhale deeply, filling my lungs with Evan. He buries his face in the crook of my neck. His skin is so warm against mine, and I feel him inhale too.

"I'm doing great, El," he responds softly, pulling himself away and kissing the top of my head. "You look amazing…and still the last to arrive, I see."

I shrug lazily as his eyes travel down the length of me before shooting me a wink. "Was held up at work."

"Awww… Eleven is back together at last," Kat teases.

"Shut up," I hiss, her words tickling my insides. My cheeks warm again. I kiss James on the cheek. "James, you're looking very Clark Kent-ish tonight," I add, knowing he hates when I make any reference to his favorite superhero, even though the resemblance is uncanny from the deep brown—almost black—hair, to his light blue eyes, strong jawline, and dimpled chin.

"Cut the shit, Els." His voice is stern, but his smile says otherwise.

I make my way to Kat, giving her a kiss hello before taking the seat beside her. Normally, I'm just as excited for our weekly Friday night happy hour, but tonight is special. Evan is here, live and in the flesh. I can't think of anything that could pry this smile off my face.

Kat looks at me next to her. "Sexy mama, te ves caliente hoy. Special meeting today?" she asks with a playful tone, already knowing the answer.

I drop my head, not wanting anyone to see me blush again. I hate that she knows the specific buttons to press to get a reaction out of me. She isn't as easy to embarrass, unfortunately. I think her caramel skin camouflages her humiliation. Then again, when you have her exotic features, curves in all the right places, and the most gorgeous pair of brown eyes, what's there to be embarrassed about? I've literally seen her fart in front of a guy, and he didn't even blink. He was too swept up in her looks, it didn't matter that she could clear a room with the right amount of Chipotle.

"You're totally bangable in that outfit. The sexy office look is hot," James says before gulping down half his beer. When he comes back up for air, he goes on, "I'd take you home, but I wouldn't want to make Kat jealous."

She rolls her eyes, and I do the same, knowing he'd take anything with legs home—it's not exactly a compliment.

"You going to let him talk about your girl like that, Evan?" Kat asks.

"I don't need Evan to protect me. I'm not his girl." The words sting my mouth, because one of the statements is a lie, and the other is a truth that hurts.

"What'd I miss?" a female's voice asks.

I look up from my fidgety fingers and see her. Genine Watson, Evan's actual girlfriend.

"El, you remember Genine, right?" Evan asks as she approaches. Of course I remember her. I enjoy her almost as much as I do my annual pap smear, tooth extraction, or when I bang my pinky toe on the coffee table.

My throat constricts and drops into my stomach, so I just smile and nod. Once she gives me the fake air kisses, I know any hope I had of a fun time has been vanquished.

She sits next to Evan, taking his hand in hers, smiling at me. She's never liked the relationship Evan and I have, and when left alone, she makes no attempt to hide her true feelings, but then again, none of his girlfriends have ever liked me. I know every loving gesture she makes toward Evan is solely to piss me off. And it does.

"So how have you been, Elana?" Genine asks with a pleasant tone, but I catch the sneer on her fake lips.

"I've been great," I say with a shit-eating grin. "How about yourself?"

"Oh, everything is great in LA. Evan and I are great. Our careers are great. We couldn't be happier."

I look at Evan while she talks, and he smiles politely while looking subtly uncomfortable with their fingers still laced together. I want to reach across the table and smack some sense into him, but that would be far too unladylike in this outfit. James might get a kick out of it though.

"So, James, how did your presentation go?" I ask, not even bothering to comment on her intentional emphasis on their happiness or overuse of the word *great*. What would be great is if she played golf in a thunderstorm, or was ravished by a pack of rabies-infected wolves. Or maybe pelted in the face with a stun gun. Now *that* would be great. Any number of things would be great, but she and Evan together is definitely not on any of my top ten lists of great things.

"Went well. I'll find out if they want to send the game to a focus group, or if they want me to make more changes." The last game he created turned out to be one of the hottest-selling video games of the year. Creatively, he's a genius, and physically, he's been blessed by the Krypton gods. Too bad he can be completely conceited and chauvinistic. Most times I swear it's an act, because when it's just he and I, he's a total sweetheart and loyal to the core.

"Heard you snagged that Miller film. How'd you manage that one?" Kat asks Evan.

"He's a complex character, and you know me," he says, shuffling facial expressions to show his range while I shake my head at his dramatics, "I'm a complex guy. We start production at the end of this year."

I eye Genine as he talks. Other than wrapping her talons around Evan's hand, she's not really here, too busy smiling and texting on her phone. Clearly, whoever is on the other end of those texts is more engaging to her than her own boyfriend.

Evan notices, too. She must feel the four pairs of eyes on her, as she looks up, saying, "Sorry, that was my manager." She clears her throat, and puts her phone down.

"So, what's new out here?" Evan asks the rest of us.

Kat goes into detail about how she dodged another bullet with her latest love interest when she found out he had a fascination with Pokémon Go.

I sneak a peek at Evan as he listens intently to her story before stealing his own glances at me. He offers an unspoken apology, knowing Genine's presence was unexpected. I turn my attention to James as Kat's story progresses into the next guy who apparently brought his teacup poodle on their date. She proceeds to go into the third and presumably fourth before I tune her out and watch Genine. Her lack of interest in any of us is evident as her phone is back in her hand, texting away.

James listens, but it's hard to tell if he's bored or annoyed. Knowing James, he's uninterested in Kat's love life and thinking more along the lines of which girl at the table across from us he's planning on shagging tonight. In my own daze, I watch Genine again, clicking away something to someone. Next thing I notice, everyone is looking at me.

"Sorry, I wasn't paying attention," I admit, taking a hefty sip of my lemon drop martini, not really caring what anyone thinks about my indifference.

"Whatever happened to that guy at the supermarket?" Kat asks for a second time, trying to get the attention off her love life, especially after James ragged on her because of her choice of guys.

Not wanting to go into details, especially in front of Genine "I Don't Want to Be Here" Watson, I simply lie. "Nothing. One date wonder."

Kendall, my supermarket date, was probably a decent guy. We went out to eat one night and it wasn't a total bomb. He, like myself, is an artist. On our second date, I went to his studio, interested in seeing his paintings. We were staring at one piece when he leaned in for an awkward hug or kiss.

I've never been one to like physical contact, especially from someone I barely know. I started freaking out, hands shaking, tears beginning to fall. I ran out so fast, all he saw was my trail of dust.

"I've changed stores to avoid running into him." I shrug. "Never mix dating and your favorite store. Now, I'm paying $1.75 extra for my coffee to avoid the guy."

"I know what you mean. I had to change gyms twice for that same reason," Kat admits.

"Just don't date asshole losers and it'll solve everything," James adds, looking at Kat directly, as if it's that simple.

"Not everyone can be with someone perfect like you," Kat jokes.

"I'm glad you are finally admitting I'm perfect. One date with me and you'd be mine forever."

Kat rolls her eyes in her usual dramatic fashion. "Unlike all of your other girlfriends, I don't put out on the first date, and I'm of legal drinking age."

James doesn't laugh, but the rest of us do. He feigns hurt feelings, but his expression shifts quickly as his eyes divert to a group of girls across the bar.

"Whatcha lookin' at, James?" I ask playfully, knowing already which of the girls he's eyeing—the brunette with tanned skin. If she's already locked in his crosshairs, he's not backing down.

"Just spotted the lucky lady I'll be kicking out of my bed in a couple of hours." The chauvinistic pig has returned, and he leaves the table to try and reel her into his little net of broken hearts.

"Are we going for A, B, or C?" Evan asks him.

"Definitely B. Give me three minutes," he responds.

Genine takes her eyes off her phone and says, "What's A, B, or C?"

"It's a wing man thing. Depending on the girl, the degree of the wing man's duties increases. A 'B girl' is one that needs a little assistance. Evan will go over and pump James up to her, make it seem like James is the cool one."

"You told her?" James asks Evan, holding his hand over his heart. "You broke the guy code, dude, not cool." He takes his tattered heart and heads over to his unsuspecting prey.

I scoff at the insinuation. "I've known you guys my whole life. It was pretty easy to figure out."

"What's C?" Genine asks Evan.

"I'd have to be the complete wingman and do whatever it takes to make sure James succeeds. In other words, I'd have to throw out my moral compass."

"Guys are such assholes," I mutter under my breath.

"No, that's just James." Kat lets the final drops of her drink settle on her tongue.

Evan places his hands on our shoulders, "Now, now, now, ladies, that's our friend you're trash-talking. He's just looking for love. Isn't that right, El?" He gives my shoulder a little extra squeeze. I have no idea why he's singling me out.

I don't need to look for love. I know where it is. I also know it'll be something I will never have—the forbidden fruit.

"It's hopeless to want something you can't have."

I mean, the idea of love is terrific, and when you are "normal" with no demons in your past, it seems completely plausible. But when you're like me and can't stand the touch of anyone besides your family and some friends, the idea of obtaining the kind of love he's talking about is just not tangible. It doesn't help when the person I'm in love with is already so unattainable. It only solidifies my theory that fantasizing about it is hopeless.

"I mean, if you have to do all of that to get her to go out with you, is it even worth it?" I add, hoping to change the context of my words as Evan's eyes are still fixated on mine. I hope I've said enough to divert the attention back to James.

Genine gets up and says, "Everyone wants what they can't have, Elana. You just need to get over it and move on."

She retreats from the table, and I see a few girls go up to her, presumably asking for an autograph. God, I hate her.

"What's her problem?" Kat asks with a killer glare.

I give my eyes a good Cirque De Soleil roll. "She's never liked me. Feeling's mutual. She's spent more time on her friggin' phone than anything."

As I finish my rant, Kat and I shoot upright in our seats as the most delicious-looking man makes his way toward us. Just because I don't like to be touched by guys doesn't mean I don't enjoy admiring them.

"Hello, beautiful ladies." His voice is almost as sexy as his looks—deep, sultry, and as smooth as silk. He's a nice distraction from this evening's events.

"Well, hello to you, too." Kat leans forward, interests piqued.

He reaches across the table, shaking Kat's hand and then mine, though he doesn't let mine go. His grip is gentle, and while I can easily pull away, I don't. I look to Evan for relief. When he sees me, his look is all but comforting. I tear my eyes away and notice the man is still in possession of my hand. "I couldn't help but notice you when you came in. I mean, I've seen you here before, but I just had to tell you how beautiful you look tonight."

My cheeks warm, although after two of Lizzy's Lemon Drop martinis, they've probably remained ruddy for some time. "Thank you."

"My name is Donovan."

"Hi, Donovan. I'm Elana and this is Kat." I try to direct some of the focus off me.

"It's nice to meet you two."

The guys return to the table, and James is seven digits happier while Evan looks less pleased.

"So Elana, do you think maybe I could—"

"Who's this guy?" Evan interrupts, rather rudely. "Elana isn't interested. She has a boyfriend."

"Oh, I'm sorry." Donovan finally releases my hand.

"No. Don't listen to him," Kat urges. "She most certainly does *not* have a boyfriend. She needs one though."

Everyone around me shouts conflicting information while he stands there confused and uncomfortable. I jump out of my seat and grab Donovan's arm, pulling him away from the table and back into the direction he came from.

"I'm sorry about that. He's overprotective of his friends."

A corner of his mouth turns up into a playful smirk. "I get it. It's all good." He reaches into his pocket and pulls out a business card. "Here's my number. You should give me a call. I'd love to take you out sometime."

I take the card and offer a polite smile. "Thank you. Have a good night, Donovan."

I make my way back to the table, where Genine has reclaimed her seat beside Evan, but her fingers are going to town on her phone again. I smack Evan upside the back of his head, catching both him and Genine by surprise. She gives me a look, but before she can utter a single word, I say, "He knows what he did."

He rubs the back of his head, laughing.

"Looks like El got digits, too." James eyes the card in my hand and gives me a high five. "I hate to leave you guys, but I have a game in the morning, and I need my beauty sleep."

"Aren't you going to bring home your new skank?" Kat asks.

"Nah, I'll save her for another day," he responds, as if she were leftover food.

"You guys are all pansies," Evan says. "You act like you're in your sixties."

"Hey, if I'm still playing baseball and bagging chicks in my sixties, life isn't half bad after all."

"Don't you want to be settled down with someone by then?" Kat asks, as we all begin to gather our belongings and head for the exit.

James looks her straight in the eye. "Only if it's with you, Kat."

She almost trips as she swings a playful right hook at his arm. He helps right her footing before letting go. We all chuckle to ourselves. As farfetched as it sounds, I could see the two of them together. Me, on the other hand, I'll probably be alone forever.

We kiss each other goodnight and part ways, but Evan and Genine follow me to my truck. Genine is the first to approach, giving me another fake hug. She whispers, "I meant what I said. He's mine." As she pulls away, her tone brightens, saying, "It was great seeing you again, Elana."

I give her my best fake smile. "It was good seeing you, too."

I don't know how much of my fake enthusiasm she heard, because she was already halfway to the rental car by the time I finished talking.

Evan's shoulders tense up as she walks away. He rakes his hands through his hair, giving me that all-too-familiar look. He's not happy with me. "I just wish the two of you could get along," he admits, releasing a long, tired sigh.

Not wanting to get into this conversation, I unlock my truck, inch up my skirt, and hop in as quickly as I can. "I'm tired, Evan. I've had a long day." I pull on the door, but he's standing in the way, holding it open. "You have to move in order for me to leave."

He just laughs and reaches into the truck, trying to pull me out. Evan is my weakness, so I let him. "Come on, El, you can't go home angry at me." He holds my hand, pulling me into an embrace. He whispers, "I miss you, El. I just wish you got along with her. It'd make me happy."

I make a loud huffing sound. As much as I want to stay locked in his arms forever, I push away, knowing that wanting it is wrong. "It works both ways, you know." I give him a quick kiss on the cheek, unwrap myself from his embrace, and get back in the truck, slamming the door. The disappointment in his eyes breaks me. I roll down the window. "I'll try harder next time. For you."

Just Like Old Times

Every kiss burns like acid, leaving a wake of blistering flesh as he trails down my chest.

My body is frozen underneath him, and both of my arms are held in place by one of his. I can feel his lean muscle dig into me as the weight of his body pushes the air out of my chest, leaving me gasping for the life I had before all of this.

"I'm going to show you a good time," he utters between kisses.

I let out a low whimper, too scared to scream, too terrified to move.

He rips my tank top, exposing my chest. Fury builds inside, and I free my hands of his hold. I reach for his head, grabbing a handful of brown hair, yanking it as hard as my frail arms can manage. He growls in pain but doesn't budge, only sucks on my young skin with a fiery purpose.

I regain my courage and kick my legs, making it harder for him to gain access. He lifts himself up, holding his weight up with one arm, and backhands me across the face. The pain sears quickly, warming my skin.

Loud thuds ring out in the distance, and I glance toward the door as the thumping continues. This may be my only chance.

"Help!"

My eyes flutter open and relief spreads, allowing me to breathe now that the nightmare is over.

The banging I heard in my dream continues. Someone is at my door, knocking incessantly.

I quickly throw on a short robe and head toward the pounding, wondering if I was screaming in my sleep again, confusing my neighbors. My eyes roll as they peer through the peephole, but my smile is bright. "I'm sorry but I didn't order a movie star with two large

coffees. I specifically asked for a movie star with two large coffees and a jelly donut."

"I ate the donut on the way here."

I slowly turn each lock, giving myself time to get rid of the dumb look on my face. I work up my best stoic mien, but it doesn't last long when I see his cheesy grin as I swing open the door. "Wait, where's Genine?" I ask.

"Back in LA. What's with the scratch on your chest?" My hand flies up to my bare skin, feeling the raised horizontal lines. "Another dream?" he asks.

I nod slowly as I reach for one of the coffees and head to the couch. "What are you doing here?"

"Thought we could spend some time together."

He sits next to me, putting his feet on the coffee table, as if he's done it a thousand times before. I like the way he looks in my apartment, like a beautiful piece of priceless art.

"And what, pray tell, makes you think I would want to spend time with you?"

"Well," he starts. "I know how much you love shopping, and I just so happen to have to go shopping, so there's that. And then tonight, we're going out to eat with my parents."

"I have plans."

Like any trained police dog, he knows I'm hiding something, and that something is actually nothing. "Bullshit. Take a shower, get dressed, and let's go." He takes my cup, places it on the table, pulls me to my feet, and pushes me toward the bathroom, shouting my orders again.

I'm grateful for the door, and sink into the comfort of the hot water, letting the tit for tat with Genine and the horrible remnants of my dream slip away into the drain. I throw on a pair of jeans and a light sweater, and when I emerge from the bedroom, Evan is not where he was last seen. Then I hear movement in the spare room, which I converted into my art studio.

I peek my head around the corner of the doorway, and I see him going through my paintings.

"Whatcha doin'?" I sing. He jumps, completely startled.

His expression changes with each canvas he sees. Most are ones I've done after a nightmare, evoking all emotion, pain, and suffering into each brush stroke. Just seeing the corner of the painting, I can tell which dream influenced each work. I bite the inside of my cheek, watching as his expression darkens. He's never understood what he's looking at, but he can feel them as much as I can.

"If only I knew what bothered you so much in your dreams, maybe I would understand what these paintings mean," he says, not really talking to me, but himself. "These are heavy to look at. I need to get out of here." He leans the canvases back against the wall and quickly leaves the room.

We head to the mall. I refuse to discuss Genine or any of his questions regarding my dating life, or lack thereof, so he keeps the conversation light and upbeat, talking about his upcoming work, charity events, interviews, and photoshoots.

The faint wailing of my phone gets my attention.

"Hello?" Just silence on the line, so I hang up. "That woman is relentless," I say, exhaling deeply.

My mother has been a drunk since I can remember, and now she calls me at least five times a week demanding money as if I owe it to her.

Memories of Dad rise to the surface, working three jobs to provide for everyone while it was my mom's job to take care of us; unfortunately, she was passed out 90 percent of the time and the other 10 percent she was chasing Timmy and I around the house with an extension cord or wooden spoon, threatening to punish us for something we didn't do. Evan's presence had its benefits; she would never hit us if he was around. I think she had a soft spot for him, too. Her mood would brighten up a bit when he was over.

Sometimes she'll call and say nothing. Other times, she threatens me or calls me every name under the sun.

Because Evan knows me so well, he doesn't comment on it. "So you know Mom, anytime she can get out of cooking, she will, so I'll pick you up for dinner tonight. I need to get clothes, since it's at some swanky restaurant in the city, and of course I didn't pack for the occasion."

He picks out a pale blue button-down shirt, dark gray dress slacks, a black belt, and nice shoes. "Want anything while we are here?"

"Sure, I'll take a pair of Louboutins and a Hermes bag."

"Okay, where's that department?"

I look at him, dumbfounded. "How are you a celebrity, dating a celebrity, and not know what any of those words mean?"

"Wait, the Louba-thingy is a shoe, right?"

"Um, they're not just shoes. You're saying 'shoe' like they're a primitive pair of twigs you put on your feet. They are the holy grail of sexy shoes. Red bottoms."

"Okay. Where are they?"

"I was only joking. They're expensive."

"You forget who I am, Ms. Elana Parks?"

"No, I get it. You're Evan Saunders, the boy who's forever indebted to me for standing up to Tony," I joke pointing to all of the bags he's currently holding. "As it is, you just spent a shit load of money on things you already own but were too lazy to pack. Don't you have people to do these mundane things for you?"

"Don't be ridiculous. I'm not that famous yet. So where do we find the Hermes bags?"

I shake my head in shame. "You're utterly clueless, aren't you?"

"Hopelessly. Can you at least help me pick something out for Mom?" He pouts with his puppy dog eyes.

I lead Evan to the designer handbags, and we pick out a beautiful purse. His mom's been like a mother to me, too, always there for me and my little brother when we were growing up. Evan's family knew how undesirable our home life was. They basically helped raise Timmy and me.

Once we finish our shopping, I notice the trail of girls following us, whispering to themselves. I try to ignore it, but then I notice all the other stares in our direction. I always forget this happens when I'm with him, because to me, he's just Evan, my best friend, not the star everyone else sees. As daunting as the attention on us builds, it's exciting, too. Then again, any time spent with Evan is exciting, as long as it's just the two of us.

Dinner Date

EVAN WAITS IN THE LIVING room while I get dressed for dinner with his parents. I throw on a black sleeveless sheath dress, one I've worn to every funeral I've ever attended, and dig out the only pair of Louboutin pumps I own from the back of my closet. I rummage through my jewelry box, donning the diamond solitaire necklace my father gave me a few months before he passed away.

Whenever I wear it, I think of the way his face lit up as I opened the box. He was so proud of me when I graduated college, being the first in the family to graduate from anything. He spent most of his life working to take care of someone, starting with his parents when he was only sixteen. He couldn't finish high school, let alone go to college. Then he married the first girl he dated and worked hard to take care of his family. But to me, he was the smartest man I knew, degree or not.

I walk into the living room and there he is, in all his glory, staring out of the window. His blue shirt is fitted perfectly, accentuating his broad shoulders and slim waist, like a perfect, inverted triangle. The fabric is fitted just enough to see his toned arms underneath. He turns around and catches me gawking.

"See something you like?"

I give an unimpressed shrug and walk toward him. "Ya know, when I look at you, I don't see that guy in the magazines." I straighten his tie just a hair to the left. "But with you all fancied up, I see it now."

His face brightens, his gaze as wide as his smirk. He gives me a once-over and says, "Didn't you wear that to my uncle's funeral?" I nod with zero shame, "Well, you looked beautiful then and you look beautiful now."

"Thanks. Where are we headed for dinner?"

"Monet. Our car service is waiting outside."

We head downstairs, and the driver opens the door of the black Escalade. I slide inside, gliding over the buttery black leather seats. The ride is smooth while Evan and I continue to catch up, and before I know it, we've arrived at our destination. Monet, the most-sought-out restaurant for the elite few. Waiting outside are a handful of paparazzi, hoping to catch a celebrity sighting. Once they see the driver exit the truck, all their cameras are ready for the unknown that's about to emerge.

The flashes begin at once. I take a deep breath, grab his hand, and carefully exit out of the SUV, making sure I don't stumble. I'm blinded as they blurt out questions, but Evan just pulls me into the restaurant without saying a word. He gives the hostess his name, and her eyes sparkle in recognition. She walks us to our table while we wait for his parents to arrive.

Out of the corner of my eye, I see Evan's mother, Sonja Saunders. My dad once admitted that he had a bit of a crush on her. She's a beautiful woman who seemed to age in reverse, without any cosmetic surgery. She fixes her flaxen hair behind her ear as she makes her way to the table. Her other hand is tucked safely in her husband Bill Saunders's hand. He's a smidge shorter than Evan, but it's evident that Bill and Sonja's gene pool was destined for beauty and greatness.

"I'm not at all surprised that Genine bailed on dinner again," Sonja comments after the waitress leaves with our orders memorized.

"She was supposed to come tonight?" I direct my line of fire at Evan, even slapping his arm, but he just smiles and shrugs his shoulders.

"El, she's bailed on meeting us every time," Sonja adds.

I stare at Evan, still waiting for him to say something. He doesn't.

"So this is nice," his dad says, taking a sip of his wine. I look around at the swanky interior of the restaurant and try to calculate how much this is going to cost Evan. "No, I meant the terrible two-some together again," he reiterates, pointing to the two of us.

"They weren't both terrible. It was mainly Evan," his wife corrects.

"He definitely was the bad influence on Timmy and me," I joke as I sip my wine.

The truth was, Evan was our savior on most occasions. He knew what my mother was capable of, having seen her beat us into submission on more than one occasion. It wasn't until he saw her whip my calves with an extension cord, shredding my skin, that he started owning up to things he didn't do. I wouldn't put it past her to hit someone else's child, but she had a soft spot for him, too. All I know is that when he was around, my home life was infinitely better.

"How's work, Mrs. Saunders?"

"Call me Mom. You're already like a daughter…in-law to us." She shoots me a wink, and my chest and cheeks burn. Evan is too busy having a love affair with the freshly baked bread to pay attention to what she said, but Mr. Saunders heard it, too, and his smile widens. "Work is good."

Evan and his father discuss the house Evan is building, while his father oversees its progress.

"I told the contractor to send me the revised floor plan. I want to approve everything before they continue. You want it finished before Christmas, right?"

"It'd be nice, but I'll be in the UK filming."

We receive our meals and begin to eat. My broiled salmon with tarragon cream sauce is amazing, unlike anything I've ever eaten. And the presentation is like a singlehanded masterpiece with each bite better than the last. I devour my entire plate.

"So, El, are you seeing anyone?" his mother asks, keeping the conversation going.

"No, but I'm going to visit Timmy next weekend. I'm hoping to find an impressionable frat boy I can mold into the perfect man," I joke, "since your son embarrassed me in front of some gorgeous guy last night."

"Ah, were you jealous, Evan?" His mother raises a brow.

With a mouthful of food, he manages, "She's too good for that guy."

"Just like you're too good for Genine," Bill adds.

"Now you sound like Els."

Sonja and I share a look. She doesn't care for Genine either; she's made it abundantly clear on more than one occasion. She also knows about my feelings for her son. I'm not quite sure when I started looking at Evan differently, but Sonja knew before I admitted it to myself. Call it mother's intuition, or maybe I'm just horrible at hiding it. If it's the latter, surely Evan, never one to hold his tongue, would have said something. Then again, maybe he knows, but he doesn't want to hurt my feelings because he doesn't feel the same.

We enjoy the rest of the evening reminiscing about old times and filling each other in on what's going on now. It isn't long before the crowded restaurant begins to thin out, leaving only a handful of occupied tables.

We gather our belongings and head to our waiting rides parked outside. I give Evan's dad a hug. I hadn't realized how much I missed seeing his parents, reminding me how much I miss my own father.

As I hug his mother goodbye, she says, "It's only a matter of time before she's kicked to the curb." I know she's trying to reassure me, but it's a futile effort and I let out a weak laugh. "Regardless, you and Timmy are always family. We love you."

She gives me a tight squeeze and gets in the SUV.

The evening breeze sends a chill through me, leaving a wake of raised bumps on my arms. Evan notices, too, rubbing his hands over my bare skin to warm me up. Luckily, our SUV rolls up at the same time, and we hop inside the warm truck, escaping the prying lenses.

"What did Mom whisper to you before she left?"

"None of your business, nosy," I say straight-faced, which is impressive, considering I'm horrible at keeping a straight face when I'm hiding something.

"Really?" he says with a raised eyebrow.

He moves closer, and I eye him suspiciously as he reaches over and tickles my waist. My body starts to wiggle out of his reach, retreating closer to my door, as far away from him as possible, but there's nowhere else to go. He's relentless. As I squirm in my seat, my stomach tightens and hurts from laughing.

"What'd she say to you?" he asks again, tickling me to my impending laughing death.

"Never telling."

He slides back to his side of the seat. "There's a lot of things you don't tell me. I thought we shared everything with each other." The playful Evan has been replaced with the "We Need to Talk" Evan.

Coming down from my tickle high, I clear my throat, sensing a serious conversation on the horizon. I'd much prefer to be tickled to death.

Even though I can't see his face, I can tell all his perfectly sculpted features are tense and scrunched, a state they should never be in. "What's this really about, Evan? You've been off all day. If it's about last night, I told you I would try harder next time."

"It's not about Genine. This is about you. Why don't you ever date?" He turns and looks at me curiously. There isn't any anger in his voice, only genuine concern. "I don't hear about you going on many dates like Kat. I just want you to be happy, you know, find someone who makes you happy."

"Didn't we have this conversation last night at Lizzy's? I'm un-dateable, and I haven't found anyone worth my time. I'm content with the way things are. Besides, I've got issues." I wave it off like it's no big deal, just one big joke.

"I'm serious, Elana."

"Fine," I say, crossing my arms like they'll have the power to shield my heart. "I'm just waiting, I guess, for someone that is willing to wait for me. I don't do the whole 'showing affection' thing very well, which has everything to do with my childhood, so usually guys our age don't like waiting. Most guys wanna get laid, not blue balls. If I could find a guy—tall, dark, handsome, and asexual—it'll be a match made in touchless and sexless heaven. Happy now?"

The confusion is written all over Evan's face. He waits patiently, knowing I can read his thoughts. I try to figure out how to explain it better.

"You wouldn't get it, would you?" My words come out more hurtful than intended. "I mean, you wouldn't understand; how I'm with you is different than how I am with anyone else. Other people freak me out. I don't trust many of them. It's hard for me."

"So, you're guarded?" he asks, as if it's just that simple.

I nod to appease him.

"You know, for a while, I thought you were gay. You never showed an interest in guys. But that didn't seem accurate either." He stares out of the window again, watching the buildings go by, one concrete block at a time. "You just seem so coldhearted when it comes to relationships. You blow people off before even letting them in."

A vortex of emotions courses through my veins, anger being the leader of the pack. I've loved more people than I've ever hated, and it's because of the love I have for my small circle that I've been able to get through certain ordeals. "Why is my dating life so important to you?" I seethe inwardly, but appear calmer on the surface. "Until you've been through what I have, who the hell are you to judge me?" I move closer to my side of the car, but it still doesn't feel far enough away from him.

"El," he says softly, "I didn't mean to…" His voice trails off. He doesn't even bother finishing his sentence.

The silence between us is deafening. As soon as the truck comes to a stop in front of the lobby doors, I take off my shoes and run to punch in my key code. The door is just about to latch before Evan grabs it and lets himself in, but I'm already in the elevator pressing for the doors to close, and they do, right in his face.

Old Secrets

MY BLOOD BOILS, BUT WATCHING the doors close in his face provides a little gratification. The tears start to form, and I want to punch something. As I exit the elevator, Evan barges through the stairwell door, fully out of breath. I release a loud huff as I unlock my apartment. I storm into my bedroom wanting to tear my funeral dress off, slamming the door behind me.

As I change out of my clothes, his words infuriate me more and more, and I begin to pace the length of my bed. Suddenly there's commotion in the spare room. Evan is either rearranging my furniture or trashing it. It's probably the latter. I swing the door open, ready to blast him for destroying a perfectly good evening with questions when I see a bunch of my paintings scattered throughout the living room.

"What the hell are you doing?" I yell.

"What's all of this about, Elana? Huh?" He points around to the various paintings I made after violent dreams of *him*, all embodying the emotions I felt that day. Having them all staring back at me, they look horrible, intrusive, torturous. "I'm no art critic, but I think these speak for themselves. What the hell happened to you? Maybe coldhearted is wrong, but something bigger is going on here. What did your mother do to you that I don't know about?" He walks over to a painting, picks it up, studies it. From where I'm standing I can't see the painting, but the way his body sinks in on itself, I know which one it is.

"You were snooping?" I accuse. The heat rises off my body. The feeling of betrayal pierces my heart. The painting he's holding was hidden behind a desk, never to be looked at by anyone.

He turns away, blocking me from snatching the painting while he continues to study it, tightening his grip and refusing to put it down.

"What is this, El?" he asks, still averting his gaze.

My voice breaks. "It's a painting." I haven't looked at it in ages, but I know the emotion it evokes, especially from me. It's not a painting I wished to share with anyone. Ever.

He turns with a strained look on his face, flashing the painting as if I weren't aware which one he was referring to.

"Elana, *what is this?*"

The tears pool in my eyes as all the memories flood my mind like a scary movie, the same one that haunts me at night. I clench my eyes shut, hoping I can block out the image, but its permanently embedded in my brain. The tears slide down both cheeks as I try to push all thoughts aside. When I finally open my eyes, the painting is down by Evan's side, and he's standing right in front of me.

I back away from him, pressing my back against the wall, tilting my face to the ceiling as I slide down to the floor, drawing my knees to my chest, giving me the comfort I need. The tears continue to fall—just tears, no sobbing, no hysterics, just sadness, pain and the horrible memories that flood to the surface.

I try to lock my fingers together to keep my hands from shaking, but it's no use. Evan sees it for what it is—fear.

"Please say something," he begs, softly but firmly. "You're scaring me."

Then he sees what's written on the back of the canvas.

Stolen Innocence

"El, did your mother do this to you?"

"Turn it around and have a seat. I want us both to look at it." The words have a frost to them, colder than I intended, but I make no attempt to apologize for it.

It's a self-portrait, not as a happy thirteen-year-old but as a bruised, battered child. My nose is bloodied, my eyes are swollen, tears are streaming down my face, bruises adorn my neck and arms, and there's a faint hand print on my cheek. My top is ripped, barely hanging onto my petite frame, and one of my breasts is exposed with a bite mark just above it.

I was young when I painted it, and even though I had no experience with paints back then, it remains a powerful piece, one I had intentionally tried to forget but couldn't find it in me to destroy.

"I was thirteen. You remember my cousin, Dana. She brought me to Max's house for a party. The moment we stepped foot into the house, she went off with her friends, leaving me alone. I went upstairs and found a room to watch TV in because I didn't know anyone. Everyone was so much older than me, and I didn't want to leave because they would have thought I was being a baby. Then he came in." Blurred images of him flash behind my eyes, sending chills through my core. "He was about sixteen or seventeen, I guess." I pause, feeling the bile rise. His blurred image focuses a bit, but his eyes are missing. For a while he didn't have a face, but through the years, little by little, memories come to the surface…but never his eyes. "A wall of smells hit my face, a very floral, perfumed scent, so strong and thick you could cut it with a knife. It nauseated me. As he got closer, it became so tangible I could choke on it. And he reeked of alcohol." I look to Evan.

He stares back, bulging eyes filled with terror, like he knows the rest of the story. "El, stop."

"No." My anger at his earlier comments fuel me. "You're the one who brought all of this shit up, asking all types of questions about my dreams, my dating life, pulling out all my paintings. Just because it wasn't what you expected to hear doesn't mean it can go away that easily. You're going to sit here and listen to every fucking word of it. You want to know the reason why I am this way. You're going to find out." I take a deep breath.

"The next thing I know, he tried to kiss me, but I turned my head and his lips ended up near my ear. He laughed at me and said, 'Anyone in a bedroom by themselves is looking for a good time.' I didn't know what he meant. He tried to kiss me again, but this time, he wrapped his hands around my throat, so I couldn't move if I wanted to. The tears came down like a waterfall, but I was too scared to scream.

"His wet, sloppy kisses tasted of alcohol and cigarettes, and that smell, there was no escaping that smell. It was all over him—his hands, clothes, hair, everywhere. He pinned me down and got angry as I struggled under him, so he slapped me. I tried to scream, but nothing would come out. He ripped my tank top, exposing me. Then he licked me like a dog. That's when he bit me. He said he wanted to leave his mark, so I will *always* remember him. I could feel his teeth sliding out of the wound as he raised his mouth from me."

I reach for my chest, and I can feel it all over again. Just reciting the story reactivated the scar. It feels alive, throbbing and burning under my T-shirt. "When he looked up at me, there was blood in his mouth, all along his teeth. I swear I was looking at the devil." I wipe away my tears, and take a much-needed breath. "He muffled my screams with one hand, using the other to touch me everywhere. I laid there as stiff as a corpse, frozen, paralyzed."

I stop to regain my composure. This is the nightmare I relive each night, the reason why I wake up and paint my pain away. This is the reason why I can't trust any guy to get close to me, let alone touch me without freaking out.

I raise my head and stare at the painting again, losing myself in its memory. "I tried to kick, but his body was so heavy on top of mine. When I'd move around too much, he'd wrap his hand around my throat. I heard him pull down his zipper, then the real pain began. It was excruciating. I thought it was never going to end. I wished for death. I was numb inside, confused and disoriented, but physically...physically, I felt everything, every part of his skin that touched mine hurt like he was made of fire. I could feel him tearing my insides.

"His sweat was dripping on my face and in my mouth, as he panted away like a feral animal. It couldn't have been more than seven minutes, but at the time, it felt like an eternity. He backhanded me across the face to get my attention. My nose started bleeding. I remember it hurting, but I don't think I flinched. I think that may have freaked him out, because he looked nervous. He picked up speed and finished. He raised himself off me and told me not to tell anyone. He said he'd know if I did. Then he said, 'Ya know, kid, you're a good fuck. I'll be seeing you around.' He left the room like nothing happened.

"My whole body ached from trying to fight him off. I took off my tank top and threw on a T-shirt I found, cleaned myself up, and ran home. I locked myself in my room. I didn't see or talk to anyone for days, just cried, morning, noon, and night."

We sit in silence for a minute before his voice makes me jump. "I called and went to your house, but Timmy said you were sick."

"I told Timmy I had the cooties, so he wouldn't bother me," I say with a slight chuckle. "The handprint on my face went away quicker than the ones on my neck. That scar on my chest is from him." I soften my voice for Evan so he knows, without a doubt in his mind, he's the reason why I'm still here. "The only reason why I left my room was because I missed you and felt safe when you were around. All of those times you helped with Mom, all of those times you protected me from her, I knew you'd protect me from him, too." I look at the painting one more time, still afraid to look in his direction. "That, my friend, is the reason for all those nightmares, why I don't have a boyfriend, why I can't have one, and why I will probably never have one. I've tried dating. I've gone on a hundred first dates, but rarely ever make it to date two. What guy will stick around when their girlfriend won't even hug them goodbye?" All of the emotions I've tried to suppress start spilling out, making me choke on my own words. "You think a guy is gonna want to be with someone this broken, this fucked up?"

The silence in the room answers my question. He rises from the couch and disappears into the bathroom without a word. I stand by the window, gazing out, lost in my thoughts when I feel a hand on my shoulder. I practically jump out of my skin. A look of horror spreads across his face, finally seeing how I act when touched unexpectedly. My jolted movement crushes him as he backs away from me, but I edge closer, reassuring him that I'm okay, practically throwing myself in his arms. The tears are gone and I'm back to reality—the one where it's okay to be touched by Evan.

"I'm sorry," I beg, "I was caught off guard. Please don't be mad at me."

"Mad? You're worried about me being mad at you?"

The anger I felt when he brought up these memories dissipates like a fine mist on a sweltering day. A faint sniffling takes me by surprise. I raise my face off his chest and glance at him. All the years I've known Evan, I've never really seen him cry. It takes everything in me not to break down all over again.

I grab Evan's face in my hands. "No. No. Please don't cry," I say frantically. "I'm okay now." I point to the painting. "I'm not that girl anymore. I just haven't seen it in a long time, and I've never talked about it to anyone."

He takes my hands, kisses each of them, and gives me the warmest embrace imaginable. I'm like putty in his arms, molding my body into his. We stand there for a while, and every now and again I feel him wipe away his own tears. Right here is where I feel the safest.

"Now you know why I'm different. Maybe I come across cold, but there's a reason for it."

"I don't think you're cold." He pushes me away so he can look at my face. "Why are you so different with me?"

I step away from him, busying myself, gathering the scattered paintings, leaning them against the wall. "It's not obvious to you?" I'm too exhausted to care if he knows the truth at this point.

"Obvious?"

The loud ringtone on my phone breaks the tension. I rush toward it, hoping it will put an end to the conversation.

"Hey, Els, you still coming next weekend?" Timmy asks, sounding chipper. His voice helps settle my mood. "We have a title to defend. I hope you've been practicing."

"Of course. I'm excited to get the hell away for a little bit," I answer, looking over my shoulder at the massive amount of black and blood-red paintings that currently fill my living room.

Evan retreats to the couch, sinking into the cushions, looking just as tired as I am.

"You okay? You sound like you've been crying." I assure Timmy I'm fine. "Cool. I'll let the guys know to bring their wallets." He laughs. "I'll talk to you later in the week to square out the details."

I hang up and finish putting away the paintings while Evan sits motionless on the sofa. Kiki meows, vying for his attention, but he ignores her as he reaches in his pocket and pulls out his phone.

"Hey. No, I'm at El's apartment. She came with me." He lets out a low moan. "No, just listen," he whines, the frustration reeking off him. "No, Genine," he says before pulling the phone away from his ear. "And...she just hung up on me."

He holds his head again, his phone still clutched in his palm. I wish I could do something to make everything better. I do what he asked me to do, and I give her a chance even though it'll sever my own heart in two.

"You should call her back and talk to her," I say in a low whisper, half-hoping he doesn't hear me.

He looks to the ground. "I can't just leave you after everything you told me."

I let out a low chuckle, and he raises his head, staring at me like I'm crazy. "I mean, I have to clean up this mess that you made, but otherwise I'm fine," I insist, straightening my shoulders and back, making it look like I'm fully in control and not an emotional wreck.

He stands in front of me. "What's that supposed to be obvious to me?" He searches my face for clues, but I give him none this time.

"I'm different with you because..." I offer a small smile as I look into the clearest blue eyes of the most clueless man I've ever known. "You're like a big brother to me."

He nods his head and swallows noticeably. The one time I want him to call me out on a lie, he doesn't.

"Yeah, we're like family," he replies, clearing his throat. He wraps his arms around me and kisses the top of my head softly. "Thank you for coming to dinner tonight. I'll call you when I get back to LA."

My heart tears slowly along the center as his true feelings are revealed. He kisses my cheek a final time before heading out of the apartment. I lock myself in, like I'm so used to doing, guarding myself from people on the outside.

I lean all my weight against the door. The lump of my lie sits in my throat and I must clear it. "Because I'm in love with you. I always have been."

Pleasant Distractions

Just as I do every Saturday, I clean, throw in a load of laundry, and run some errands. Today, though, I rush to get everything done so I can pack an overnight bag and leave on time for once. With everything done, I throw on a pair of comfy ripped blue jeans, a cute plaid shirt, and some Chucks for the drive upstate.

I feel excited and renewed, trying to put everything that happened behind me. I blast my music, roll the windows down, thinking about the trouble I'm going to get myself into tonight with a bunch of young, impressionable men. Surprisingly, this thought doesn't repulse me. The anger of the past week—not hearing from Evan since he left my apartment, and the nasty voicemail Genine left me—is enough to change my whole outlook on men. Maybe this could be a good thing.

Timmy meets me outside of his frat house with a cup ready for me as soon as I walk up the steps. I chug it down while he watches in awe before throwing me in a huge hug.

"Welcome back, Els. The guys are already taking bets on us."

"Well, we can't disappoint them then."

I race upstairs to his room to change into my party clothes—a cute top that reveals some cleavage, skin-tight jeans, and knee-high stiletto boots. The warmth of the drink sinks into my stomach, and I can't wait until I get more in my system. As I descend the stairs, I see some familiar faces and hear the hooting and hollering in my direction. My brother awaits eagerly at the bottom of the staircase, ready to defend our title. Tonight, I'm feeling particularly friendly, giving out hello kisses to some familiar faces and some of the sore losers from the last tournament. I plan to make them sore losers again.

Timmy fetches us new Solo Cups filled with some type of punch, but neither of us drink yet.

"These two are the competition?" a homely-looking guy asks while staring at me and Timmy.

His friend wraps his arm around him. "Nah, bro. She's the competition. Her brother sucks."

I let out a little chuckle while Timmy pretends to be insulted.

Since I arrived, my smile hasn't dropped. I knew coming here would be the distraction I needed to put the past week behind me. The promise of a dozen shots and the company of my brother and his friends doesn't hurt the cause either.

"Can we get this started," I ask as Rob, a frat brother, throws his arm around me, "or do you, ladies, need to put a tampon in first?"

I met Rob, a stockier version of James, on Timmy's first day at college. They shared a dorm room together, having been close ever since. He's kept a secretive eye on Timmy for me through the years, and has become like a second brother. I'm not sure if my threat of castrating him in front of everyone was the cause of his loyalty, but I'll take it either way.

"Someone's a little cocky."

Rob jumps on a chair and calls out over the crowd, "Welcome, ladies and gentlemen, to our second annual pool tournament. The rules are as follows: At the start of every game, all players must take a shot. Whoever wins the coin toss breaks. If you miss on your turn, you guzzle from your cup. If a team sinks two in a row, the other team must guzzle from their cup. Three in a row, the other team takes a shot. If a team makes four in a row, the opposing side guzzles and takes a shot. Let's be honest, we've never had five in a row, so we'll wing it if the time comes. Now, let's get this tournament started."

Rob jumps off the chair and the room erupts into a loud and drunken chaos—people start banging on furniture, walls, and other people. It's a madhouse, and I'm glad I don't have to live here. The stench of beer is imbedded into every fiber in the house.

The pool table is surrounded by guys and a few random females, waiting for the competition to begin. They bet amongst themselves while someone racks the balls. Timmy and I defend our title while Johnny and another guy pick their pool cues. Four shots are lined up, one for each of us, and we all quickly throw them back.

Timmy and I win the break, and I do the honors since his breaking skills are horrendous. I lean forward, holding the pool cue seductively, laughing to myself as the guys all whistle while Timmy gets pissed. I break with force, sending the balls scattering across the table and sinking two in the process, a solid and a stripe. I gauge the layout and choose stripes, knowing Timmy can easily sink the nine ball. The other team chugs from their red plastic cup.

I step up to the table and sink a ball, causing the other team to take a shot each. Our opposition gets a break when Timmy misses on his turn.

I feel my phone vibrating in my back pocket. I check the text, which is from my long-lost friend, Evan.

You know how crazy those parties can get. Be careful.

I roll my eyes and type away.

I can take care of myself. Great to hear UR alive

The alcohol I've consumed so far is starting to warm my body, but I know it'll take a lot more than that to affect my game. Our competition on the other hand, isn't fairing too well in their current state. Even the drunken spectators notice their demise is coming soon. I use their glassy-eyed condition to my advantage, missing the next shot on purpose, placing the cue ball flush against a stripe and on the rail, solidifying a definite miss on their part and an automatic guzzle down their gullets. I gladly accept my drink. I was thirsty anyway.

Evan's text fuels my anger, but I play better angry anyways. I haven't heard from him all week, and now he decides to reach out. I pull out my phone again.

The dating drought might be coming to an end.

Timmy and I win our first match with only taking a total of three drinks between us and no shots. We wait while another match starts. I make a small wager on the winner and double my money when my bet pays off. I sit back, watching our competition, and guys approach me on occasion, but Timmy gets rid of them quickly, which is good because I'm in no mood for awkward drunken conversation.

By the time Timmy and I are in the final rounds of the drunken pool tournament, he and I are buzzed, but I notice our competitors are way worse off than us. During their turn, I bend over in their line of sight, trying to distract them, although I'm not quite sure I need to. They can barely stand on their own, using their pool cues for support.

Timmy and I are victorious yet again.

My little brother, who is not so little anymore, lifts me up and spins me around in a hug. "I knew we could do it."

He and I pose for pictures that I know are going to be posted online in a matter of seconds. I feel surprisingly good and relaxed for the first time in a long time. I even dance with a couple of Timmy's frat brothers, not a care in the world.

I pull out my phone and see all the pictures I was tagged in, some of Timmy and I, some of me and a couple of his frat brothers dancing or taking shots together, and some I don't even remember taking.

I notice a bunch of texts, too.

Kat's says,

SAW UR PICS ON IG, SCORE A YOUNGIN'
FOR ME. NEXT PARTY, I'M COMING

James writes:

Timmy & El, reigning champs!! U & Timmy
are the only ones that look sober. Have fun, missed
u last night.

Evan's says,

Don't accept drinks from anyone but Timmy

I respond to his text even though I know one should never drunk text.

For someone so smart, ur soooooooooooo dum.
It's obvious to every1 but u. But it's all gooood

I put my phone on silent and go back to having fun, partying with Timmy and his brothers. Before I know it, the party starts to die down, girls are pairing off with random guys, but thankfully, everyone is respectful of me because of Timmy and Rob. I head upstairs to Timmy's room and throw myself on his roommate's bed, enjoying the effects of the buzz that still lingers, keeping my mood jovial and renewed.

****

I blink furiously, trying to get the images of my nightmare out of my mind while the remnants of last night's booze-fest still loiters in my bloodstream. My brain feels fuzzy and heavy all at once as my breathing levels out again. I glance over to Timmy's side of the room, the messiest side, and he's not sprawled out in his bed. As my brain starts to process my awakening, I find I'm in desperate need of a bathroom.

Forgetting which door leads to the bathroom, I crack open random ones on the floor in hope of finding it. With only one door left in the hallway, I hear the faint sounds of a shower behind it. Normally I'm a patient person, but between getting wound up from my nightmare and the fullness of my bladder, I'm anything but patient. I pace back and forth, stalking in front of the door.

The door swings open, and a half-naked frat brother crashes into me, practically knocking me off my feet. He quickly reaches to catch me, letting go of his towel in the process.

My hands slip as I try to hold onto him, any part of him, for support, but he's so slick with water that my hands slide off his skin. A faint squeal escapes my mouth, and my heart nearly jumps from my chest. If it weren't for his arms around my waist, I would have completely fallen to the floor.

Our bodies frozen in a dip pose, he says, "Hey, good-looking. Nice of you to drop by." His wet, nude body is pressed flushed against mine.

"Morning," I mumble, trying my hardest to not think about the towel pooled around his feet.

"Um, what's going on, El?" a curious Timmy asks from down the hall.

We—Naked Frat Boy and I—look down the corridor while I'm still half upside down, spotting Timmy by his doorway with a bagel in hand. Naked Frat Boy stands me up straight, and I pull my wet and now virtually see-through blouse off my skin. My face warms as Timmy stares at us, waiting for an answer.

"I just plowed your sister," my naked cohort answers.

"What?"

"Yeah, that didn't sound right," he adds. "Into. Plowed into your sister."

"It was my fault," I interrupt before Naked Frat Boy says anything else that might cause my face to turn the color of a boiled lobster. "I was pacing because I needed to use the bathroom, and I bumped into him as he was coming out. He saved me from falling," I stutter hurriedly.

"Okay?" Timmy watches us, relatively calm under the circumstances. "So...why are you still standing there naked, Sebastian?"

We both look at the fallen towel and simultaneously bend down to retrieve the only piece of fabric that can salvage this already awkward moment from becoming increasingly scandalous.

"Ow!" we both shout as our heads collide.

"You guys are a bunch of idiots. I brought you a bagel, El." Timmy retreats into his room before I embarrass myself or him any further.

Sebastian and I rub our heads as I hand him his towel. My cheeks burn red again.

"Thanks." His voice is confident, with not a hint of embarrassment, but smooth and sweet, like caramel. His skin is perfectly tanned and glistening with water. His wet, tussled, almost-black hair drips down his neck like little rivers, cascading down his torso, creating lines that disappear into the white towel. He's panty-dropping sexy. As he towers over me, I imagine he's got to be at least six feet five inches easy, with a body like a Roman god, cut to perfection.

"I hope I didn't ruin your shirt," he says as he secures the towel low on his hips, tucking the material firmly.

"It's fine," I assure, pulling the now-sheer fabric away from my chest.

He reaches toward me, rubbing the back of my skull where the assault took place. "I hope I didn't hurt you." I lean into his touch as his large but gentle hands stroke the base of my head, closing my eyes, enjoying the free massage. Not a single part of me wants to pull away.

"I've taken harder hits than that by smaller men."

"Babies don't count."

"What?" I ask utterly confused.

"Babies. You know, because they are small and vicious. My baby brother almost knocked my dad out with his Thomas the Train toy once." He drops his hands, ending my massage. His smile widens with a wink. "Vicious animals, they are."

I laugh at the visual. "I'll be sure to stay away from small children."

"See you around?"

I nod, moving around him and throw myself into the mercy of the bathroom, unable to hide the already formed smile on my lips.

Sebastian

TIMMY SITS ON HIS BED, thumbing through his phone when I get back to the room.

"What was that about?" Timmy asks at once.

"Wrong place, wrong time."

He puts the phone down and leans back on his palms. "We were unstoppable last night. We should have shirts made for next year."

"The woman, the myth, the legend," I joke. "I want that on mine."

I sit on the bed next to him, taking a bite of the bagel, needing the carbs to soak up any booze that may be left in my stomach. I lean my head on his shoulder, missing my little brother. Growing up, I never felt like I was stuck with him. Even though I had to practically raise him, I genuinely loved spending time with Timmy. Never once did I feel like I missed out on something. Besides Evan, Timmy was my best friend, too; one that got on my nerves, but a best friend just the same.

"How've you been?" I ask, having realized that we haven't quite spoken as much as we used to.

"I work, go to classes, occasionally drink and party, but mainly just work and go to class," he lists, but I know that can't be all. "I need you to do me a favor though. There's this girl," he starts, and there it is, one of the reasons he doesn't call as much. "So, I need a signed picture of him, or give me his new number. He changed it and forgot to tell me."

I make some sort of a mixed breed sound—a cross between a moan and a grunt.

"Please, for your little brother." He attempts a pouty face but ends up looking a bit deranged—too much excitement in the eyes, with a lot of pout in his bottom lip. It's weird, and I wish he'd stop making that face.

"I'll give you his new number, you can ask him." I jump off the bed and shove my wet clothes into my bag. "But Timmy, if you have to do all of this to impress her, she's not worth it."

He scoffs. "We've been dating since last semester. Why do you think I stayed here on break?"

I've only ever heard about his flings through Rob, but Rob has neglected to share this tidbit of info. He and I might have to have a word before I leave.

As Timmy sends Evan a text, I watch him. He's changed since the last time I visited. He looks as if he's matured, and I stand there feeling like a proud sister. I give him a quick hug and sling my bag over my shoulder, ready to hit the road.

"You're leaving?" He jumps off the bed and follows me out of his room. "So, let me get this straight, you drive four hours to hustle my frat brothers, drink our booze, check out my frat brother's junk, then assault him with your huge head, eat my bagel, and leave?"

"I didn't check out his junk." My words are freckled with embarrassment. "It just happened to be out when my *average-sized* head hit his huge head." Blushing, I hide my smirk with another bite of the bagel. With a mouth full of bread, I remind him how much I needed this trip after the week I had.

We head downstairs, stopping in the kitchen to get a bottle of water for the road. A bunch of his frat brothers are huddled around the large kitchen table eating breakfast, most of them still drunk from the night before. Sebastian is the first to glance in our direction. The smile on his face doesn't go unnoticed, and I find myself grinning, too.

"Hey, good-lookin'." He flashes a wide grin, nods his head, and offers a quick wink. His teeth are so perfect and white—he's a tooth fairy's fantasy.

My brother nudges my side, and I'm snapped back into reality, hearing the volume in the kitchen for the first time—loud and full of taunts hurled in my brother's direction.

"She's my sister. I'll kill all of you if I have to."

The teasing continues as Naked Frat Boy, Sebastian, gets up from his seat and strolls towards me. Timmy continues to defend our victories while Sebastian leans casually against the fridge looking like a high-end model selling low-budget appliances. All I can think to do is fidget nervously with my water bottle.

"Leaving already?"

My neck cracks looking up at him. God, he's tall. Now that he's fully clothed, I'm able to get a better look at him without the distraction of watching the water drip down various toned portions of his body, especially when said body was pressed against me. His masculine features seem almost too perfect for one mortal being—strong jawline, chiseled cheeks, perfectly shaped chestnut-colored eyes with accompanying thick lashes. Damn, he's good-looking.

I clear my throat, taken aback when I realize his proximity isn't sending me on a trip down horrible memory lane. My breath hitches when I say, "I have to get home to take care of my cat."

"I can help take care of your kitty," Sebastian amuses, barely able to keep a straight face.

My face burns bright, and the room instantly feels warmer.

"What the fuck are you guys talking about?" Timmy interrupts, startling my thoughts.

Sebastian and I burst into laughter. "Yeah, that didn't sound right either," Sebastian replies while Timmy glares at us both. "I'm really good with cats. They usually love me for some reason."

Without thinking, I raise my hand to his forehead and touch the subtle lump that my hard, not-huge skull caused. "You should put some ice on this." I press a little too hard. He winces.

"Your big head gave me a concussion. You have to stay and nurse me back to health." He flashes his bright smile while pretending to feel faint.

"Why does everyone keep saying I have a big head?" My brow furrows as I think about these horrible allegations against me. As I eye Sebastian, I don't doubt he has a harem of women at his beck and call. Some probably already come fully-equipped with the sexy nurse's uniform. "If anything, I'm the one that needs a nurse. You have a hard head." I felt my brother's presence before anything else, so I add, "We aren't talking about *that* head."

My wording catches the other fraternity brothers' attention, and they all erupt with various forms of playful taunts. My face burns again, but Sebastian's massaging hands on the base of my skull distract me from the immature chaos surrounding us. His massive palm almost covers my whole head, and my eyes close to his soothing touch. Now I know how Kiki feels when I pet her. If I could purr, I would.

The faint sound of the house phone rings, and Timmy's name is being shouted from the other room. All the room's energy shifts to him as they rag on him, knowing who is on the other end of the call.

He hesitates to answer the phone, and I know why. "Take the call," I insist. "I'll text you when I get home."

"I can walk her to her car," Sebastian offers.

Timmy looks to me for approval, and I nod without thinking. We say goodbye, and he disappears into another room.

"You parked far?"

I wave him off. "I'm fine, you don't have to."

He gives a dubious stare. "You can't dismiss me that easily." He picks up my overnight bag off the kitchen floor and swings the strap over his shoulder. It's a simple motion, but one that he made look effortless. "Tim is very protective of you. He'd kill me if anything happened from here to your car. Plus, we did kinda get to second base, so it's the least I can do."

We walk out of the kitchen, and the remaining brothers start chanting his name as if he had just scored the winning touchdown. All I can do is shake my head at the shenanigans.

"Ignore them. They're a bunch of knuckleheads," he says. "You think any one of those guys would carry this enormous weekender bag for you? What the heck do you have in here? It weighs a ton." He wasn't lying. I don't know how it ends up that way, but it always does. "Weren't you only here for a night?" He raises the strap off his shoulder and tries to calculate the weight of it.

"My brother carries my bags for me, and I carried it in. It's not *that* heavy."

"Your brother and I are cut from the same cloth."

"So that would kinda make you and I like brother and sister?" I give him a curious expression with a whisper of a smirk.

"I doubt what happened this morning would be good for the family dynamic. It might make Thanksgiving dinners awkward and confusing for Little Timmy." We both laugh as we head toward my parked car down the street. He continues, "What I was going to say was that he's a good kid—focused, respectful, and a gentleman. He's not a party animal. He's got his head on straight."

I've never doubted Timmy's focus and drive, but it's nice to hear it from someone who didn't grow up with him. It's hard not to feel proud.

"I heard you and Tim hustled your way to the top of the tournament last night. You were all anyone is talking about this morning. I'm mad I missed it."

"There was no hustling going on. Everyone knew what they were getting themselves into, and if they didn't know before, they know now." I dust the imaginary hate off my shoulders.

He lets out an airy giggle. I notice our pace has slowed, and I'm glad it has. There's something about Sebastian that sends all my regular reflexes on vacation to a distant land. I feel comfortable around him. Maybe it's that lazy sexiness that he doesn't even try to achieve, it just comes naturally. He's funny and charming, but I'm sure he's got a hoard of beautiful women lined up to be with him. Whatever thoughts that begin to rise, I instantly push them away.

He catches me eyeing him and winks again, causing a mild flutter in the pits of my stomach. I drop my head in embarrassment as we inch closer to my car. Secretly, I wish I parked farther away while I unlock my doors.

"So are you planning any more trips to visit Tim anytime soon, preferably with less baggage?" He puts my bag in the back seat and rotates his shoulder as if it hurts.

"Like you said, he's a good kid. He doesn't need me checking up on him."

"I'm sorry. I misspoke before. He's horribly unfocused and parties like an animal. He needs sisterly guidance constantly." Sebastian's smile reaches all the way to his eyes, and his teeth sparkle in the morning sun. "You could always just come and check on my injury." He rubs his forehead and frowns.

I give an apprehensive smile as he walks with me to the driver's side, opening the car door for me.

"Thanks for walking me to my car. Sorry about your head." I stand on my tippy toes, reach up, and touch the lump. Realizing how much I keep touching him, I pull back even though he doesn't seem bothered one bit.

"Well, I hope you visit soon." He hands me a piece of paper. "Here's my number. I'd like to talk to you again."

His fingers linger on my hand a little longer than necessary, but I don't flinch away. There's an effable calming aura about him. The only other nonrelatives whom I've allowed to touch me, even in the most nonsexual way, have been Evan and James.

His hands, although large, are delicate and warm against mine. I look up at him. The warm browns of his eyes soothe me, putting me at ease. I raise myself on my tippy toes, hold his face in my hands, and without giving it a second thought, I kiss him.

My lips catch him off guard, and he stumbles back, but he's quick on his feet and steadies us both. His hands slide down, resting on my hips while I hold his face to mine. Sebastian's soft lips caress mine, and he tastes of cinnamon. When my brain finally realizes what I've done, I break away, utterly mortified.

"Well, alright." He exhales, surprised by my mouth assault.

"I'm so sorry, I don't know why I did that," I babble. "Don't get me wrong, you're beyond gorgeous and charming and sweet and built like a Roman warrior god," I blurt, shifting my hands down to his biceps, feeling his hard, corded muscles. I jerk my hands away. "And I keep touching you and invading your personal space, and I literally almost gave you a concussion. And then I kissed you. You're a great kisser and you taste like cinnamon, which I'm sure you've heard a million times before, well, maybe not the cinnamon part and…and now you probably think I'm insane." I take a baby step back, suddenly overwhelmed by our proximity, while silently wishing I could toss myself off a very steep cliff and preferably hit every rock on the way down.

He laughs at my longwinded mish-mosh of words and run-on sentences. "I don't think you're crazy, and I don't mind the 'touching me and invading my personal space' part at all, but I think we could both do without the assaults. You might be the one with the concussion." He takes a small step toward me, closing the gap once again. I don't move where I stand. "Regardless of what you think, and I know you're thinking it, I don't have hot girls literally throwing themselves at me, until this morning." He steps a little closer again, but that anxious feeling I had moments ago fades quickly. "And you're a pretty good kisser, too. I would like to get to know you better." His hand cups my cheek, and he leans down and kisses me softly one more time, rubbing my lower lip with his thumb.

"I really do hope you call me, good-lookin'." He grabs my hand and kisses my knuckles before heading back to the house.

I sit in the truck for a moment thinking about everything I've been through in the past week, all the one-date wonders of my life, and Evan. Since the moment Sebastian and I literally crashed into one another, he had my attention, and conversation with him feels easy and not terrifying at all. I haven't found that with anyone besides Evan. I push all assumptions I've made about Sebastian aside, and pop my head out of the sunroof.

"Hey, Sebastian," I shout, and he turns quickly. "Would you like to get a cup of coffee or something, I mean, if you're not busy?"

A Chance

Sebastian and I sit at a nearby café, sipping on hot, overly priced beverages. He orders a shot of wheat grass. I never understood people's fascination with liquid grass, but maybe that's why he's six feet six inches; it does a body good.

He tells me about his large family; he's the second oldest of five, and I'm intrigued about his childhood. Growing up with that many siblings sounds like fun. He seemed to have normal games of hide-and-go-seek while Timmy and I would be hiding from our mom with a cigarette in one hand and a belt in the other. His stories of his youngest brother truly make me belly laugh. I'm not sure if it's that funny of a story or if it's just his delivery.

Hearing him talk about his parents, I feel it's hard not to get a little jealous. Timmy and I lost our father almost five years ago, but we lost our mother way before that. Even though she's still breathing, the moment she chose the bottle over her family, she was gone to us.

He asks about my childhood and what it was like having to raise Timmy while being a kid myself. It isn't my usual conversation, but he has a calming presence, making it feel less like a therapy session, full of heaviness and emotional distress, and more like two people exchanging pleasantries. "She'd be drunk most of the time, and if we weren't hiding from her, we'd be tiptoeing around the house so we didn't wake her up. Playing created noise, noise disrupted sleep, lack of sleep meant someone would have to suffer." I shrug my shoulders as if it's all just memories now, even though I can still feel the extension cord whip my legs over and over.

"I figured that's why Tim rarely drinks."

I nod. "So tell me why you're so different from the other guys at the house?"

He takes a sip of his tea. "My mom lost a baby when I was sixteen, a girl. She was premature and only lived for two weeks. It made me realize how precious time was. I wanted each day to have a purpose. I have fun, don't get me wrong, but I don't party that much. And I don't want to waste my time entertaining any of the girls that frequent those parties. I guess, like you, I grew up quicker than everyone else. Why waste precious moments with irrelevant girls?" His voice trails off. I watch him as he runs his finger along the edge of his cup repeatedly. His nose begins to redden, and it's clear he's fighting his emotions.

Without thinking, I extend my hand, hoping he'll take it. He does. His long fingers find mine and we share a silent moment.

He surrounds my hand with both of his. "You've got big hands for a girl."

"A big head and now man hands?" I say, bemused. "If these compliments keep coming, I'm going to leave here with a complex." I start to pull my hand away, but he holds it firmly.

"All of my sisters are five feet six and under. They'd kill themselves to be your height."

"You mean, the Hunter family aren't all giants?"

He lets out a boisterous laugh, causing everyone around us to stare, but he doesn't care and neither do I. "No, I'm the black sheep, so far. The little ones still have time. I didn't hit my growth spurt until eighteen." He's still inspects my hand against his. "So, what's your story?"

I let out a small laugh, because there's not enough time in the day to dive into my story. My phone vibrates, and I quickly check my text.

Just checking to make sure you are okay. Thinking about you.

I roll my eyes and put my phone back in my pocket.

"That can't be good," Sebastian comments.

"It was just my friend checking up on me."

"You could have brought her to the party."

"She's a he, and he's in LA. We're kinda going through something at the moment. The main something is that his girlfriend is a bitch, and she's affecting our friendship. But maybe it's for the best that I separate myself from him."

"Interesting." He rests his head on his hands and eyes me briefly. "So you have feelings for him." His smirk widens.

My eyes fly open, and I choke on my coffee, almost spitting it across the table.

"I'll take that as a yes." Sebastian laughs lightly while I cough the coffee out of my lungs. "Yet you're here with me. And we got to second base. Nice."

"Seems so."

"I'll take it." He shrugs lazily. "You're different than most girls. I like you, good-lookin'."

He has no idea how right he is. I'm unlike all girls. "I like you, too," I blurt, but the embarrassment I thought I'd feel admitting it doesn't surface.

I sit back in my chair, listening as he tells me more about himself. He's not the shallow jock that his appearance would tell you. He's intelligent and takes his studies seriously, and it's evident when he talks about his side passion, studying Reiki.

He explains how Reiki, the ancient Japanese art of palm healing, is about transferring universal energy through the palms, energizing the physical, mental, emotional, and energetic levels with twelve hand positions. It's intriguing to hear about, but like with most things these days, I'm skeptical.

Everything about him oozes confidence and intelligence, but nothing about him intimidates me, other than his height.

Growing up with Evan, I've always considered myself inferior— lack of self-esteem will do that to a person, along with everything else I've been through. For some reason, I've always put Evan on this imaginary pedestal, too out of reach. Maybe it was all the whispers about how unworthy I was compared to him. After a long while, it brainwashed me into thinking there was an element of truth to it, but here I am, sitting with someone who looks like a model and is extremely smart, and I don't feel an ounce of inferiority toward him.

We sit talking in the café for hours, so effortless and fluid, never a dull moment or awkward silence between us. Our butts grow numb from sitting, so we drive to a park that he frequents, walking around for a little while until I absolutely cannot stay a minute longer.

I pull up to the frat house, engine idling in park. It's that awkward moment when you say goodbye to someone and you don't know if you're going to kiss or not, so you look uncomfortably at one another, smirking while waiting for the other person to make the first move. I shouldn't feel awkward, considering I kissed him already, but now that my brain is finally back at the steering wheel, it feels different.

"When I woke up this morning, I thought it was just going to be another dull Sunday. But thanks to you, good-lookin', this day was definitely a pleasant surprise."

"You ever going to call me by my name?"

"It's a lovely name. Your parents did an excellent job picking it, but *good-lookin'* suits you just fine, too."

My cheeks blush for the hundredth time. "If you saw me thirteen years ago, you'd think differently."

"Thirteen years ago, I would have gone the effortless way out and found something that rhymed with Elana."

"Yeah," my lips form a crooked smile, "because *good-lookin'* is so—"

"Clever, I know right? It was the first thing that came to me when I held you in my arms."

I roll my eyes, trying to hold back my urge to smile again. I notice the time. "Get out."

A sad expression washes over his face, like I've just kicked his dog.

"I want to give you a hug, and it's not easy to do that in the car. You may be clever, but you're awfully sensitive."

I jump down from the driver's seat and hear him mumble "bossy" under his breath, but he's all smiles as he meets me on my side of the truck. There's a gang of butterflies fluttering in my belly as he gets closer.

I lean against my black truck as he approaches, trying my hardest to look as relaxed as he did when he leaned against the fridge this morning. He's got a devilish grin on his face like he knows that a hug isn't all I want. How can I go from never wanting to be touch by anyone, except Evan, to wanting someone I barely know to put his hands on me in all the inappropriate places?

I grab his hand, wanting to see the size difference, but mainly just wanting to feel his warmth against my cooled skin. Sebastian pulls me closer, removing his hand from mine, placing it on the small of my back. He looks into my eyes.

"Thank you for a surprising day."

"Well, I can't afford your medical bills, so," I look into his beautiful brown eyes, getting lost in them, "I thought this would be sufficient." I rest my arms around his neck, pulling his mouth to mine again.

My breathing hitches as his hold on me tightens. I want this kind of nervousness—I need this kind of nervousness.

His soft lips press against mine, and it's not rushed like when I kissed him. He still tastes like sweet cinnamon and not wheat grass, thank God. His tongue runs across my lips, parting them slowly. I pull him closer, and he deepens our kiss all while maintaining that gentle quality. I feel like a high school girl, making out in the open—except when I was in school, I didn't act like this at all.

I detach my hands from his neck and find his waist, hooking my fingers in his belt loops, pulling his body toward me more. We fall back, and my shoulders slam into the side of my truck. But all I could feel was his lips on mine and his warm hands on my lower back, warming my whole body like a heating blanket.

"You okay?"

"Mmmhmm," I hum, wishing he didn't break away.

He presses his lips harder while my hands explore his terrain. He breaks away again, catching his own breath. "I know I'm going to be cursing myself later, but you have a long drive home, and your brother is going to kill me for keeping you so long."

Unfortunately, he's right. His hand cups my face tenderly while his eyes search mine for a rebuttal, but I can't give him one.

"So does this mean you're going to give me a chance?" he asks tentatively, but he still has that smooth confidence laced into his words that signals he already knows the answer.

I let go and step onto the footboard, placing a final kiss on his sweet cinnamon-flavored lips. "This is me giving you a chance."

Changes

Two months elapse, and I hear from Evan less frequently, but the pain of it dulls the more time I spend with Sebastian. There isn't a day that goes by that he and I don't speak or text. All fears and apprehensions I had about dating no longer loom over me like black clouds of doubt; he's managed to strip them away, one layer at a time, with just his voice or the gentle touch of his hand.

There is no pressure to be intimate with Sebastian; it's as if he knows I need to take things slowly without asking why. There's a relief in knowing I can trust a person I've only met recently, giving me a feeling of normalcy that I haven't experienced before. I always wondered what the big deal was when Kat would get so excited about dating, and now I get it—the excitement of learning new things about him or seeing his face brightens my days, and our connection grows like flowers in the spring.

James and Kat noticed something was up the first time they saw me after the frat party. Even though I've craftily avoided answering any questions about my change in mood, I know they aren't dumb. I never thought I was sad before, but compared to how I've felt these past two months, I wake up with a smile on my face, even after a bad dream, because I know he's only a phone call away.

I like keeping Sebastian to myself though. I'm afraid if I talk about him to anyone else, it'll make it real and easier to destroy, and I'm not ready for it to be tainted just yet. Everything feels so dream-like and perfect, giving me a real chance to get over Evan and find happiness.

I say good night to my coworkers, thankful that Friday came and went quickly, and head over to Lizzy's. My mood isn't as bright, because Sebastian will be with his family, celebrating his little brother's birthday, but I know I'll hear from him. Besides, I've neglected Kiki and my apartment long enough.

As I make my way to the table, Kat sits alone with an inexplicable look on her face.

"What's the matter with you?"

"I'm golden." She gives a wicked smirk. "So before this evening takes a turn for the worse, and it will," she assures, "when do you plan on dishing the dirt on who you've met? I love Timmy as much as the next person, but I know you aren't going to visit him every weekend."

I knew it was coming. Kat's patience meter only lasts so long before she'll start berating me with questions. And I have every intention of quenching her thirst.

"Why would it take a turn for the worse?" I ask, confused.

"It just will. Now spill fast." She leans forward across the table, eyes wide with anticipation.

"So I met someone," I admit.

An arm hooks around my shoulder, and I jump, quickly shrugging off whoever thought it was okay to touch me.

"You met a guy?" His slurred words spit out with shock.

I spin around and Evan wobbles in front of me with James close by, ready to help his inebriated friend in case he stumbles over his own feet. My jaw drops, and my stomach does a quick somersault.

"You're too late—wait, no, I'm too late."

Kat motions James to sit Evan down before he falls. "Everyone was late, but we're here now, so sit."

James pushes Evan into the seat beside mine while I try to swallow the thick lump in my throat.

"Pay up, James." Kat holds out her hand, and he begrudgingly hands her a $20 bill.

"What are you doing here, and why are you drunk?" I ask Evan while Kat holds the bill to the light, verifying its authenticity.

"Was nervous. But you were right, Els." He throws his arm around me, but this time I don't shrug him off. "She was cheating the whole time. Pictures will be released any day now. It's a PR nightmare." He pulls me closer and drops his voice, "I shouldn't have left you that night, but you broke my heart," he adds, his voice cracking. Evan presses his lips firmly to my cheek, wetting it with his drunken kiss. "I think I need another drink," he yells, raising his hand to get the waitress's attention.

I'm left dumbfounded. Broke *his* heart? Maybe it hurt him hearing what happened to me, or maybe given the fact that he appears to have drunk half a bottle of Johnny Walker, he meant to say "she" broke his heart. I look to Kat and James for any nonverbal explanation, but they just shrug and shake their heads in their own confusion. I'm glad he's rid of her, but seeing him so distraught is equally painful to watch.

"Why is James giving you money?" he asks Kat.

"James and I bet whether or not her chipper mood was because of a man, and I won." She pops her collar with triumph while my insides turn to knots.

Evan looks at me with a furrowed brow, giving me a look I've never seen before. "You're dating?"

"I thought no one could put a smile on her face like you, but clearly, I was wrong," James admits, and Evan shoots him a gaze that appears to be new to all three of us. "I was hoping she got a new vibrator or something."

Evan diverts his eyes back to me as if I'm center stage, and all of a sudden I feel uncomfortable in my own skin. Luckily, the waitress arrives with a fresh round of cocktails. I grab mine and annihilate it.

All questions about my secret relationship cease, courtesy of Kat and her interest in the juicier topic, which is Genine and her trifling ways. After seeing Evan's face shift from sad to indifferent to irritated, we try to keep the rest of the night's conversation light and fun. Before we know it, final call is announced, and we're the last ones to leave.

"Give me your keys, El. I'll put his suitcase in your truck," James says.

"I'm staying with you, unless you're expecting company," Evan spits out, as if the words left a bad taste in his mouth. "You know

I always have dibs on your bed. He can stay in the guest room," he slurs, almost tripping over an imaginary crack in the ground, even bending down closer to get a better look, and almost falling in the process.

James puts his things in my truck and hugs me good night. "I'll walk Kat to her car. Get him some Tylenol, and put his ass to bed."

The shock of Evan's presence hasn't worn off as I watch James and Kat walk away. I guess I never made it crystal clear to anyone that Evan and I haven't exactly been on the best of terms lately. He's slumped in the passenger seat, staring out the window as I start the car.

"I don't want to go back to your apartment yet," he mumbles.

Without him saying anything else, I know where he wants to go. The silence is welcomed because I have no idea what to say to him, not that it matters much. He's so drunk right now, I doubt he'll remember anything from tonight anyways.

We pull up to our park and he gets out, stumbling over to our table, plopping down onto the bench. He looks broken, betrayed by someone he loved that tore his heart in two. My own heart aches seeing him like this.

I sit on the table, dangling my legs over the edge, and he gets up to stand between them. Evan pulls me closer, wrapping his arms around me, hugging me so tightly it's hard to breathe.

"I'm sorry, Evan."

"Don't be," he mumbles, mouth pressed against my shoulder. "I shouldn't have left you."

I let a moment pass, allowing his words to seep in. "She was your girlfriend."

He yanks away, and I'm finally able to get a breath in as he looks me in the eye. "You're all that matters to me."

I let out a light laugh. "You're so drunk right now."

He nods in agreement, then grabs my hand, pulling me off the table, dragging me behind him. He pulls me down as he lies face-up on the grass. He cages me in his embrace, making me stare at the stars with him.

"What are you thinking about?" I ask.

"You know she hated you," Evan says, still taking in the cloudless expanse.

I sit up, drawing my feet to my chest as he scans the starlit sky. "The feeling was mutual."

He laughs. "Every person I ever dated has disliked you."

"Well, I can't help your choice in women." I shrug off. "That's your issue, not mine."

I lie back down next to him, but I keep a little distance between us as I admire the night sky.

He props himself up on his elbows, looking down at me while I'm lost in the sea of bright, twinkling lights. There isn't a cloud in sight, only a blanket of stars spread as far as the eyes can see.

"I know one woman good enough for me."

"Yeah? She'll probably hate me, too." My eyes remain fixed on one star, and I think about all the wishes I've asked for over the years, ones that included Evan, but now I think about Sebastian, hoping he's thinking of me, too.

Evan's face hovers over mine, blocking the sky above us.

"She's pretty amazing, the most beautiful woman I've ever seen, and I know she loves me."

The concentrated look in his eyes terrify me. For once, I have no idea what is happening as he inches closer.

He whispers at a close and uncomfortable distance. "I live for her laugh, her smile, her voice. She's all I've ever wanted and so much more."

I put my hands on his chest, stopping him from getting close enough to kiss. My palms can feel his heart racing under his clothes. "She sounds wonderful," I admit, "but I think it's time to get you to bed." I push him away and crawl out from under him.

"Now you're talking, Elana Parks." He plops back on the grass like dead weight. I shake my head, trying to figure out how to get him back to the car. All ideas evaporate when my phone starts to ring. "Tell your mom to fuck herself," he says.

I see the caller ID and instantly feel better. "Hey."

"Hey, good-lookin'. You still with your friends?"

"Um, yes and no." Evan tries to stand, but I can tell he thinks the grass is moving under him as he grips clumps of earth between his hands. "It's an interesting evening. I'm still kinda dealing with it."

"Go suck a lemon, Mrs. Parks!" Evan shouts from the ground, trying to roll onto his feet.

"Who's that?" Sebastian asks.

"Evan. Genine just broke up with him. He's completely hammered."

"No," Evan barks. "That's not what happened." He stumbles. "And I'm not hammered." He loses his footing again and falls. "Okay. I might be a little hammered."

"You okay?" Sebastian asks.

"I'm fine. Glad to hear your voice." He doesn't respond, but I can sense his smile forming on those soft lips of his. "How's the family?"

"Everyone's good. I dodged a flying train walking in the door, so no injuries to report. Yet."

I let out a giggle, and I notice Evan staring at me, completely quiet, hanging onto every single word. I turn my back to him and talk more softly into the receiver. "I'll text you when I get home."

"I miss you, El."

A smile spreads as he says exactly how I feel. "I miss you, too."

"She'll be busy tomorrow, so don't expect to hear from her," Evan shouts.

"What'd he say?" Sebastian asks.

I spin on my heels, giving Evan my most murderous glare before responding. "I'll text you in a little while."

I hang up the phone and look to him. Evan wears a proud grin.

Bittersweet

EVAN IS A LOT HEAVIER than he looks. I lug his duffel bag on one shoulder while trying to hold his drunken weight with the other.

"You smell good," he whispers, his mouth barely grazing my ear. My eyes are sore with all the eye-rolling I've done this evening.

We make it to my apartment, and he falls onto the couch. The weight off my shoulder is a relief. I drop his bag to the floor and take in a deep breath.

"I'll make the bed in the spare room. *Don't* fall asleep," I command.

After I clean the clutter and make the bed, I rush into my room to quickly change out of my work clothes. I head back into the living room, and there he is, sprawled out on my couch, fast asleep with Kiki curled between his legs. I could stare at him all day.

When we were younger, I actually did. It was the fiercest staring contest ever, and I won. I could hypnotize myself just by looking at him, and that's how he was defeated. I studied every feature of his face, concentrating as I memorized each curvature, his almond-shaped eyes and dark, long lashes. The way his mouth naturally turned upward, and his full, supple lips always looked soft to the touch, like velvet.

His chest rises with each breath. I quietly tiptoe to turn the light off, but I trip over his sneakers.

"Still clumsy as ever," he mumbles, half asleep. "I love that about you."

"Shut up," I hiss. "You wanna sleep here or in the other room?"

"In your bed."

I don't bother arguing with him. I just lead him into the spare room, knowing his eyes are half closed anyways. He pulls me down on the bed with him. "Sleep with me."

I've been around drunk Evan before, but this one is funny. I manage to wiggle out of his grasp, and he makes a loud huffing sound as his arms drop to the mattress with a thud.

"You'll see, I'm going to prevail."

"You sure will," I say, giving him a thumbs-up, not having a clue what the heck he's talking about.

I walk to my room and release a huge sigh of relief that he's in bed and sleeping it off. I hop into bed and shoot Sebastian a quick text. As soon as his reply comes through, my body sinks into my mattress, finally able to relax for the first time in hours. The night's events were enough to completely exhaust me, and slowly my vision fades to black.

****

It wasn't the sun peeking through the blinds that woke me up. It wasn't even a dream that tore me out of my sleep. It was the excessively warm body draped over mine. He looks as if he's been here all night, but I don't remember him ever coming into the room.

It's not odd that we've shared a bed together. We used to sneak into each other's room all the time growing up. I purposefully kept my small room on the first floor because it was easy to get in and out when I wanted.

After what happened to me, the nightmares started, and Evan became my safety blanket. Whenever he was next to me, I'd have the most peaceful night's sleep. Now, his body is dug into my mattress, and it explains why I didn't dream last night.

I carefully lift his arm and leg off me and slither out of the bed. The coffee can't come quick enough as I wait for the stream of dark liquid to fill the base. The kitchen stool moves behind me. I jump, now fully awake, my blood pumping fast through my system.

"Did I wake you with my snoring?" Evan asks with a dazed, still-hungover glaze in his eyes.

"I didn't even know you were there until a few minutes ago, but it explains the dreamless night." I raise my glass to him. "Thanks."

"Just like old times."

"Eleven is in the house," I say, amused, raising the cup to my mouth.

He signals that he's going back to bed, and I head into the spare room, feeling the itch to paint. I sit on my stool and stare at the blank canvas, slide in my earbuds, and slip into my painting trance, brushing whatever emotions rise to the surface.

****

Unaware of how much time has passed, I'm pulled back to reality with a light kiss on my shoulder.

Evan stands above me, staring at my work.

"Whatever it is, it's nice. It looks happier than the other ones." He tilts his head to the side as most people do when they look at a painting that isn't immediately obvious. "I have to leave tomorrow morning, so what do you want to do for the rest of the day?"

I head into the bathroom, where I clean my hands and gaze into the mirror. I wasn't expecting to have any plans this weekend, let alone plans with Evan whom I haven't really spoken to since he left my apartment months ago.

"We could go watch James's game. He's been feeling neglected lately."

"Works for me."

I find him in the kitchen, eating a bowl of cereal. I sit down across from him with another cup of coffee in hand. "I'm sorry about Genine."

"Are you really?"

"I'm sorry that you're hurting. How's that?"

He stands up, puts his bowl in the sink, and gives me a quick hug from behind, kissing the top of my head. His cologne from last night still lingers on his skin. The woody scent is warm and familiar, and I sink into his embrace.

"I'm fine. I'm gonna get ready."

He disappears into the other room to change, and I'm left with my thoughts. I know he's a good actor, but there's no way he could be fine. He almost drank his weight in whiskey last night. What I do know is that he'll open up when he's ready. Maybe when the pictures are released, he'll want to reveal his true feelings. But it's nice to feel like things are back to normal again.

We head out of the apartment and run into one of my neighbors, Mr. Sam.

"Good morning. How are you?" I ask.

"Morning, Elana. Good morning, Evan."

Mr. Sam gives Evan the ol' once-over. "You know, Evan, she's a good kid. Don't break her heart."

"Oh no, Mr. Sam," I interrupt, waving him off, "I told you, Evan and I are just friends."

Now it's his turn to do the waving. "I know love when I see it."

"We're like family," I reiterate.

"Yeah. She loves me like a big brother," Evan adds, and I feel the knot in my stomach, twisting and turning my false words against me. Hearing myself tell the lie was one thing, but having it being told again, in his voice, hurts worse.

He waves us both off again. "Nonsense. You two have something special."

"Okay, Mr. Sam," I give in, wanting to put an end to this conversation. Evan's eyes drift to the floor. I'm sure the last thing he wants to hear is another conversation about love right after he broke up with Genine.

"Well, I'm glad I ran into you. I'm going to be visiting my sister in October. Would you be able to look after Jack while I'm away?"

"Of course, just text me the details."

****

Evan and I make our way to the park. We take a seat on the bleachers. I close my eyes and soak up the sunrays, letting them warm my face when suddenly it stops. The warmth is gone.

"Well, hello, Eleven."

I don't even have to open my eyes to know who it is. I can tell by the condescending tone and the chill in the air.

"Amber Cummings, wow, you look great." Evan stands up, leaning over me to give her a hug. I sit there silently wishing she'd fall off the bleachers, hitting every step along the way, but my wishes rarely come true.

"What are you doing in town?" She twirls her hair in an attempt to flirt, a move that didn't work for her in high school and certainly isn't going to work now.

"Just a breather from Cali chaos."

"You could be vacationing anywhere and yet you're here," she says in amazement, "with Elana. Where's Genine?"

Amber has never liked me, and she's never pretended to either, much like Genine. She sneers in my direction, giving me her infamous condescending smirk. I do my best to ignore her and watch the batter swing, the bat, narrowly missing the ball. I wish he'd hit it into the stands, right where Amber is standing. My smile is instantaneous as I daydream about the various injuries she could receive.

Evan waves away the idea of Genine, as if swatting at a fly. "Publicists set that match up. Actually, I tried to convince El to come with me to St. Tropez, but she couldn't get off work, so I came to her."

I look at him with confusion written all over my face. He knows my hatred toward her runs deep, but now he's just telling tales.

He sits back down and goes on, "She's the love of my life. I'd do anything for her. Everyone knows that."

Evan places an arm around me, pulling me close to his side. His eyes wander over my face, and he leans forward, laying his lips on mine. It catches my breath, and I feel my body tense up against his, but once he places his hand on my cheek, stroking it with his thumb and holding the kiss, I melt into him. The lips I've ogled growing up are softer than my imagination could have ever devised. And doubts I've had of him as an actor are washed away in this moment.

Amber clears her throat—she's seen enough. "Well, I guess I'll leave you two lovebirds alone then."

"It was good seeing you, Amber," he says with a wide grin, but his eyes haven't left mine. I'm still trying to catch my breath and figure out what the hell just happened when he says, "It was nice seeing her, don't you think?"

"Um, yeah, she's always a pleasure." He drops his arm from around me, and all his warmth is gone again. "Why'd you do that?"

"I figured it'd piss her off, and you'd find enjoyment in her misery. She was always jealous of you."

"Seeing her miserable *is* a secret joy of mine."

He laughs so hard his shoulders shake. "Who are you kidding, El? It's no secret."

We sit through the entire game, but my mind keeps thinking about the kiss. I know he only did it for show and it meant nothing to him, that he was playing a part; but while he can easily move on as if nothing happened, I'm left feeling guilty and confused.

****

"Great game, James," I congratulate him once it's over.

"Guess if you didn't stay out so late, you wouldn't have had that era in the fifth inning," Evan adds, playfully punching his arm.

"Probably, but my friend was a bit drunk last night, and I couldn't leave him alone in his time of need."

Evan's cheerful mood drops quickly. I think about when I divulged my innermost secret to him and he left my apartment in my time of need. Maybe he's thinking about that, too.

"Wanna grab a bite to eat?" Evan asks.

"Can't. I got a call from my boss about my game. I have to fine-tune some things again. I feel like it's all I ever do these days. When's the next time you'll be in the area?" James asks, packing up his equipment.

"Not sure, but I'll be visiting more frequently."

This is all news to me. He never said anything about coming to town more often; frankly, I find it hard to believe with his busy schedule. As we head back to the truck, Evan sees Amber and once more throws his arm around me, giving her a playful wave goodbye. I smile and wave, too, playing my part in this soap opera. If looks could kill, I'd be suffering a horrible, painful, slow, torturous death. But even after Amber is out of sight, Evan's arm doesn't drop.

****

We start devouring our food like ravenous beasts who had been starved for months.

"About the kiss…," Evan starts.

"It's fine," I say, waving it off. "I appreciate why you did it. Her misery does bring me joy."

He looks at me with a falling glance. "You never used to hate her that much in high school."

He's right, I didn't. I wasn't a huge fan of hers, but it wasn't until college that my indifference grew into disgust.

"She spread rumors about me. When people found out I wasn't even loose giving out high-fives, I got a new title around campus."

"You and your secrets," he says, shaking his head and sucking his teeth.

The conversation steers toward everything but Sebastian or Genine, and it feels like old times, reminding me of how things used to be when it was just the two of us, Eleven, together. The warmth from his words hit me like sunshine on the brightest day, and I can't stop smiling.

We hang out in the apartment, watching old movies, laughing and throwing popcorn in each other's mouth. His demeanor changes only after a call from Sebastian, but I know it's just because he's protective of me like I was of him; plus, he's never had to deal with me dating before.

****

I wake up in the morning alone in my bed, half-expecting Evan to occupy the space next to me. As I walk through the empty apartment, I secretly wish he was still here. I head toward the most important invention ever made, and there's a note taped to my coffee machine.

*Thanks for a great weekend. I needed it, and I
needed to see you, but next time I won't be drunk, I
promise. I'll let you know when I land.*
I love you.

                                                    Ev

I busy myself with all the chores I was supposed to do yester-day, and before I know it, Evan is calling me, keeping me on the phone for over an hour. The pictures of Genine have surfaced, and the media frenzy has begun, but he seems unbothered by it.

When I finally get him off the phone, I finish all my chores. Before I can question why I haven't heard from Sebastian, he too calls. My day feels complete hearing both of their voices in the same twenty-four-hour span.

Exhaustion takes over, and I can't even think about picking up a brush to paint. I decide to lie in the warmth of my sheets, inhal-ing the scent of Evan's cologne that still lingers on the pillow. With Sebastian's goodnight text putting another beaming smile on my face, the last thing that comes to mind before drifting off to sleep is Evan's kiss.

New Territory

Weeks pass, and I try to return to my routine of visiting Sebastian on the weekends, but Evan's renewed presence has infiltrated any unoccupied thought, throwing all feelings I have for both into a state of confusion. His frequent calls and talks of visiting again, and that kiss, oh that kiss—I can't get it out of my mind, as hard as I try to convince myself that it was just a kiss out of a movie scene, one simple lip embrace to make the villainous high school bitch jealous of the not-so-popular odd girl and nothing more. But it felt like something more.

The only way for me to figure out how I truly feel about Sebastian is to throw him into my world and make him real to the people around me. We make the arrangements, and I start to remove any and all paintings that could lead to questions about their meanings from the spare room.

It's hard to keep the plans secret from Kat. Her constant poking and prying for information is getting harder to dodge. I give little morsels of information about Sebastian, just enough to sate her appetite and keep the hunger at bay. After work, I rush into the bathroom and change out of my office clothes, throwing on a pair of dark skinny jeans, a draped neck top, and a black moto jacket. The cleavage alone will undoubtedly spark raised brows. I stand in front of the mirror, fluff my hair, and touch-up my makeup, absolutely giddy with excitement.

I check my phone for updates on his arrival time before I head inside of Lizzy's, elated that he'll be here in a matter of minutes. I stroll over to the table with a little extra pep in my step and both Kat and James's eyes are wide with wonder.

"He's coming tonight, isn't he?" she asks. "C'mon, tell me."

There isn't a crowbar for sale that could pry the smile off my face. I can't remember a time where I felt this alive, this elated to share something new with my friends, the people that mean the most to me. My stomach twists and turns in anxious knots, and I'm utterly impatient to see Sebastian. That's when he walks in.

The blue-and-white plaid button-down fits him perfectly, showing off his fit body, with jeans that fit just right. And I know before he approaches that he'll smell divine and taste even better. A smile flashes across my face. It doesn't go unnoticed.

"Is that him?" Kat asks loudly, slack-jawed. "That's him, isn't it?"

James groans to himself. "Jesus Christ, Kat, keep your panties on."

She backhands his arm, an automatic reaction she has whenever he says something she slightly agrees with but won't fully admit out loud.

Without a word, I jump off my seat and glide over to him. He notices me at once, and hurries his pace. We practically run into each other, just like the first day we met. As predicted, he smells amazing. He throws his arms around me and leans in.

"God, I've missed you." He places a gentle kiss on my lips before pulling me into a hug. His lips graze the skin on my neck. I breathe deeply, filling my lungs with his scent, letting him soothe my senses.

"So," I start, trying to hide the guilt that's starting to surface, "I never brought anyone to meet my friends before, like ever, so be prepared for combat. It might get ugly," I warn him with a smile. "Don't show your fear. They'll feed off that." I playfully nudge his hard, flat stomach, and he gets a kick out of my enthusiasm. "But it should be fun."

"Yeah, thanks for that uplifting pep talk."

I reach for his hand and pull him toward the action, hoping he's ready for the barrage of questions headed his way. Kat is on the edge of her seat while James is busy on his phone. I formally introduce Sebastian to everyone, and when we sit, he places his hand on my bouncing knee. I'm a ball of excitement and nerves, but I know they'll like him as much as I do.

"So, Sebastian, how did you two meet?"

"I'll take this one," I jump in. "If he answers, he'll say, 'I plowed her,' and everyone will think it was one thing, but it was really nothing like what you're thinking, oh God. I should have just let him answer. Damn it." I drop my head in my hands, and Sebastian is the only one who laughs. He pulls my head into his chest and kisses the back of it, the spot where our heads collided on that day.

He lets out a low chuckle. "Ah, isn't she cute when she rambles?"

I raise my head, hoping that, by a miracle of God, no one is looking at me, but only half of them are. James is staring at me, while Kat is watching Sebastian.

Kat leans her chin on her hands, inching closer over the table. "I wanna hear his version."

"It's actually really funny," Sebastian starts. "I'd just gotten out of the shower, still wet, only in a towel when…"

I cut him off. "Let's just put it this way—the situation looked more scandalous than it was."

"Shower and scandalous, you say?" Kat can hardly contain her enthusiasm. "I like where this is going already."

"So, you work at the school or something?" James interrupts. I'm surprised he's not trying to hear the titillating details.

"No but I have a few places lined up after I graduate. I'm in the same fraternity as Tim."

"And you're how old?" James questions in a fatherly tone. I immediately balk at him.

Sebastian laughs, not particularly bothered by the question. "I'm twenty-three. The only reason why I haven't graduated yet was because I took a few semesters off to help my family when my father lost his job."

I start noticing a pattern with James. He looks at his phone and then asks a question, types, waits, asks another. It happens a few times until it hits me. He's been texting Evan. If Evan was so curious about Sebastian, he's had ample time to ask, but he barely acts like Sebastian exists when I'm on the phone with him.

I look at Sebastian and mouth the words, "I'm sorry." He offers me a wink and squeezes my knee. As with Evan, I'm drawn to Sebastian, too, leaning my head on his shoulder, hating the distance between us, however minor. I've seen Kat lean against plenty of men in her past, but never once did she receive the expressions I'm seeing now.

Both Kat and James have only ever seen me with Evan and no one else. Without knowing why I'm not a serial-dater, and without any questions regarding my nonexistent dating life, they've accepted it as if it were normal to be single. This particular scenario is undiscovered land for us all.

I try to give Sebastian a reprieve, directing the conversation toward James's video game; luckily the two of them start up their own side dialogue. James's demeanor is less aggressive when he's not doing Evan's bidding. Then I get Kat talking about her photography, and since Sebastian's sister is taking a photography class, the two of them go back and forth until finally the discussion flows more naturally, veering away from the initial interrogation.

Kat starts arguing with James about something, but he's busy on his phone again. The brief interruption gives Sebastian enough time to whisper, "I want to kiss you so bad right now. It's driving me crazy."

The smile creeps slowly when I realized that I need the kiss as much as he does. Our eyes lock. "Well, I don't want you going crazy or anything," I tease.

I lean in and lay my lips on his, tasting the remnants of his drink. It's not a deep or passionate kiss, but that doesn't take away from how it feels. It's like an awakening, a new Elana Parks. I need this identity. It's almost essential for my future survival.

Sebastian goes to the bathroom, and as soon as he's out of hearing distance, James starts. "You're acting like a little high school girl." He looks at his phone again.

Kat hits James's arm and lets out a sigh. "I'd be a high school girl, too, if that was my man."

"Did Evan tell you to say that?" I let out a low, annoyed groan. "You think I don't know what's going on here? I thought you guys would be happy for me."

I remind them of all the times they've heckled me in the past about my dating life. Here I am, finally with someone, finally happy for a change, and it's still a problem.

James places his phone on the table, annoyed. "Look, all I'm gonna say is that Evan is concerned. I admitted that I thought Sebastian seems cool, and he wasn't happy with my opinion. I think you two need to talk."

I feel the anger bubble, bursting every pleasant feeling I had moments before. "He's got some nerve, after we all had to put up with Genine."

James agrees. Still, he has a look on his face that makes me think he's hiding something.

"What'd I miss?" The chair beside me slides out, and Sebastian reclaims his seat at the table.

"Everything." Kat relishes the drama.

"I was just telling Elana how her friend Evan Saunders has been asking about her," James replies.

I spot what he did right away, and Sebastian catches it, too.

"Evan Saunders, like *the* Evan Saunders?" he asks, and I nod. "That's the Evan you and Tim are always talking about?" All I can do is keep nodding with a tinge of guilt over having never mentioned it before.

The turn of events has disrupted my pleasant mood, and I fear if I open my mouth, someone will get cursed out.

"Interesting," he says with a bit of indifference, as if he isn't fazed at all knowing my best friend is famous, the same friend he knew I had feelings for that day in the café. He squeezes my knee again, then leans in to kiss my neck. The softest touch sends a vibration throughout my body. He whispers near my ear for only me to hear, "And yet here we are."

Every move Sebastian makes goes noticed. Kat is practically drooling while James looks completely bothered as he answers yet another text before finally shutting his phone off and placing it on the table.

As a person walks to my rear, Sebastian's cologne wafts toward me. I look to him as he sips his drink, listening to Kat go on about something. As he swallows, I observe his neck, thinking about the water traveling down his body. Images of our first encounter rise to the surface—the liquid trickling down his taut flesh, glistening on his body in the dimmed bathroom doorway, the droplets that fell on my face from his dark, saturated hair, his stomach flat against mine. Suddenly, I want nothing more than to trace the tips of my fingers along his bare skin. My mind starts to burn with forbidden thoughts, and my body follows slowly, tingling with desire.

"I think Sebastian and I are going to leave now."

Sebastian eyes me mid-sip, and follows my lead.

"Wait, where are you guys going?" James asks as I give him a goodbye kiss on the cheek. "Stay."

"Why?" I inquire. "So you can give Evan an itinerary of my evening? I know he thinks he needs to be super protective of me—calling me every day, trying to make plans to come here and keep tabs on my relationship—but Sebastian is a good guy."

"You're wrong."

I can tell James is hiding something, but all I care about is that Sebastian is waiting for me, and I've been waiting for someone like him to come along for a long time now. With his hand in mine, I decide to move forward, tearing myself away from the confusion in hopes that Sebastian is the only answer I need.

The Only Exception

I POUR US BOTH A glass of wine, and we talk for hours in my living room. Kiki has curled herself on his lap. He must be right about cats liking him, because like her mother, Kiki dislikes most men. She must also see something in him, because we're right where we both want to be.

"So, Evan Saunders, huh? Figures my competition is a celebrity," he jokes. "I mean, Roman god, celebrity, at least you have a type."

I almost spit out my Chardonnay, and Kiki scowls at me for waking her before she lowers her head. "We've been friends since forever. He's just looking out for me."

"I knew coming into this that you had unresolved feelings." He holds his hand up to stop me from interrupting. "But I also knew that there was something about you that I'm drawn to, and I think you're drawn to me too. Otherwise, I'd have walked you to your car and that would have been the end of it."

He's not wrong. Sebastian has a way about him that draws me in. He manages to obliterate all my insecurities and fears with just his voice, touch, or simply his presence. He and I have both had to deal with things in our past that made us different people, and we understand each other without words.

I lean into him, running my fingers through his hair as he watches me closely. If I can do this, it's because of Sebastian alone. My heart starts beating quicker, and my body feels like it's getting warmer the more my thoughts start running wild. Kiki wakes up, eyes me a final time before moving off his lap and onto her pillow.

Sebastian thumbs my bangs away from my face and tucks them behind my ear, letting the tips of his fingers linger.

I look into his eyes, and it feels right. A warm confidence washes over me.

"I have to tell you something," I say, meekly. He strokes my hand with soft, steady motions, hypnotizing me into a state of calm. "Something happened to me when I was younger, something that I haven't been able to move past on my own. I thought Evan was the only one I could be comfortable around, but then I literally ran into you, and all of that changed. You don't mind taking it slow, and when I'm with you, the fears I usually have aren't screaming for my attention. I can't deny that I've loved him for years, but you've given me feelings I've never dreamed possible."

Thoughts of Evan and how he's been acting the past couple of weeks—calling me daily, saying things that just don't make sense, even for us—run through my mind. And then there's Sebastian, who's managed to break down every wall I ever built around my heart and body, making me feel like a *normal* woman for the first time ever.

Sebastian lifts my hand to his lips and offers a kiss. He pulls me closer and holds me in his arms for a minute, holding the weight of my words between us. The only thing that could make me feel better is his lips comforting mine and just like that, he gives me what he couldn't possibly know I wanted. A kiss.

His lips are sweet like candy as I run my tongue over them, playfully biting and feeling the corners of his mouth turn up. I straddle his lap, and his hands rest on my hips, occasionally running his fingers through my hair before gradually sliding them down my arms and torso, but always retreating to my hips.

I run mine through his dark hair, pulling myself closer to him. Our tongues explore one another's until I break away, guiding his mouth to my neck, where he kisses and sucks gently on the tender skin below my ear. Before I can overthink anything, I move off his lap and pull him to his feet, leading him into the bedroom.

"Elana, we don't—"

"Shhh…" I push him lightly onto the bed and get on top again.

His arms wrap around me, and we continue where our kisses left off. His patient hands hold my hips as I lower my body onto his. Sebastian slowly runs the tips of his fingers along my sides, then tangles them in my hair, not once retreating from our kiss.

At last I break the kiss and unbutton his shirt. My fingers are slow but steady, pushing all thoughts away as quickly as they fight to the surface, refusing to let anything ruin this for me. His body is exactly how I remembered—tanned, hard, defined. I run my hands over his muscles and start kissing and licking his neck, slowly working my way down to his chest and then back up to his lips.

His breathing grows heavier, and his hands feel hot under his touch. My breaths are controlled, but I know it's only because I'm setting the pace. He kicks his sneakers off and wraps his arms around me, rolling us over, our lips still locked.

He lifts himself up as my body begins to tremble underneath him. His soft, gentle brown eyes help keep me steady. He places soft pecks on my neck, then works his way back to my waiting lips as my heart races faster than before, no longer in the driver's seat. The fear is starting to bubble up, but I want to forget about everything—the rape, the nightmares, Evan. I want to get lost in the moment with Sebastian. But first I must let go of myself and shed all the layers of damage that's weighed me down for so long.

The trembles roll over my body like a wave pool, and he notices immediately. "We don't have to do this, Elana," he whispers softly, with that soothing voice of his.

I feel completely vulnerable, but for once, I don't care—I want him to see the true me, so I let the desperation of my words ring through the air, no longer wanting to hide it.

"You're wrong." My voice cracks as I begin to deteriorate. "I want to. I need to. If I don't do it now, with you, I never will. For the last twelve years, I've never let anyone get close—physically or emotionally. You're the only one I've ever allowed to touch me. Ever. I need it to be you," I plead.

The tears start forming, but he's there to catch them as they fall. My breathing increases as each quiet second ticks away until he kisses me again.

I kiss him back with everything I have. The repulsion I associated with sex fades, and all the desire I wished to feel flows freely. As I undergo my transformation, I feel a difference in him too. For the first time since meeting him, he feels nervous and timid as if all the confidence he had had just been sucked from the room. There is an unspoken understanding of what this moment means, not just for me, but for him, too.

He lifts my shirt over my head and stares at my skin. The tips of his fingers run over my stomach, leaving a trail of want in its wake, but his eyes never break from mine, watchful for any signs of apprehension. His fingers travel over the scar above my breast, and he closes his eyes. His breathing levels out again as mine toes the line of an erratic rhythm.

I run my hands over his taut skin, leaving goose bumps along the way. Every motion between the two of us is slow and delicate. He reaches around and expertly unclasps my bra, but isn't quick to remove it. He waits until he reads my eyes to make sure it's okay.

Yearning for his lips, I pull him close and discard my bra on the bed. With our bare chests pressed together, the skin-on-skin contact is welcomed and—oddly enough—comforting.

"You're so beautiful, Elana. I'll never hurt you."

Another tear escapes, and he's there to catch it again, kissing where it fell. He leaves a trail of kisses down my neck to my bare chest, and then they stop. I feel his breath against my breast. The glow of the moon hits my bare skin like a spotlight, and all I can see is the faint white lines of the scar. He sees it, too. Mortified and ashamed, I pull my hands up and cover my face.

Before I lose it totally, he tugs at my hands. "What's the matter?"

"It's hideous." I try to stifle my sobs, but it's futile.

"Hideous? No," he protests. "I know how important this is. I'm just scared as hell I'll fuck it up." He pauses for a moment. "Look at me, Elana." He places his hand over my scar. "You trust me, don't you?"

"Yes." My voice is breathless yet as sharp as glass as I stare into his eyes.

"Okay. Close your eyes and concentrate on your breathing—in through your nose, and slowly out of your mouth."

I do as he says and close my eyes, trying to get my heavy breathing under control. He shifts on the bed, no longer touching me. After a few moments and a lot of inhaling, he rests his hand over my breast, right where the scar lays.

The sensation is dull at first, but then it builds, slowly, increasing in strength. An outpour of relaxation consumes me, and I realize what he's doing. He's using his training.

When he explained Reiki to me, I remember being skeptical, but I can feel this. His palms feel hotter than before, and the tingling sensation keeps building, but the energy is welcomed, flowing smoothly through my body, discarding the pent-up emotional stress. When his hand rises off me, I still feel his energy cycle through, balancing my senses.

I open my eyes, wary, but his eyes are the complete opposite. Any apprehension he thought he had is gone. He leans down and kisses my chest, taking my breast in his mouth. My back arches, lusting for more, but he remains careful and slow. His hands reach for the waist of my jeans, and he looks up. I nod in approval.

He's steadier now, with a focus in his eyes. As he removes the rest of my clothes, the tips of his fingers glide along my smooth legs and thighs, causing my skin to prickle.

"You sure about this?"

Without a sliver of doubt, I nod, and I pull him on top of me, feeling his skin on mine, his erection is pressed against me.

"Just don't stop looking at me...please," I say with desperation. "I need to see your eyes."

His heart races under my palms, or maybe it's my own heart beating a mile a minute. I match my breathing to his, trying to connect our bodies in every way possible as I become electrified with desire.

"You'll stop me if it's too much."

I let out a little chuckle, breaking the tension. "It looks kinda average to me."

He laughs to himself before saying, "You know what I mean, Elana. Just say the word." I pull his face close to mine and offer a kiss, brushing my tongue along his, telling him without telling him that

I'm okay. When the kiss ends, he whispers, "Lord Hardwick takes serious offense to that, by the way."

I manage to stifle my laugh, but I pull him close again, crushing my lips against his. He holds me with such intensity that a diamond could form between us. He reaches down my body, placing his fingers between my legs. I close my eyes and truly feel Sebastian's every move. My breaths hitch in my throat, and my heart races like fast-moving traffic that I can't wait to hit head-on.

****

I wake up alone in my bed. No dreams and no Sebastian. I lie still for a moment, revisiting the night before, running my fingers over my swollen lips as I think about Sebastian's fevered kisses. I throw on some clothes and head toward the kitchen, hearing Kiki's soft murmurs. As I walk, my body feels sore but renewed, having that heaviness lifted off my spirit.

"Morning, good-lookin'." His smile is infectious, and I can't help but grin back.

He stands near the coffee pot in a pair of dark sweatpants that hang low on his waist, advertising his washboard abs and the deep indentations of his pelvic muscles.

As he walks to the kitchen table, the wind from his swift stride knocks a picture off the fridge. When I pick it up, I see which one it is. My heart feels shredded. It's Evan.

A monsoon of emotions batter me. I know he and I have no romantic ties, but the guilt feels like a vise on my heart. I still feel tied to him whether I like it or not. I miss his laugh, I miss the way his hair looks when he wakes up, I miss the way he looks sitting on my couch, playing with Kiki. I miss Eleven. Then the guilt of having this amazing man sitting in my kitchen smacks me in the face. He's precisely what I need in my life, and yet it doesn't feel right.

Sebastian sits at my little kitchen table with his steaming mug, making it look even smaller against his large stature. I sit across from him, knowing he deserves the truth.

"You don't have to say it, Elana." The shock must've registered on my face, because he lets out a little smile. "I can't hear your thoughts, but I can see it in your face when you looked at the picture."

He reaches for my hand across the table, and I give it freely. His thumb strokes my knuckles, and our eyes connect.

"I wouldn't trade last night for anything, but I know you still love him."

I look down, too much of a coward to face the truth, watching his thumb soothe me with hypnotic precision.

All I can say is, "I'm so sorry, Sebastian."

He rises from his chair and pulls me up from mine, locking me in his embrace. Sebastian lifts my chin up, holding it between his fingers as my eyes begin to well. I wish I could be different, but until I can shake Evan from my heart and thoughts, and truly look at him as just a friend, I must let Sebastian go. He deserves more than I can give right now.

The tears trickle down my cheek, but he doesn't try to catch them this time. "You don't know what last night meant to me. I owe you my life. You shouldn't have to wait for me to get over someone else." Sebastian doesn't let me go right away. We stay connected, holding each other for comfort. He leans down and grazes his sweet lips over mine. Then his arms drop and he disappears into the bedroom, leaving me standing in the kitchen, cold and alone.

I place the picture back on the fridge and allow myself to sob quietly, but I know I did the right thing. By the time Sebastian returns, he's fully clothed with his bag slung over his shoulder, and I've wiped my tears away.

"Walk me to my car?"

Sebastian and I walk hand in hand. He strokes my knuckles with his thumb, soothing me still, even though I'm setting him free. His arms wrap around me one last time, and his lips come in for one last kiss. I'll miss his sweet cinnamon taste.

He holds my chin between his thumb and forefinger and says, "I'm always here for you, Elana. Who knows, maybe one day, I can be the one that fills your heart."

"I look forward to it," I admit. The lump in my throat makes my voice waver. "Let me know when you get home."

"Will do, good-lookin'." He flashes me his perfect smile, and I try to give him one back as he gets into his car.

As he pulls away, I fall to the curb and break down, crying hysterically into my palms. I allow myself to sob, but only for a moment. With this sorrow also comes a hidden blessing. I was able to trust someone again, a feat I never thought possible.

Can't Hang Up

THE DAYS DRAG LIKE A full week of Tuesdays as time moves in slow motion around me. When Friday finally rolls around, I'm too drained to be social and I blow off my friends, refusing to hang out at Lizzy's. I provide texts to everyone, so no one harasses me to the point of annoyance. They've known me long enough to know not to press the issue further. I need time to myself, time to work through all the emotions that flood to the surface about Evan and Sebastian.

I paint to keep myself sane, taking my inner chaos out on the canvas. Sebastian has helped me in ways that he couldn't possibly imagine, using his Reiki skills, or maybe it was just Sebastian being Sebastian. Either way, I've grown to care for him in ways I cannot describe. But then the force that is Evan always rears its head, reminding me of the connection I feel toward him. And that kiss. That kiss ruined all hope I had of tucking away my feelings for him.

I decide to focus on a piece to give to Sebastian, as a thank you of sorts, when I'm interrupted by the wailing of my phone. Evan. I send it straight to voice mail. I'm not ready to talk to him, and I find myself enraged because he is the cause of all of this.

Everything was going great until he and Genine broke up, and I briefly wished they were still together so he wouldn't be calling me constantly, stealing my thoughts of Sebastian and replacing them with him.

New voice mail.

"Hey, El." A moment passes as his voice fades out. "Everyone is worried. You bring some guy to Lizzy's and then the next week, you want space from your friends?" The concern is woven in his voice, a situation all too familiar for him. "Did he hurt you? I'll kill him if he touched you. I need to know you're okay. Talk to me," he begs, "I need to talk to you."

The heat radiates off from my skin hearing him talk about Sebastian like that, as if Sebastian would do anything harmful to me. If he wanted to get to know him, he had plenty of chances to. Little does he know, I'm the one that did the hurting this time.

Sebastian was there to pick me up when I needed it. And he was careful with me as if we've known one another our whole lives, the way Evan should have done the night I confided in him. I don't know how, but Sebastian understood me better than anyone I've ever met, and was delicate with me both emotionally and physically, without question or judgment.

I stare at the phone, wishing I could crush it in my hands.

I retreat to the studio and put my earbuds in, cranking up the volume and watch as my phone continues to light up. Caller ID: Evan. Caller ID: Evan. Caller ID: Evan. Caller ID: Evan. Caller ID: Evan. Caller ID: Evan. Six calls go through with no new voicemails. As the phone lights up again, I answer it and disconnect the call immediately. I turn my volume louder, trying to drown out the ringer, but more importantly Evan, something I should have done a long time ago.

I shouldn't have let Sebastian go.

****

Another Friday afternoon finally rolls around, and I'm emotionally drained and in desperate need of a drink or five or ten. It might not be the smartest thing to do in my frame of mind, but I couldn't care less. I let Kat know that I'll be needing a designated driver because I'm getting wasted, and she is more than accepting of her duties, grateful that I'm rejoining society. I want to drown my tears and anger in tequila, rum, vodka, or anything with a high alcohol content.

I pull up to Lizzy's and rush through the doors like a patient whooshing through an emergency room. The only cure for my ailment is a tray full of martinis.

"Hey," Kat says warily, "did something happen with Sebastian?"

I say nothing, just hand her my car keys. The waitress comes over, like the saint that she is, and I place my order.

"Two double shots of Patrón and two lemon drop martinis," I say with urgency, like a surgeon demanding his instruments in an operating room—except instead of a scalpel, I need a steady intravenous drip of vodka.

Kat waits patiently as the waitress jots down her order and leaves the table. "Okay, Els, spill it. I know you have this whole hang-up about your secrets and blah blah blah, but seriously, we're all worried about you."

"I want the drinks first." I tap the table, drumming to the beat of the music in the speakers overhead. Kat mumbles something about me being stubborn and frustrating, but I don't waver.

The waitress carries over our drinks, and the moment the first one hits the table, I chug it down. She's barely gotten the second martini off the tray, and I've already guzzled the second double of Patrón, going straight for one of the martinis.

"Is everything okay, hun?" the waitress asks.

I finish the first martini and hand her the empty glasses. "It will be if you keep these coming. I'm gonna need another martini and another double of Patrón, please?" I take a deep breath, and right as I'm about to tell her what's been going on, James walks up to the table.

"Ah, you've finally decided to rejoin the world again. We've been worried." Not the warmest of welcomes, but with my belly full of warmth, I don't care that much.

"You just missed the drink-a-thon." Kat raises her brow and eyes me as I try to taste the martini instead of inhaling it.

"Let me guess." James points to his chin. "Sebastian is out, and Evan is back in?" He relaxes himself at the table, deeply satisfied with his theory.

"What?" Kat and I ask in unison.

He stares at us incredulously. "We all know Elana has been in love with Evan since eighth grade. Sebastian was cool, but he's not Evan."

I gulp down my drink, needing all the liquid courage I can get. The only thing I can think to say is, "Eighth grade. I don't think so." It wasn't the best comeback, I admit. "And I don't love him like that, so there, you're wrong." I stick my tongue at him and take another hefty sip.

I feel humiliated, realizing my true feelings have probably always been obvious to everyone while I thought I hid them so well. And if James could figure it out, Evan couldn't be that oblivious.

"That kiss probably didn't help, huh?" James adds. Apparently, this whole time, he's been moonlighting as a relationship therapist, analyzing every interaction between Evan and me.

I tried so hard to forget that kiss ever existed, so I do what I can to provide an alternative remedy to his theory. "He only did that to piss Amber off. She implied he should be spending time with someone more worthy, you know, the usual reaction when people see us together and we aren't even *together*."

"Girl," Kat starts, flipping her hair, "that's the face of jealousy. Welcome to my world."

"I don't even know why we're still talking about this. What matters is that my drink is practically empty, and I need a refill. I'm over it all. I just want to move on."

"All I'm saying is that you and Evan need to talk, and I'll leave it at that." James wipes his hands clean of the conversation and resumes drinking his beer.

Kat waits a beat and asks, "So is it over with Sebastian then?"

"Yeah. He was amazing," I admit. "It was me. It's always me, I'm the problem."

Kat looks to James, who shares her demeanor. "Did you know about this?" she asks.

"Nope."

"Oh, don't act like you guys don't know I have issues. Everyone knows. Just let me drink my weight in alcohol so tomorrow I'll wish I was dead when I'm throwing it back up in the morning." I grab her drink, and it's wolfed down before she even knew I touched the glass. Luckily, my refills are right on schedule.

James leans on Kat. "Well, this just got interesting."

I look at the table full of glasses, some empty, and others that soon will be, when I feel a tap on my shoulder. Anger boils in the depths of my gut, and I'm ready to knock out whoever's taking away my precious drinking time.

"Hey, Els."

Seven Too Many

MY THROAT DROPS INTO THE Patrón and vodka pool in my stomach. Before all of this, I would have been swinging on a star and over the moon with joy, but right now, I just see someone who broke my heart and turned my world upside down.

What makes it worse is the fact that he looks so damn good and smells even better. Thankfully for me, that woodsy scent stirs my fury, because if he weren't here, I could enjoy my drinks and wallow in my own misery. If he weren't here ever again, I could get over him and be with Sebastian.

"Not happy to see me?" he asks, holding a bouquet of mixed flowers.

Normally I cringe at the first sight of a petal. The smell has always reminded me of that infamous night, but these barely have a scent. Lucky for him, or else I would've expelled the contents of my stomach on his worn Converses.

I give him a once-over, checking him out from his disheveled hair to his scuffed-up sneakers. "If you would excuse me, friends, I'm thirsty."

I stand up from my seat, a little shaky on my feet, but I shoulder past him and stumble my way to the bar. Evan asks how much I've consumed so far, but before Kat can calculate the total, he starts trailing behind me.

"Two lemon drop martinis, please," I ask Lizzy behind the bar.

"You know I don't drink martinis, El."

"They aren't for me." The buzz starts kicking in, hampering my speech. "I meant, I'm not for you. *They* are not for you."

I give my head a little shake, hoping my mouth and brain will work together properly now. Fixing my eyes straight ahead, I chomp on some bar mix to keep myself occupied, because I know if I look at him, I'll break. The amount of alcohol I've imbibed so far is keeping me good and mad—a little wobbly, but good and mad all the same. I just have to keep reminding myself why I'm angry at him.

It's a little hard to remember through the fog of it all, so I make a mental check-list of the reasons: (1) he left me after I spilled my deepest memory; (2) he wouldn't leave me alone long enough to get over him; (3) I want him and can't have him; (4) that kiss meant everything to me but was just a joke to him; (5) that kiss—that soft yet passionate kiss, feeling his tongue dance with mine. I moan aloud thinking about it, reliving the pleasure all over again until the loud bell above the bar rings, snapping me out of my reverie. I grunt now, frustrated with myself again for thinking about that damn kiss.

"Lizzy, can you get the guy behind me a Black and Coke? Add it to my tab. He hasn't been working, unless meddling into my love life pays better than I think."

Lizzy laughs, which I'm not too happy about either because I wasn't joking, but I'm in no mood to argue with another person tonight, especially one that makes my drinks.

"Sure thing, El."

"You know, that's how rumors get started," he says as I wait impatiently at the bar. I can feel the smirk on his face when he speaks, poking at me like a stick covered in honey. I can also feel the desire to slap that smile right off that gorgeous face of his.

"After you hung up on me, which was pretty rude, by the way, you never called me back—also very rude. I thought I would come and talk to you in person. You can't hang up on me this way."

"No, but I can walk away." I grab his drink and shove it in his flowerless hand, getting some of it on his shirt, which he doesn't seem to notice or care. "You shouldn't have come. I really don't feel like talking to you. And you're actually the last person I want to see right now." I grab my drinks and head back to the table, drinking one and spilling the other as I walk.

"Elana, wait," he cries out as I'm halfway to my destination. "Can we go outside and talk for a second?"

I turn to him and the room spins a little, halting me momentarily. "Now? Now you want to talk? How about when I poured out my deepest secret and you left me for her? Or when you rarely called me for months afterward? That's when I needed my friend, Evan. That's when I needed to talk or just know that you weren't going to throw me away for some piece-of-shit actress. And guess what, Sebastian taught me something very interesting about myself. All this time, I thought you were the only one, but I was wrong. I was so wrong."

The liquids slosh in my belly, eroding away my defensive walls, burning them like acid. My emotions are clawing their way to the surface, but I need them tucked firmly below. I need to stay strong, and hurling in the middle of the bar while crying hysterically will defeat that purpose. And the last thing I want is to become an emotional drunk, like my mother.

"Can we go outside to talk, please? There's an audience gathering."

"You're an actor," I boast. "Isn't that the point, to have an audience?" I point casually to the groups of eyes staring at us from various points in the bar, Kat and James among them.

"Elana, c'mon, let's just go outside so I can explain, *please*." There's a pleading tone to his voice that wears slowly at my armor like centuries of water on metal, destroying it beyond repair. As fast as I can rebuild my walls, he's faster at knocking them down.

"Ugh, fine," I groan. "You have five minutes." I finish the other martini and set the empty glasses on some random couple's table.

I storm out of the front door, blasting it open. At least that's how I wanted it to look. It was more of a stumble and less of a storm as I rush past the smokers. I head over to the side of the building, crossing my arms, annoyed that I let him talk me into this.

"What?" I ask impatiently. His explanation is taking entirely too long, and it hasn't even begun yet.

"I'm sorry. I shouldn't have left you that night, not for anyone. Never in a million years did I think you'd ever tell me that, and to think it happened to you, my best friend, it devastated me."

The way he says "friend" makes me gag. I hate that word. It feels like a barred cage, wanting what's on the outside and knowing you can't break free of the bars keeping you trapped in.

"But you left, for her of all people," I remind him. "I never wanted to tell you any of it. But you kept insisting and prodding, pulling my paintings out and questioning me. You couldn't just let it be, Evan. And then you walked out. I wasted too many years thinking you were everything and I was nothing, just like everyone always used to say." The tears form, and there's no stopping them.

He stares at me angrily. "What?" He raises his voice, like he thinks I'm deaf, not drunk. "You aren't nothing, Elana."

"No, I'm not nothing, but I sure as hell felt like it when you shut me out for months and then started blowing up my phone because Genine cheated on you. Am I only a necessary fixture in your life when it's convenient for you? Because ever since I can remember, I've always been there when *you* needed me."

"Now you're just talking out of your ass, Elana."

I roll my eyes, almost losing my balance. "Am I? Well, the one time I thought it would be a no-brainer for you to stay, you bailed, hurting me more than any guy ever could."

"I told you I was sorry," he says with mounting frustration. "I know I was an asshole, and I'll do whatever's necessary to make it up to you, as long as it takes." He rakes his hands through his hair, and I'm left in a daze. I watched him touch every strand, but as soon as he was done, his hair looks the same. Perfect. He must use a special gel, one made only for celebrities, because there's no way a product like that exists in CVS. "Hello? Are you even listening to me?"

I snap out of my reverie. "Look, if you're here because of Sebastian, you're a little late, Evan. He's already gone."

"Gone? Did something happen?"

"Oh, like you don't know," I slur.

"What happened?"

"You're looking at her," I point to myself in a grand gesture. "And…a bit of you and a whole lot of us. Why am I even telling you this? It's none of your business anyways."

"You're my friend, El."

"Friend." There's that word again. My heart sinks in my chest like a brick in water. "Great." I look at the concrete, realizing the cracks seem to reflect how my heart feels. "Then be my friend and go home," I order, "no questions asked."

I try to walk away, but all the shots and martinis have kicked in at once. I shake my head, but the swirling dance my eyes are performing stop me where I stand. It takes me some time to get my bearings in order.

"You okay, El?"

"I'm fine, I'll be fine." I'm not fine and I won't be fine. I'm hurt. I feel betrayed, not just by him but by myself. Why do I have to love him the way I do?

I plop myself on the cool, cracked concrete. It seemed like a great idea at the time, although thinking about it now, I'm realizing it's not going to be an easy task getting up—at least, not without some assistance.

"I wish I could change how I feel," I sob to myself, my exterior crumbling quicker than I can restore it, "about Sebastian. About all of this. Just go, Evan."

"Go? I'm never making that mistake again." He walks toward me. "I need to tell you something, but not when you're like this."

I wipe my runny nose on my sleeve like any classy inebriated girl does. "Like what? Sobbing hysterically, getting snot all over my sleeve, or completely mad at you?"

"Two sheets to the wind. And mad at me, I guess."

"How old are you, fifty-seven? No normal twenty-six-year-old guy says that, Evan."

I want to hit something to feel pain anywhere but my heart. Maybe this is why Mom always drank and hit us. The thought of my mother and I having anything in common sends a bolt of fear through my body and my stomach into a frenzy. I sway back and forth like I'm on a boat, but I'm most certainly not on any body of water.

"Ah, my girl is back." He starts pacing in front of me, back and forth, back and forth, over and over and over again.

"Can you stop fucking moving? You're making me dizzier than I already am."

"Sorry, I'm just nervous," he explains.

I blink hard, trying to focus on where I am and how to stop the wave I feel like I'm riding. I rub my palms against my eyes, hoping it will stop the dizzying effect. It doesn't.

"The last time I was here, I came to see you. Genine was just the excuse I gave. Do you remember what I said at the park?"

"I can barely remember my name right now, so nope, sir-eee-bob," I stammer.

"I remember everything about that night."

I interrupt again. "Oh, look at you, Mr. Memory Man." I pick up a rock and toss it a few feet in front of me.

"Can you let me finish? The dinner with my parents, hanging out with everyone, the baseball game, just being around you, it was what I've missed and what I want."

"That's normal stuff, Evan, nothing special about it," I slur.

I try to stand up, and on the third attempt, with Evan's help, I'm as upright as my body allows. I walk to the swaying image that is Evan, holding out my hand. He takes it, but I shake him off.

"No, give me your phone, not your hand. I want to call Timmy and tell him I love him. Timmy is a good kid, Evan. We raised him well, even Naked Frat Boy thinks so." I start snorting to myself and move a little too fast, losing a little balance.

Kat told me once that when I have a bit too much Patrón, I want to talk to Timmy and tell him how much I love him. Apparently, she was right. She also said that I ramble about things I should keep to myself. I'm not going to do that tonight. Nope.

"Naked Frat Boy?" he asks, perturbed.

"Pay attention, will ya? Fraked Nat Boy," I burst out laughing again. "I said Fraked Nat Boy...ahhh... I love being drunk," I shout at the moon. "Sebastian is my Naked Frat Boy. He's tall and sexy, built like a Roman warrior god and he likes me even after he plowed me and offered to take care of my kitty." I start laughing again, not caring how it must sound to someone sober—or drunk for that matter. I don't care much about anything right now, and it feels wonderful. "We almost gave each other a concussion. His head is very hard and thick," I enunciate for no reason in particular. "Did you know that? And why does everyone keep telling me my head is big? Do I have a big head, Evs?" I try to wrap my hands around my head, seeing if the tips of my fingers meet. They don't, and I frown. My eyes find Evan's. "Why do you look so angry?"

Before he can answer, I wave my finger, summoning him to come closer, and he does. "The first time I met him, he was naked and wet, and I didn't even flinch when he touched me," I boast with an ounce of pride. I hold my hand up to whisper to him, but my volume is as loud as ever. "I totally peeked, but promise me you won't tell him. Promise me, Evan." He promises nothing, just maintains his gaze, eyes bulging with curiosity and a sprinkle of anger or disdain or both. "And then we got to know each other, and he was amazing and blah blah blah, but you know that part already because you had James be your eyes and ears. Didn't you?" But I don't wait for him to answer. "And then he was so gentle and held me with such care." I release a long sigh, thinking about it now. "He helped me get over my fear, ya know. He was a beautiful distraction from—" I don't finish my sentence, only tap Evan on the tip of his cute little nose.

I take a step back, putting some much-needed space between us, because being this close to him is dangerous, especially with him smelling so damn good.

"What was I saying?" I ask, losing all train of thought. "Do you hear that?"

He looks at me confused, considering I'm the one doing all the talking.

"What exactly am I listening for?" he asks.

"Ticktock, ticktock. Your five minutes are up." I walk away from him before he can break my heart anymore.

"Elana, are you done rambling about nonsense? I think you're just telling me this stuff to piss me off." I can sense the frustration in his voice as his steps quicken behind me.

"I get it, Evan—you're sorry and blah blah blah blah, but I'm still mad at you, and I wish you never came here."

"Why are you so mad at me?" He raises his voice. "Is calling you and telling you how much I miss you and want to see you such a horrendous thing?"

"For me, yes. I still have one more secret that I don't plan on revealing, no matter how much Patrón I consume, so quit trying to interrogate me and go home."

"I've barely asked you anything."

I look him straight in the eye. "Exactly."

I walk as fast as my drunken cement feet will allow, trying to get away so he can't see the tears collecting, but he's right behind me, grabbing at my arm, pulling me into him. The sudden movement makes everything spin. My eyes get all starry, and the lights in the parking lot start to dim. I try to reboot my sight by blinking faster, but my body starts to feel heavier by the minute, making any movement I attempt more and more difficult.

"Elana, I'm in…" His voice fades out, and my eyes fade to black.

No Answers

I WAKE UP IN MY bed. My mouth is as dry as the Sahara Desert, my head throbs uncontrollably, and my stomach churns violently. Even with the blinds and drapes closed, my room is still entirely too bright.

Why did I drink so much? I think to myself as I rub the sleep out of my eyes. I suck in a quick breath, the slightest contact of my palms to my sensitive sockets causing unnecessary pain. They feel swollen like I've been crying all night, and nothing would bring me more misery than thinking I'm a sad drunk.

I head into the living room, another room too bright for my condition, dragging my feet as I walk. A relaxed Evan is draped casually on my couch, reading my newspaper. The smell of coffee penetrates my nose, and I know I'm going to need an intravenous drip of it as soon as possible.

"What the hell happened last night?" the sound of my own voice causes my brain a whole lot of suffering.

"You had about seven drinks too many and passed out."

I hold my head in my hands. It doesn't help the throbbing, but it helps keep the light from penetrating the thin layer of skin over my eyes.

"What are you doing here?" I ask, remembering I was mad at him, but not recalling if he ever answered this question already.

"I came to talk to you. Want some coffee?" He pours me a cup and gets Tylenol out of my cabinet. "Can I borrow your car for a little while? I need to pick something up in the city."

I don't have the energy to argue or question it. "Whatever." His absence will give me time to call Kat and maybe get a few answers about last night. Plus, I could use a nap, and the only way I might be able to get some rest is if he's out of the apartment.

"Do you still like Sebastian?"

"I'm not having this conversation with you right now." My voice trails off as my stomach performs a perfect triple front flip that would make Gabby Douglas proud.

He studies my face, then looks at his feet. "Are you going to be okay by yourself for a little while?" He stands by the front door, staring at me while I'm trying my hardest to remember anything from last night, especially anything pertaining to my mentioning Sebastian.

"I'll be fine. Don't get into any accidents with my truck."

"I'll just buy you a new one if I do." He leaves my apartment, and I perform my signature eye roll, but the slightest motion invokes extreme pain and nausea. I race to the bathroom, expelling the contents of my stomach.

Since cleaning and painting are out of the question with a hangover, I throw myself back into bed, hoping to sleep off any remnants of alcohol that remains in my system.

When I wake up from my nap, I decide to throw in a load of laundry. Oddly enough, doing laundry has always been soothing for me, even with a massive hangover. When my mother was on one of her drunken rampages, Timmy and I would hide in the laundry room. The smell of fabric softener was a soothing scent because I knew we'd be safe there. It's the one chore that relaxes me. I bring a book to the laundry room, but my eyes become increasingly heavy as I try to get through the first page.

Charli Thorton walks into the laundry room.

"Hey, El. You look like shit."

"I feel like it too."

We chat about random things while we do our laundry. She's one of the few people my age who lives in this building. When she first moved in, I remember seeing her by the pool and gawking at her bikini body and perfect chocolate skin. We got along quickly, sharing a love for art.

"Word around the complex is that Evan Saunders is staying with you again."

"I'm still amazed at how quickly information spreads like wild-fire around here." I hold my head in my hands; it's suddenly become too heavy for my neck. "I'm sure his stay will be brief. Did everyone see me passed out drunk last night, too?"

She lets out a squeak of a laugh. "You know people are nosy, present company included, so yes, it was mentioned that Evan carried you into the building." Her laugh continues, sending my ear-drums into overtime. "I heard he and Genine aren't dating anymore."

"Trust me, he's better off without her." I grab my clothes out of the dryer, one article of clothing at a time. The movement makes the room spin like the dryer drum.

The words aren't out of my mouth for two seconds when Evan strolls in. "Mr. Sam was right, here you are." Evan looks at us and notices we stopped talking the moment he entered the room. "You were talking about me, weren't you?"

"Speak of the devil." I take a quick seat, feeling dizzy on my feet. "Evan, this is Charli Thorton. She lives in the building. She's a fan." I wave away at the air and bury my face in my hands again.

"El has mentioned you before. It's nice to finally meet you. What do you do for a living, model?"

Evan isn't the type of guy to say something he doesn't mean. Charli is absolutely gorgeous and could easily be on the cover of a magazine. Her face drops down, flattered at his comment, looking away shyly.

"I work for an art gallery in the city."

"Really? Did you know Elana is an artist?"

"Yes," she boasts, "but she conveniently locks her studio door when I come over." I feel her eyes on me, but I don't pull my head out of my hands to make sure. "I tell her all the time about our new artist showcases, but you know El, she's stubborn."

"I'm sitting right here, ya know." The buzzer of a machine startles me in my seat. I tear my head away from my hands for the first time in minutes. "I've never really shown my work before. Don't take offense."

"Why don't you stop by tomorrow? I'll make sure the studio is unlocked." Evan's grin widens, and Charli cheers with excitement, causing me great pain. "Come by around 11:00 a.m."

"Great, I'll see you guys tomorrow." Charli grabs her laundry basket and practically skips out of the room.

I stare at him coldly, in disbelief at what he just did. "How do you know I'm free at eleven, and why would you think I would want to show my paintings to people?"

"How great would it be if her gallery featured your work?" Evan enthuses, ignoring everything I've just said.

I unleash a frustrated sigh. "I've never painted because I wanted to show people. I paint to keep myself sane, and I could sure use a paintbrush right about now, mainly just to stab you with it."

"You're so dramatic."

"Ughhhh." My head drops into my hands again, trying to soothe the dull pulsating of my brain. I need to get him back on a plane as soon as possible. "How long are you staying exactly?"

"How about we get some food and stay in tonight? We can watch…" Evan reaches into his back pocket and pulls out a DVD case, purposefully refusing to show me the cover. And he said I was the dramatic one. Finally, he does the big reveal. "*Spaceballs.*"

I'd be lying if I said I wasn't thrilled. "I haven't seen that movie in forever," I admit, snatching the box out of his hand. I try my best to ignore the spinning room again.

He throws the rest of my clothes in the basket, and we head up to the apartment and order food. I wait for the delivery downstairs, needing the fresh air for my headache. I sure hope they include a fortune cookie that explains what the hell is going on, because I'm still clueless. Worst-case scenario, I'll learn how to say "duck" in Chinese.

I wait on the stairs, just outside of the lobby door. I guess I hadn't realized how long he was gone when I notice the sun is starting to set. The cool air feels good on my skin, easing some of the tension that has tortured my brain all day long. With a clearer head, I try to reach for any memory of last night, but only bits and pieces come to me—flowers, the burning tequila going down, wanting to call Timmy, and James bringing up the kiss.

That kiss. Its memory alone is like heroin, just one time and I was hooked on it, except I only got to try it once, leaving me jonesing for it ever since.

There's only one common denominator for the way I'm feeling—the grumbling of my stomach, the pounding of my head, and the aching of my heart. Evan. The sooner I get this weekend over with, the quicker I can get over him. I just have to get through it first.

Confessions

I FEEL TRAPPED IN THE elevator with the scent that reminds me of him, overwhelming all my senses like it did that dreadful day. Even the bags of Chinese food aren't strong enough to mask it. When the elevator doors open, I throw myself out and rush into the apartment, slamming the door behind me.

I look at Evan. He paces the living room, holding his chin between his fingers, deep in thought.

"Why are you white?" Evan asks, as I breathe in my scent-free apartment. The only thing I smell is Evan's cologne, which smells fantastic, and I still hate him for it.

"Well, when two Caucasian parents are in love and the sperm enters the—"

Evan interrupts, "I'm being serious. What's the matter?"

"That smell, the one I told you about, was in the elevator." My breaths are heavy as I try to wrap my head around it, but from the safety of my locked apartment. "A mix of flowers or potpourri and alcohol." I take a whiff of myself. "The alcohol stench might be me, but someone must've gotten a delivery of some sort."

I sit on the couch with my head in my hands, trying to calm myself down. A whirlwind of images flash in my mind—his mouth on mine, the pain of each thrust, all the visuals I'd kill to forget. I shake my head to try to regroup and focus on my present reality— the one that involves me still hungover and completely confused as to why Evan is here.

"I hate that it still freaks me out. I'm sorry," I admit, trying to shake it off. "I guess being hungover doesn't help things."

111

"Don't be sorry, El. I guess now is as good a time as any." He takes a deep breath and slogs toward me. "I should be the one saying sorry. It was my fault that it happened to you at all. You called me to go with you to that party, but I stayed home because your cousin always ragged on me. If I just would have gone, none of it would have happened." He throws his shaking hands to his face, trying to cover up the fact that he's about to start crying.

"Evan, stop. Don't blame yourself. Is this why you've been weird since I told you?"

"No. Yes. But no. After Genine left you that nasty message, I kicked her ass to the curb. No one is allowed to talk to you like that. The magazines didn't know it was over before they published the pictures. I hated myself for leaving you, and the more I thought about what you told me, that's when I remembered I didn't go with you. I couldn't bear talking to you knowing I could have prevented it."

"Listen—"

"I'm not done yet. I spoke with a few people, and I get it now. But I know you lied to me that night, too. I just realized it too late. Well," he says, raking his fingers through his hair, "I hope I'm not too late."

"What?"

"James and Kat said you ended it with Sebastian, but the way you were talking about him last night, I don't know what's true. Do you still have feelings for him?" He studies my face, searching for an answer that feels impossible to give. He looks as if his next breath is dependent on my replies.

"It's complicated."

Evan drops his head. "I'm so confused."

"You're singing to the choir, Ev."

"It's 'preaching to the choir,' not 'singing to the choir.'"

"You're really going to correct me right now?" I give him my infamous glare. "What are you trying to get at?"

"Normally, I can tell when you're lying, but that night, I guess with everything you told me, my mind was all over the place and I didn't spot it. But the more I replayed it in my head, seeing your face as clear as day, I remembered it. Your eye twitched."

I've never felt more confused than I do right now. He must see it. He hands me a box, and when I open it, there's a single key inside. "What's this?"

"A key."

"Really, asshole? Does it open a door that I can toss you through where you'll have to fight off sand worms? I'll settle for my front door if I have to."

"I love that movie, too. And no, it doesn't. The only door it opens is the one to the new house in LA."

"Why would I need a key to your new house?"

"Not really *my* house. Here," he says, handing me another box. His hands look shaky as he fidgets in place.

The second box contains a beautiful necklace with a number "1" attached to the chain. The platinum pendant is encrusted with brilliant, sparkling diamonds.

"It's beautiful," I say, awestruck by the shiny metal and precious stones that sparkle in the living room light.

"I have a matching one." He sits next to me on the couch and pulls the chain out from under his shirt. I can't believe I didn't notice the glittering chain that rested on his neck before now. "Well, mine isn't as girly because that would be a little out of character for me." His voice is full of light and air, soft as a feather. "When we aren't around one another, we are just 'one' person, but when we are side by side," he says, placing our pendants next to one another, "we are better, we are light, we are 'Eleven.'"

"So you got us an updated version of best friend charms?"

He ignores my sarcasm. "I want these necklaces… I want us to be around each other more often."

"Fine, I won't be mad at you anymore. Are you done being dramatic?"

"I'm serious, Elana," he says more firmly, taking the necklace from my hand, holding the pendant between his fingers. "Why are you different with me? The truth." The nervousness he exhibited before is replaced with a look of wanting, and just a splash of fear.

I swallow hard, sensing his emotions, and I owe him the truth. "The truth. The truth is that I have *some* feelings for you."

"*Some?*" he asks with a hint of humor.

"You know I love you, so shut it. But for me, I don't know. I guess my feelings run a little deeper than that."

"I was hoping you'd say that." He grips the pendant tighter, looking at it with a smile. "I'll admit I'd hoped for some telenovela-type of admission, but I'll take it." He prepares himself for my playful tap. But he looks at me completely serious. "You've always been the number one woman in my life. You're all that matters to me, Elana Parks."

It's not the first time he's said those words, but it's the first time he's said them sober. My knees feel weak even though I'm sitting. I've dreamed, fantasized even, about this moment for the better part of my life, for him to utter those words. I'm rendered speechless.

"At the baseball game, I only used Amber as an excuse. I've wanted to kiss you for years, thinking about it day and night. I guess I was too scared to tell you because I didn't want to ruin what we had. Then, when you said I was like a brother to you, it killed me until I realized you're a big fat liar."

The small smile on my lips blossoms into something brighter. He reaches for my hand, and his touch feels different now. There's an intimacy to it, unlike how he's held my hand in the past. It's like he's trying to convey his feelings through this one simple touch, and it gives me goosebumps over every square inch of my body. He lets go of my hand and brings his up to my cheeks, cupping them in his palms, rubbing his thumb over my cheekbone. His eyes watch me, searching for answers, and he's found it.

"I've been dying to do this again." He leans in closer and presses his soft lips to mine. Slowly and sweetly, he kisses me.

His mouth parts as his tongue lightly strokes my lips. The kiss is passionate and loving, sending sensual vibrations throughout my body as our tongues play in each other's mouth. It's better than the kiss at the baseball game. Then he releases me, and I'm left dazed, almost panting, but wanting more, always wanting more from him.

"I'm in love with you, Elana. I have been for a long time." His hands drop, but his gaze doesn't. Still reeling over what just happened, he continues, "Every happy moment or memory I have is because of you."

I look down at our interlocked fingers, thinking about what I could possibly say. My nerves cripple every part of my body, but I've waited too long for this moment to let it slip through my fingers because I was too scared to tell him the truth.

"I've been in love with you for—" I start, but he's heard all he's needed to hear, and he kisses me again, ramming his lips into mine.

Lips locked, I reach for him as if this is all just a dream and if I let go, I'll never have it again. I pull him closer, lowering myself back on the couch, and our kiss deepens. My insides turn to jelly, as I'm finally able to kiss the man I've been in love with for so many years.

He lies on top of me, stroking my hair with one hand, gazing into my eyes like he's never seen me before. Every tooth in my mouth is showing. My smile is a mile long.

"So, does this mean that Eleven is official?"

"We are most definitely in the house," he jokes with his own wide smirk. "Is kissing okay? I mean, I know you are tentative with affection…" His voice drops as he gazes down, looking at me steadily, stroking my hair.

I put my finger against his lips to shut him up. "With you, everything is different."

"I want to do this right, El. I want to take you on dates, make you laugh, keep a smile on your face until your cheeks hurt. I could be content with just kissing you and lying next to you until you're absolutely ready. Or eleven days, whichever comes first," he jokes.

Before I know what's happening, the tears slide out of my eyes. He's said all the right things, and I'm overcome with emotion.

I wipe the tears away. "I'm sorry. I know we just started dating like thirty seconds ago," I say, half-laughing and half-crying, "but I love you, Evan." The freedom of being able to say the words to him is unlike any feeling in the world, and I can't help but laugh at the ease of it all after having kept it locked away for so long.

He lets out a chuckle. "I've never loved anyone like I love you."

He gets off the couch and reaches for my hands, pulling me into his arms, locking me safely against him. We kiss again only briefly before he puts the other half of "eleven" around my neck.

****

The two of us cozy next to each other, watching the movie, a smile tattooed on my face the entire time. I ache to kiss him again, but laying my head on his shoulder is almost as satisfying as he holds my hand in his, rubbing my knuckles softly with his thumb.

Before we know it, we both start yawning, and retreat to my bedroom. He crawls into bed next to me, holding me in his arms. I find his lips in the dark.

His breath deepens as I run my fingers through his hair before wrapping my arms around him. The nerves I thought I'd have with him seem nonexistent even as his hands travel up and down my body. The urge to have his hands touch my bare skin fills my entire being.

I straddle his lap, and his hands automatically find my hips, digging into them as I kiss his neck, running my tongue along his sweet skin. He moans on my mouth, and my smile widens as his grip tightens.

His fingertips run up my body, creeping under my tank top, touching my skin. It gives me chills. His magical touch makes my stomach flutter.

I ease his T-shirt over his head, exposing his chiseled chest and ornate tattoo work, leaving a trail of kisses down his torso as he whispers my name with approval. Before I can think twice, I sit up and take my top off as well, leaving the thin lace of my bra to cover me. I instantly regret it.

He looks at the scar above my breast, then back at me. He sits up on the bed. I can feel it starting, the trembling I get when I feel vulnerable, and he senses it, too. Before I can move, he embraces me in his arms, pulling me toward him.

"I'm not going anywhere."

I try to get my breathing under control, try to bring myself back to the moment, feeling his arms around me, breathing his scent into my lungs. It's then I realize that Evan Saunders, my best friend, is holding me and loving me the way I've always desired.

He lays me down next to him, fitting my body against his as he places gentle kisses on my neck, stroking my hair in soothing motions like he used to do when we were younger. I find myself melting into the mattress, feeling the warmth of his body and breath beside mine until I let the exhaustion take me, blissfully happy. How could I not be? Evan is here with me, and he's all I ever wanted.

Talent

I'M WOKEN UP BY A pounding sound, and for once, it's not from the hangover or a dream.

"What the hell?"

"What time is it?" Evan mumbles.

"Shit, it's Charli," I shout, eyes bulging, fully awake. I jump out of bed and throw on some clothes, not caring that my shirt is inside out and possibly backwards. "Get out of bed, Evan," I demand, "you're the reason why she's here." I race to the bathroom, swish some mouthwash, hoping it kills my morning breath before I kill Evan, who's taking his precious time dragging himself out of bed.

"Morning, Elana. Did I wake you?" Charli asks unapologetically, with a hefty dose of enthusiasm.

"No, no," I answer, waving her off while I try to lean casually against the door, hoping she doesn't see me out of breath. "I was just in the bathroom."

She wears a colorful smirk as she walks inside. I quickly suck in the air my lungs so desperately need before she turns toward my bedroom as Evan trudges out of it, barely dressed.

"Morning, Evan."

"Morning," he yawns, stretching his arms out wide. "Glad you're taking the time to see her work. She has some amazing pieces."

Unlike us, Charli looks well slept. Her skin glows as if she's already had a light morning run, followed up by a facial, and finished with expertly applied bronzer, blush and highlighter. She's radiant. Her perfectly coiled hair is pulled into a high ponytail, elongating her slim neck and jawline. "I'm super excited. I spoke with my boss yesterday. She's been dying to find some new, raw talent." Charli claps her hands with elation, just like she did yesterday.

"I've never painted with the expectation of them being shown, so—"

"Stop being modest, El," Evan wraps his arm around me and kisses my temple. I shove him away, so Charli doesn't make any assumptions. He checks his breath against his palm, and throws me a bit of a scowl.

The three of us head into the spare room. "I really should have organized them for you, but I was a little out of it yesterday."

I start pulling canvases out of the closet, displaying them against the wall, leaning some against the bed, trying to show Charli a mixture of small and large pieces. There's more than enough variety, not only in size but with the assorted styles that I've used over the years.

She gasps, but I don't know if it's a good or bad thing. "These are great, El." Her jaw drops and her eyes go wide. "I think my boss is going to love these. Are you willing to sell them?"

"I guess, I don't know."

"What's that one?" She points to the infamous painting that's no longer hidden behind the desk.

"No, no...that one isn't for viewing." Evan darts over to the painting in question.

"Actually, Charli," I interrupt, snatching the painting from Evan's hands, "this one is an old piece, but it's very graphic."

"I don't mind if you don't."

I turn the canvas around. She remains stoic. There's no quick inhale or dramatic clutch of her chest, her expression a blank canvas of its own until her head shifts to one side and she releases a breath. Waiting to hear her opinion, I think about how far along I've come since I was that little girl. I could have fallen down my mother's path, relied on the bottle to get through each day, but I didn't. I survived, not without issues, but I survived nonetheless.

The strings that connect me to the painting are still attached, but since Sebastian, they don't seem to pull at me the way the used to. Having Evan know every part of me makes this painting easier to consume.

"I painted that when I was younger, just beginning with paints. It's not very good, technically speaking, but it's still commanding, I guess."

Evan holds up a different painting, "What about this one? Good, right?" I see his gesture for what it's worth. He's trying to divert her attention elsewhere.

"You're right, El, it's a powerful piece," Charli says. "I'm sure there's a story behind it, but I think I've seen enough. Can I take some pictures to show my boss?"

"Sure, we'll be in the kitchen. Do you want anything to drink?"

She shakes her head and pulls out her camera, snapping pictures of various pieces.

Evan and I head into the kitchen, and I know what he's going to say before he opens his mouth.

He leans in close, dropping his voice for only me to hear. "Why'd you show her that painting?"

I hop onto the counter, popping a grape in my mouth. I soak him in. His gorgeous eyes and lips stare back, hanging onto the silence until I break it, but all I want to do is kiss and hold him like I did last night.

"You helped me realize something. All my secrets have been hidden for far too long. I didn't do anything wrong, yet I lived like I had. If I keep feeling ashamed of it, he wins. For me to heal, I have to let the darkness come to the light and move forward and stop looking back."

He stands between my legs and hugs my middle, offering a light kiss on my neck without a word.

"Ahem."

I quickly push Evan away, jumping off the counter. "Sorry, Charli." I stroll over to the doorway as she glances at me with the most curious smirk on her face. "Did you get everything you needed?"

"Yup." She laughs. As I walk her to the door, she says, "I'll call you and let you know what she thinks."

As I start to put some of the paintings away, I feel his eyes burning a hole in the back of my head. "What?"

"Why'd you push me away when Charli came into the kitchen?"

I think about it for a second. "I don't know. You're Evan Saunders. You date Hollywood starlets, not a nobody from New York. I didn't think you wanted people to know."

He glides in my direction and takes the canvas out of my hand, leaning it up against the stool. He closes the space between us, holding me once more, locking his eyes with mine. "If I ever hear you call yourself a nobody again, I will tickle you into submission." His arms tighten just a touch. "I don't care who sees us, El." His arms drop, but his hands find my cheeks. "We aren't hiding from anyone, not anymore." Evan lays his lips on mine. When he's finished, I see that the corners of his mouth are turned up. "Unless," he starts, dropping his hands, "you're the one ashamed of me?" His mouth parts with dramatic shock.

"Well," I admit, "since you mentioned it." I eye him up and down, but I can't hold in the laugh long enough to convince anyone. "So when do you have to go back to LA?"

"Tomorrow afternoon."

I don't know why I was shocked by the sudden departure. He normally only stays the weekend when he comes to visit, but it doesn't curtail my disappointment. He wears his own sullen expression.

For the remainder of the day, we lounge in the apartment, enjoying each other's company as a new couple, making up for years of suppressed kisses and cuddles. I couldn't be happier.

****

The friendly GPS lady gives me the directions to Monarch Art Gallery, where Charli works. What the GPS neglected to say was that there was absolutely zero parking anywhere near the building. I park about what feels like twelve city blocks away.

Over the phone, Mrs. Monarch, owner of Monarch Art Gallery, sounded so enthused about my work. She said there was a severe drought of talented, emotion-struck painters. If it's emotions she's looking for, she hit the jackpot with me. I've got enough bottled-up emotion to drown her.

When I walk in I see some empty walls, some with exposed, aged bricks, and some with regular walls painted with the brightest white finish, as if sent from the angels of purity. The overhead spotlight shines on a few random pieces in one corner of the room.

Before I'm able to fully scout the whole gallery, an eccentric woman approaches me with a wide-armed welcome gesture. Her tall, thin frame make her limbs appear lanky. The image of her bright red lips against her ivory skin reaches me before she does, and those glasses…man, they're big. They're the largest, blackest frames I've ever seen. The tops cover half her forehead, while the bottom stretches past half her cheek. And if there were any hairstyle in the world that would match her persona, it's the exact one she has now, a perfectly coiffed bob, super sleek, cut so razor sharp it could prick your skin. It's the color of oil, and just as slick.

"It's great to meet you," I say. "Thank you for taking the time to see me."

She reaches out to shake my hand, with both of hers. "Darling, you must show your work here. You are what I've been lusting for—those brush strokes, the emotion—just thinking about it gives me the bumps." She holds out her stretched arm, showing me the raised skin. "You're so raw, untouched, not influenced by some half-wit professor trying to teach you how to feel. You are the epitome of emotional outcry."

She glides toward a section of the gallery I had yet to explore, and I trail behind. "I prefer to do these showcases with artists like you. Opening night is the first Friday of the month, and the event lasts for two weeks."

She continues to walk through the different nooks of the gallery, each one feeling a little different than the last. I can imagine some of my pieces spread out as I follow behind.

"In the extremely likely event that someone wishes to purchase your work—and they will—we also handle the transaction for you, as most artists feel weird negotiating, seeing how each piece is priceless to them, as you know. I had Charli prepare a package for you. It lists our fees for that service. Feel free to ask other galleries what they charge. You'll find we are the fairest, and honey, we have the best clientele. I feel like you were born to show your work here." She grabs my hands and shakes them enthusiastically before releasing me.

She isn't entirely wrong. I've been to art showcases and galleries before; most felt drab or stuffy. This place has character, and the exposed brick walls give me a sense of being outside, not like an outdoor type of way, but as it it were a feeling unto itself. The feeling that I've always been outside of the norm, often cold and lonely, weathered and vulnerable.

She watches as I shift my head, really soaking in the surroundings. She grabs my hands from my sides. "You can feel it too, can't you?" She inches up the fabric of my shirt and underneath my sleeve, revealing the raised skin on my arm.

Charli comes out of a back room with a large white envelope in her hands. She greets me with a hug and a kiss.

"Ah, Charli, I was just telling Ms. Parks that she loves this place," Mrs. Monarch says.

Charli and I give a little chuckle. "She's not wrong," I admit.

She grabs the envelope and hands it to me. "That one piece of the little girl, darling, the focal point of your whole exhibition," she exclaims, clutching her heart as if to hold it. "You really must showcase it."

That one piece, an image of me trapped in time, did start it all.

My head is swimming with thoughts and excitement as I head home. The moment my butt hits the couch, I review the documents repeatedly. Fear hits as I think about the impact this could have on me, Timmy, and my friends. If I decide to showcase *Stolen Innocence,* I know I'll have to reveal the part of my life I've kept hidden for years.

After careful and strenuous thought, I decide to just go for it. I include the piece that started it all, trusting Mrs. Monarch's vision. From just one meeting with her, she seemed more in tune with me and my work than I ever imagined possible.

****

"Noooo!" I scream.

His body is heavy, like he's been weighed down with cinder blocks, too much for my sore, struggling arms to push off. I can't move, no matter how hard I try to wiggle out from under him. The salt of his sweat drips onto my face, burning my eyes and entering my mouth. I can feel him inside me. The pounding, the tearing of my flesh searing through me like electric jolts.

"You are a good fuck!" The guttural tone of his voice shakes my insides.

I try my hardest to ignore the overpowering floral scent, gagging on the taste of it before he wraps his hand around my throat, preventing any air from getting into my lungs. Our eyes meet before he sinks his jagged teeth into my skin.

I scream, waking myself up, clutching the spot above my breast, gasping for oxygen. My heart thunders in my chest. Although my cheeks are stained wet with tears, my mouth is as dry as ever, gasping in quick breaths. My muscles burn as if I've done a full circuit exercise, probably from fighting in my sleep.

"It's just a dream, it's just a dream," I tell myself, hugging my sides as I rock back and forth on my mattress, even though it felt so real.

I reach onto the nightstand for my bottle of water, terrified that if I look at the clock it'll curse me from falling back asleep. After knocking most of my belongings off the nightstand, I look for my water, and my eyes betray me, catching a glimpse of the time. Now there's zero chance of falling back asleep.

I think about the dream and head into the studio with Kiki hot on my trail. I try to paint what I see, but at the same time, I want the images erased from my memory, not frozen on a canvas for a lifetime, so I paint how I feel instead.

I squirt some cadmium red, crimson, and black on my palette. I pick up my brush and cover the white canvas with various shades of deep, rich blood-red. With my palette knife in hand, I scoop up a little black paint, and in quick, short motions, swipe the knife over the reddened canvas, laying smears of darkness everywhere. Every motion is harsh and abrupt, almost violent, like the tearing feeling of my dream. The tears fall with every unforgiving movement. It's painful to paint, but the pent-up anxiety in me is spilling over, and I need to release it so it doesn't haunt me every waking minute.

I sit back, wipe my hands on a rag and admire my work, absolutely drained. As the sun begins to rise, I start getting ready for the work day. After getting my cup of fuel, I see my phone vibrate on the counter, I check my email, noticing the reply I was waiting for:

Elana Parks,

I received your signed contract. Opening night will be October 5. There will be hors d'oeuvres and an open bar. Please invite as many people as you wish. Your paintings will remain in the gallery until October 20. If there is a continuous turnout, we can discuss an extension period toward the end of the second week.

I will speak with you further as the date nears. During that time, I will have a team receive your works, and when you come to the gallery, we can discuss placement.

I also ask artists to write something about themselves—your background, inspirations, or motivations behind your pieces, etc. If you have a photo of yourself to accompany the summary, please provide, or I can have Charli make arrangements to take a few photos if you prefer. Congratulations again, and I look forward to working with you.

Mrs. Linda Monarch
Owner of Monarch Art Gallery

Unexpected Surprises

"How the hell do you get here first all of the time?" I give Kat a quick kiss as I put my things on the chair beside me. "I left fifteen minutes early and you still beat me."

A simple shrug of her shoulders is all she offers. "Sorry I didn't call you back the other day. I was on a date with this hot guy I met at Starbucks. Els, he was smoking, like that sexy lumberjack look, full beard, manscaped perfectly. Mmm," she hums, "caliente. He was magical in bed, you have no idea. He broke my uterus, like literally broke it. I had to go to the doctor and everything." Her eyes drift to her lap, adjusting the cold pack. "I'm off the market for a while. My vagina has PTSD, but it was so worth it."

The curious part of me wants to hear all the spicy details about how he was able to injure her baby-making machine, but the smarter half of me knows I should tread carefully. The less I know about her sexcapades, the better off I'll be.

"Anyways, that's why I've been quiet on my end. Please tell me you and Evan are good now? Like *good good*, if you know what I mean."

"Yeah, we're good," I say plainly. But it isn't long before my poker face cracks under the pressure of her stare. "Yes. We are *good good*."

"It's about fucking time," Kat shouts, slamming her hands against the table. "I thought you two would never get your shit together."

I laugh at her theatrics. She goes on about watching us both pine over each other, clueless about how the other truly felt, pointing out things I didn't really see, but makes all the sense in the world now. Hindsight is a real bitch.

James arrives, looking relieved that the work week is finally over. "How are my favorite girls doing on this blessed Friday evening? What'd I miss?" Kat offers up her newly given information, and all James says is "I know," shrugging as if it's yesterday's news.

"How do *you* know already?"

"Well, Katarina, if you returned some of your calls, you wouldn't be finding out this late in the game."

Before she can offer her rebuttal, I answer, "Trust me, James, you don't want to know why she didn't call us back." I eye her lap.

James looks down at her lap and says, "I definitely don't."

We discuss the past week's events, and I mention my news about the art gallery. James orders a fresh round of drinks to celebrate. My phone starts buzzing.

"Hello," I answer mid-laugh.

"Elana…it's your mother."

I hang up abruptly and watch my phone light up repeatedly, each time sending it to my mailbox. She won't ruin my night, not tonight.

****

As I head home, I go through my messages, deleting the ones from my mother before I can hear any of her slurred, drunken words. As exhausted as I am, I can't wait to call Evan and see how his day went, but mainly, I just want to hear his voice before I go to bed. I'm in the middle of texting him and turning the knob to my apartment when I'm taken aback.

There are beautiful white candles lit everywhere inside. I could feel the warmth of them hit me as I swung the door open wider, and smack dab in the middle of all that warmth is Evan, holding a bunch of white calla lilies wrapped together with a wide golden ribbon. He's too good to be true.

"Hey, beautiful."

I run to him and throw myself into his arms. He lifts me off the ground while I kiss him madly. Those butterflies arrive in time to make an encore performance as he holds me around my waist, gazing into my eyes. He smells divine, I'm liquid in his arms.

His warmth is contagious. I'm not sure if it's all the candles around my apartment or the desire that burns inside us both. He leans in with a kiss. "I have some good news."

"Tell me, tell me," I say, dancing with anticipation.

"I just got word that I got the lead in Louise Bradley's new movie. And the best part is that it films in New York in March."

I jump with excitement into his embrace. No words are needed to express how happy I am for him, and to know he'll be in town for weeks launches me into the clouds.

He holds my hand and leads me into the kitchen, where the table is set with more candles and two settings equipped with fancy silver lids. Even Kiki seems impressed, humming as she walks past Evan, grazing his ankles. He pulls out my chair and removes the silver lid off my plate, presenting me with a healthy stack of pancakes—my favorite.

Evan lifts his lid, revealing his larger stack, and sits across from me. "Now eat." He points to my plate, I won't ever win a battle if pancakes are his weapon of choice.

As I finish the last bits on my plate, I lean on my fist and watch him eat, no longer caring if I get caught. Being with him still feels like a dream, one I don't mind staying trapped in.

We clean up the kitchen together, and I playfully squirt him with water from the sink. Before I know it, it turns into a full-fledged water fight. Kiki takes cover in the living room, leaving me to fend for myself.

"Traitor!" I shout as her black tail escapes perfectly dry.

He turns the faucet against me, soaking me from head to toe. There isn't a single part of my clothing that isn't soaked through. My side hurts from laughing, and he clutches his, too.

"I remember filming a scene similar to this. I left the set and dried off, and the crew had to clean up."

"Welcome to the crew," I say, throwing him a towel before grabbing one for myself.

Before he begins his first day on the job as a crew member, he strips off his wet shirt and rings it out in the sink. He must feel my eyes on him, because he turns just enough to give me a sexy sidelong glance.

His hair drips onto his damp chest, and my eyes follow each droplet as it travels along his skin. My hands glide over him, tracing the dark lines of the tattoo that covers his chest, working my way to his shoulders and down his bicep. He watches without a word until I feel his fingers on my chin, tilting my head up.

"You are so beautiful, Elana."

I raise myself on my toes, placing a single kiss on his lips. "You're the beautiful one." My hands follow the contours of his body and the deep indents of his muscles while my eyes search his. In this lighting, they are more blue than normal. "Why does this feel like a dream?" The words are feathers on my tongue.

He cups my face. "You don't have to worry about waking up from this one." His mouth is so close to mine, not even a grain of salt could fit between us. "I'm here to stay."

I pull the hem of my shirt over my head, standing before him in only my bra and jeans. I reach for his hand and close my eyes while I place it over the scar. I know he can feel my heart race because I can hear it in my ears, a loud bassline that vibrates through us both.

I think of what Sebastian did that night, holding his palm over the scar, transferring his energy to me. I know Evan is no expert on Reiki, but deep down I wish he were. If only he could heal me the way Sebastian had for that moment, I could give Evan what he deserves, not just my heart, but my body, too.

He removes his hand, but I don't open my eyes, too scared I'll lose it in front of him again. I feel his lips on my neck, tender kisses that travel down to my chest until finally he places one sweet kiss over the scar. I open my eyes, looking down at him as he continues laying a trail of his warmth along my cold, damp skin. My hands clench to keep them from shaking. My breaths deepen as he makes his way back up to my neck, while his hand cups the back of my head, tangling his fingers in my saturated hair.

"Can we just do this tonight?" I ask sheepishly.

"We can do whatever you want," he says between kisses, his voice just as soft as his lips.

I retreat into the bathroom to change, then join him in the bed. I get lost in his sensual touches and kisses. Our lips lock, tongues dancing together as we test my limits carefully.

Eventually, Evan falls asleep, and we are a tangled mass of clothed limbs, draped and hooked around one another. I relax hearing his even breathing against my skin, knowing I can't disappoint him while he's sleeping. But I'm left wide awake, bothered by the fact that I'm not healed after all.

All I've ever wanted was him. For years, I've thought only about his touch, and now, when I try to give myself to him, the panic floods through my veins like a tsunami. Evan knows all my secrets, and yet there was so much Sebastian didn't know, but I was able to let go and relinquish the power that held me back. The relief I thought I had from knowing I was able to move past my restraints is gone, and the fear of intimacy returns, with the last person I ever thought I'd have a problem with.

I move my head on the pillow and notice it's wet with my tears, even though I had no idea I was crying. Silently, I let them continue to fall until my exhausted body is too strained to stay awake.

****

"Again?" I ask as he kisses my neck.

"I love you, Elana," his voice says.

"I love you too, Evan."

His tongue runs along my neck, working his way down to my chest. He kisses my naked breast, sending shivers down my spine, and I moan in anticipation. Evan's touch is delicate as his hands run over my body. I'm erupting with pleasure. His mouth finds my breast again, savoring the taste of it, and then a sharp pain rips through me as he sinks his teeth into my skin.

I jolt out of bed in one swift move, standing over Evan, shaking. His eyes are wide, and his breaths are quick.

"What's the matter? What happened?"

The tears are instant. "I thought it was you. It kind of felt like you, but then…" I throw my hands up to my face and crumble to the floor, too overcome with emotion.

The bed moves, and he appears right by my side, pulling me off the floor. "It was just a dream." He holds me in his arms, and I wrap mine around his waist, squeezing it while my cheek rests against his chest.

As my sniffling ceases, he lies us down, keeping my head on his chest. He smooths down my hair, knowing the gentle motions soothe me. His body warms mine, but all I can think about is how much he deserves a normal girl, one who isn't terrified to dream or have sex with her boyfriend.

"I'm used to you waking up after a bad dream. Granted, it didn't happen often."

"You deserve someone normal."

Evan's laugh is tired when he says, "You're my normal." His hands move down my arm in a soothing motion. He lets out a low yawn. "Remember that time I did *Fear Factor?*"

We say in unison, "Coffin of…" and before we could even finish what they called it, we both shudder.

"So gross," he says. "But I don't scare easily. I'm here, El. Don't forget that."

The exhaustion weighs me down, and the motion of his fingers make my eyes feel heavy. My faint smile is hidden from his view as I hear him say those words. He kisses the top of my head, and lets out a deep exhale.

He may act like he's content with just having me, but I know better. It'll only be a matter of time before frustration rears its ugly head. It always does. Hopefully, I'll be ready before that time comes.

Kindred Souls

EVAN LOOKS AT HIS WATCH as he shovels the spoon in his mouth. "I'm taking you to meet someone in a little while," he says with a mouthful of Cheerios. "And, no, I'm not telling you who, so don't even ask."

I let out a frustrated puff of air and shove a piece of toast covered in Nutella, and bananas in my mouth. "You know I don't like meeting new people."

As he rinses out his dish, he shoots me a reaffirming grin. The smile reminds me of my dream. I blink the image away, but the fact that it even happened sends my stomach in knots, and I lose my appetite.

I head into the bathroom and lock the door behind me. Both palms on the sink, I stare at myself in the mirror. I close my eyes and take in a few deep breaths through my nose and out my mouth, just like Sebastian told me to do whenever I feel stressed, nervous, or scared. I think of a beach—the warm sand between my toes, the peaceful sounds of the waves crashing along the shore. In no time, the feeling fades.

"You almost ready, Els?"

I glance in the mirror a final time, and take another breath. When I open the door, Evan is standing on the other side of it with my keys in hand.

We drive upstate; the scenery is beautiful. The lush greenery and the trees with their changing leaves are a breath of fresh air compared to the concrete facade of the city. Even the air is crisper and cleaner.

He parks in front of a warehouse. There isn't a single sign to signify what's inside.

"Are you sure this is the right place?" I look around to see if there is something nearby, but there's not much going on in either direction. "You're going to murder me here, aren't you?"

"Not this time."

We get out of the truck, and he grabs my hand, lacing his fingers with mine before knocking on the metal door. A bald man wearing paint-splattered overalls answers almost immediately.

"You must be Mr. Saunders. Did you find the place okay?"

"Yes, your directions were perfect, Mr. Harper. Did you get the delivery?"

"Please call me George. And, yes, everything is here."

Evan looks to me and squeezes my hand with a wide grin—no teeth, just turned-up lips and big eyes.

"I'm sorry," he says with his hand extended toward me. "You must be Elana."

"Nice to meet you, too, but I don't understand…" The confused look on my face is hard to slip by him.

"I didn't tell her why she's here," Evan confesses.

"Ah…well, come in, please. I'm sure it'll make more sense if you see my studio."

We walk down a short jailhouse-gray hallway and enter the main room. It's massive. The ceiling's breadth defies measure. It's the biggest art studio I've ever seen.

The studio is very industrial, raw, and cold, but there's a metal sculpture that stands tall in the center of the room, and it's hard not to be drawn to it. For starters, it's at least twelve feet tall, branching out even taller in some areas. If the height wasn't an eye-grabber, the sunrays beaming on it through the high windows, like mother nature's spotlight, would draw any person near.

At first glance it looks like a tree, but as I get closer, I see that it's a woman made of metal scraps of ranging colors. She's breathtaking, beautiful beyond compare. I feel a draft pass through my slack-jawed mouth. I walk around her, wanting to see every angle possible, loving the intricacies of the branches that were made to look like hair, and her curvy trunk of a figure. Like a kid in a candy store, I scan his other works, and each one is made from different mediums—paintings, clay sculptures, even some pieces with blown glass. Each item is worthy of being called a masterpiece.

"Over here, El," Evan calls out.

I travel in the direction of his voice, but my eyes continue to explore. In the corner, Mr. Harper and Evan stand in conversation right next to something familiar. My painting. And then I see another. I'm sure I'm wearing the most perplexed expression, because the more I look around, the more paintings of mine I see.

"George Harper is an artist, as I'm sure you've noticed, but he also specializes in stretching canvases and creating a one-of-a-kind framework. He came highly recommended. Since you were having your pieces showcased, I figured he could help create the perfect frame for each painting."

"Custom framework sounds expensive."

Evan shakes his head in disagreement. "It's free."

"Lies."

George watches us volley back and forth like two tennis players.

"Okay. It's expensive," Evan admits, "but I'm paying so it's free." Evan gives me his award-winning smile, but it's not enough to convince me.

"Uh, no, you're not," I fire back.

Evan hands me a slip of paper, an estimate for the paintings that are sitting in the corner. I glance at it quickly, pulling the paper closer to my eyes before backing away, making sure I'm not seeing double the numbers. Evan gives the ol' "I told ya so" look.

I hand him back the invoice. "Okay, so you were saying that you are paying for it."

"That's what I thought."

It'll probably take the rest of my life to pay him back, but the thought of having him for the rest of my life doesn't seem like a dreadful thing at all.

Evan excuses himself to take a call, and George and I get to work. He shows me how different frames can complement the look and feel of a painting. We take one piece at a time, and he gives me his ideas and opinions. Together we pair the perfect frame for each work of art.

He makes all the ornate frames by hand—chiseling, carving, staining, and painting the wood—to coordinate it with each picture. Some of the paintings I opt to leave unframed, keeping its original feel. George's knowledge is astounding, and like a sponge, I soak everything in.

While Evan and George work out the numbers, I take the time to look at the tree sculpture again. In a short while, George is by my side, also gazing at his work of art.

"How long have you been doing this?" I ask, gesturing to all the works surrounding us.

"About forty years," he responds. "My father was a welder for a machinery plant. I turned his craft into my medium."

"It's breathtaking."

"It's one of my favorites, too." He smiles wide. "It's in remembrance of my wife. She passed away ten years ago from breast cancer."

"I'm so sorry."

"She was a great woman—loving, kind, selfless, full of life. Even toward the end, she was more worried about how I was handling everything." He admires his work, still thinking deeply about her. "I started working on it shortly after Charlotte was diagnosed, but she never saw it finished. I think she'd be proud of it though."

I love how from afar you think it's just a tree made from iron, but when you get closer, that's when the magic happens. Everything changes. It's so smooth and fluid, you'd never know these were sharp, rough metal scraps. The shinier metal is laid in the perfect place for the light to reflect, while the duller metals create internal shadows. Her face is flawless, as if it were a mold of the most beautiful woman alive. The branching coils create illusion of motion in her hair, bending in an organic and natural way, as if a gust of wind blew past her just moments ago. Her strong but elegant arms stretch out, welcoming any force that comes, while her feet meld into the tree's roots.

"You can learn a lot by the art people create. Your pieces remind me of Charlotte's earlier work. You have a story to tell, but you hold back because you're scared to relive it. Masterpieces are born when you just let it flow. They are one hundred percent pure."

"I thought if I pushed things far enough back, they'd eventually disappear."

"The past never disappears. It'll always find a way back into your life." I think of last night's nightmare, and his words couldn't ring any truer. "It's a part of you, but it doesn't define you." He looks at my demeanor, catching the fear and apprehension in my eyes. "You may feel like you're full of darkness, but you have that light inside of you. It comes across in subtle ways. You hold back because you are letting your demons dictate your fear, with your harsh strokes and jagged linear work. Don't get me wrong—they're beautiful, too—but it'd be interesting to see how you would fair with the other side."

"I'm not sure there is another side," I add sadly.

"The way that man gushes about you," he scoffs, unconvinced, "there's definitely another side. Charlotte brought her pain into her artwork, but each time she left a piece of her past on the canvas. You're more than welcome to come back, and I'll show you some of her work. Frankly, I don't get much company. It's nice to have other people here."

Evan walks over, bored at whatever kept him busy for so long.

"I'd like that."

****

My eyes are blinded by spots. As we left the diner, a few paparazzi were waiting outside for Evan, a surprise for he and I both.

"Is it normal to not see for this long?"

Evan laughs as I rub my eyes with my palms, trying to regain my vision. "I guess it's not a secret anymore. Don't be surprised if they start following you—to work and Lizzy's. They're going to want to know everything about you, so chances are, if you think you're being followed, you probably are." He gets stuck behind a city bus and curses. "I just hope they keep their distance. Sometimes it can get dangerous."

"That's comforting," I deadpan.

My phone buzzes. Blocked number.

"Hello?" I release a long sigh when no one answers. "Hello?" I say again, more irritated.

"El-ahn-nahhh," the slurred words dribble out of her mouth.

"Ugh, what do you want?"

"I just need a couple of dollars, maybe like $100," she says, barely able to get out the words.

"What'd you do with the last $100 I gave you?" My once-happy mood has faded into a dark abyss.

"I had to pay rent to this lady who's letting me stay on her couch because you won't let me stay at my own fucking house."

"Dad left it to me and Timmy. It's not your house anymore. I don't have anything for you."

"I'm your mother. I raised you. You owe me." Her words are a slow, messy dribble.

"Don't kid yourself. You didn't raise anyone."

"Who was home with you while your fucking father was off doing God knows what in the middle of the night?"

"It's called working, something you know nothing about. Who was there when Timmy broke his arm falling off his bike? I was. Who put the fire out when you blacked out with a cigarette in your hand? I did." I feel my hands shaking, but I don't lose momentum. "Mrs. Saunders was a better mom than you ever were. I just wish Dad kicked you out sooner."

There is silence on the other end, and for a moment, I think she disconnected…until I hear her sobbing.

"I was a horrible mom. I want to get help."

"You say that all of the time. I'm sick of your empty promises."

"I'm sorry, Elana," she says, weeping. "I just need some money, and then I'll go to a meeting."

"You need more than a meeting. You need a facility that will watch over you."

"Elana," she snaps. "I need money. That's what I need."

"I'm hanging up now." She tries to plead her case, but I just hang up.

I stare out the window, trying to recall a time when my mother was loving and not a drunk. Only one memory surfaces. I was seven and Timmy was almost two. We went to the zoo. It always felt like the best day, because there were so many shitty days that followed it. We were happy though, I remember that much. Timmy doesn't have too many fond memories of her before she fell into the bottle. All he remembers is Evan and I taking care of him day in and day out.

I dial his number.

"Hey, Timmy, whatcha doing?"

"Working on a paper. Gotta work tonight. What's up?" Timmy asks.

"Just got off the phone with Mom."

"Yeah, she called me a couple hours ago. I didn't answer. Sebastian told me to tell you he says hi," Timmy repeats reluctantly. The two of them mumble something to one another.

"Tell Sebastian I said hello, and that I'll talk to him later." I can feel my cheeks burning as Evan's eyes narrow in on me. "I only called because Mom pissed me off, but since I have you on the phone, I wanted to make sure you are able to come to opening night."

"Hell yea." Timmy holds the receiver away from his mouth and yells to his frat brothers, "The Shark is having her art showcased in the city. Who's coming?" I hear cheers in the background, but Sebastian's voice is the only one I recognize. My stomach drops at the thought of Evan and Sebastian in the same room together.

"What did you just call me?"

"Oh, that? The guys gave you that nickname after the party. Elana 'The Shark' Parks." He laughs out loud, and I hear them chanting my nickname in the background. "Trust me, there were others, but this is the only one I approved of."

"Well, now we have an idea for those shirts you wanted."

"Yup. So, email me the information, and I'll spread the word. I can bring Samantha, right? I'm ready to let you meet her."

"Yeah. The two of you can crash at the apartment."

Timmy says goodbye, disconnecting right as Sebastian says the same.

"So Sebastian, huh?" Evan ogles me before eyeing the road again. "I was never the jealous type, but now that I'm with you, I kinda am."

"There's no need to be jealous."

He's focused on the road, but I can tell he's thinking about something. "You said that he was a 'Roman warrior god.' Even I don't think I can top that, and I'm famous." He starts to laugh, then backtracks. "Do I want to know what you meant when you said he helped you with your fear?"

I really don't remember saying that, but under the influence of Patrón, I could have told him where Hoffa was buried, for all I know.

"You rambled on and on about him, and from what everyone told me, you seemed really into him." The smile on his face is gone, replaced by a tight-lipped gaze.

"We just connected, and I was comfortable with him. I can't explain why. I'm grateful that he's in my life," adding, "just as a friend."

Evan's face tenses, and I watch as he clenches his jaw.

"He knows I'm in love with you, so you don't need to be jealous."

"How'd he help you?" he blurts.

I've rarely seen Evan angry about something, but I can tell he's getting more irritated as each second ticks by. "Evan, don't."

"Let me get this straight. You knew him for all of thirty seconds and you slept with him, but you've known me your entire life and you shake uncontrollably the second you take your shirt off?"

He's never raised his voice to me in this way before. It's terrifying, because he has a legitimate argument, one that I can't explain my way out of. I stare out of the window, upset that this day has turned into the biggest clusterfuck, and once again, Evan's inquisitions have given him more than he could chew. He couldn't just leave it alone. He had to ask questions that he had to have known he wouldn't like the answers to.

Tears start to pour out of my eyes as the tension builds—thick, dark, suffocating tension.

"And now you aren't going to say anything?" he mumbles under his breath.

My voice breaks up, knowing my emotions are as thin as my boss's hairline. "What do you want me to say?" I wipe the tears away. "How do you think I feel? All my life, you were the only one I ever wanted, and now that I have you, I can't even really *have* you. It's like giving a kid a gift they always wanted, but they aren't allowed to open the box. It's cruel, I know. You think it makes me feel good that I can't make you happy the way you deserve?" I shoot him an accusing finger. "I warned you last night you should run for the hills."

He tries to comment, but I just put my palms up, dismissing anything he was going to say. He parks the car in my spot, and before he takes the key out of the ignition, I'm already out of the truck.

"Elana, wait," he pleads, rushing toward me, hugging me from behind. "I'm sorry," he says against my ear. "I'm sorry."

Trapped in his embrace, I stand there. His face doesn't leave the crook of my neck. He offers kisses of forgiveness and apologies, but I know he'll always be thinking about what I was able to do with another man and not with him. My mouth has gotten me in enough trouble, so I remain silent.

"Fuck." His arms unwrap from me as he stares at the gated entrance. "They know where you live." I follow his gaze, noticing a white sedan and a man standing outside the car, snapping pictures of the two of us. "Let's go inside."

Pushing the Limits

I FORMALLY INVITE EVERYONE TO the art show—friends, the little family I have left, coworkers, anyone I would want there beside me. Thoughts of *Stolen Innocence* come to mind; I won't be able to sweep it under the rug or hide its meaning behind a desk much longer, but I can't think about that discussion now, still too mentally exhausted from the argument in the car not too long ago.

"What are you doing?" he asks, plopping himself next to me.

As much as he's apologized, it's hard to move past it. My mood hasn't improved much. The loneliness I feel won't leave me alone. Evan won't ever be able to understand something I don't understand myself.

"Emailing everyone."

I close my laptop and place it under the couch, along with my pen and pad, and tilt my head back. All my thoughts feel heavy, weighing me down. I'm drowning in the silence.

I get up from the couch and unbutton my blouse, breathing quickly. I've been pushing upriver from this my whole life, and I'm too tired to keep swimming against the current.

"El, don't."

I move toward Evan, straddling his body. I bring my lips to his, crushing them with a timid urgency. "Take off my bra."

"Elana..." he starts to contest, but when my tongue runs along his neck, he doesn't finish, but hums with approval.

His hands find the clasp, easily undoing the hooks. He runs his fingertips along my shoulders, pushing down the straps. I continue the breathing that Sebastian taught me as I take off Evan's shirt, knowing his bare skin against mine will soothe me. It must. His hands find my breasts, cupping them as I continue to suck on his neck. The warmth of his hands against my skin causes the rest of my body to react. My nipples harden as he rubs them between his fingers, giving me so much pleasure that I stop what I'm doing and throw my head back, arching my body closer to his.

My breathing deepens as he runs his tongue over my breast, heightening my senses. His hair curls around my fingers while I hold him there, letting him lick and suck as his other hand wraps around my waist. An unexpected moan creeps out of me, and I can feel him smile against my skin.

He runs his tongue along my chest, working his way back up my neck, finding my lips again, parting them. Our kiss becomes ravenous and wild.

I feel his heat beneath me, pressing into my thigh.

"Can we go into the bedroom?"

"El…" he starts, then looks into my eyes, seeing how serious I am. He rises, my body still straddling his, carrying me to the other room. I lick the spot under his ear, flicking my tongue as he walks us.

He lowers us slowly onto the bed, but I sit up, wanting to be the one to undo his jeans. My fingers work quickly as I push them to the floor.

His hands creep up my body. I react to his touch, lusting for more. He rolls my nipples between his fingers again as he kisses my stomach. Evan's tongue moves along my skin, and I can't get enough. His fingers hook the sides of my panties, hitching my breath.

"You okay?" he whispers.

"Mmm…hmm," I lie.

He lies on top of me, searching my face for a signal, kissing me with the sweet tenderness I need.

"I want this, Evan," I whisper. "I really do."

His fingers hook my panties again, lowering them as he takes his boxers off at the same time. I look down, ignoring my vulnerability, concentrating only on him. Every muscle was carved by hand from the finest marble. The deep indents of his pelvic muscle, his chest, his abs…they all make me want to touch him more, feeling every toned muscle along the way. I want every bit of his skin flush against mine, knowing his touch will keep the demons at bay.

"Did you just lick your lips at me?" he asks playfully.

I guess I had without realizing, and I start to laugh, covering my face with my hands. His hands fall to either side as he hovers above me, also giggling. He starts to kiss the underside of my jaw, and I uncover my face, throwing my arms around his neck. His erection presses against me, and I spread my legs for him.

He reaches down, but I stop him, wanting to touch him first. I hold him in my hands, stroking his length as we kiss. He emits a moan as he reaches down my body, and his fingers find my waiting lips.

We pleasure each other with our hands. I enjoy his touch. My body reacts to everything he does, moving with his fingertips as he stimulates me. I nibble on his lower lip as his fingers continue to work their magic, sending booming pulses right through me. My legs tremble with anticipation.

I can't believe I denied him, denied *myself* of this pleasure. Before I'm about to erupt, I move his smooth, long shaft closer, raising my pelvis up to meet his. The pain of the connection fades quickly as the pleasure begins.

He moves slowly, almost tentatively, until he sees the longing in my eyes. I'm more than okay. I'm in pure bliss, finally able to give myself to the man I love.

Evan's hips pick up speed. His strokes lengthen, filling me deeper. I wrap my legs around his body, digging my nails into his back as I release another moan. Our bodies are slick with sweat as we continue to move with one another, gradually picking up speed. My thighs tremble as my insides vibrate with pleasure. Uncontrollable sounds seep out of my mouth, as his long strokes get faster, and I feel his entire rock-hard length.

"Give yourself to me, Elana," he whispers through labored breaths.

As soon as his words ring through the air, I find my release—my muscles tighten around his erection, and I let out a guttural moan from the bottom of my diaphragm. Evan's body bucks uncontrollably, releasing himself into me as both of our breathing grows erratic. Our spasms come to a stop, and he slowly lowers himself next to me. The heat radiates off both our bodies.

"What are you thinking about?" he asks, winded.

I take a moment to compose my thoughts. So many things are running through my head—elation that I was able to give myself to Evan, the feeling of pure ecstasy that's coursing through my veins, the fact that I'm still terrified to do it all over again.

I say the only thing I'm one hundred percent sure of. "I love you."

Coming Clean

WITH THE SHOWCASE ONLY A few weeks away, my mini studio is packed with beautifully framed paintings, courtesy of George. Most are packed and ready to be sent to the gallery, but a few are loose ends I need to tie up.

Evan is in Chicago, filming a commercial, and for once I'm okay with it. I want to be able to sit down with Timmy, James, and Kat, without Evan hovering, worrying about me, while I share my experience and explain what they will see during the showcase. Timmy agrees to visit over the weekend with the impression that it has to do with the house we grew up in. He obliges, but with a specific demand—a home-cooked meal. I arrange another meal for Kat and James.

Being the procrastinator that I am, I avoid thinking about that conversation and decide to work on my summary for the showcase instead.

> Elana Parks, 26
>
> Elana grew up with her father and brother on Long Island. After graduating with a bachelor's in fashion marketing and merchandising, her main love was always the canvas, where she would escape into the world of paint to cope with a traumatic incident. Follow her journey of healing in her showcase called "The Truth."

****

The week takes its toll on me, as I had to share my experience with Kat and James. Both broke down in their own way. Kat sobbed. James's fists clenched tight, his jaw looking no less tense before he pulled me into a body-crushing hug. But after having told them, it gave them a better understanding of the person they've known so many years. I never felt closer to my friends, and their overwhelming support makes me wish I would have trusted them with the truth sooner. A lot of tears were shed that night, but I know more will come as I dread telling my little brother this weekend.

I opt out of going to Lizzy's on Friday, as I'm too stressed about telling Timmy, so I try to get a decent night's rest. As if God himself knew what I needed, I got just that—a peaceful night of nothing, no dreams, just pure sleep.

While I prep for dinner, I speak with Sebastian, who called to see how I was doing. He's always been easy to talk to, giving me clarity about how I feel, offering ways to cope with certain stresses, trying to provide me with the confidence to face and defeat the monsters running wild in my thoughts and dreams.

Kat comes by with her equipment, ready to take the picture that'll be hung at the showcase along with my written summary. I want this picture to embody who I am, not some overly glamorized version of myself for the sake of a nice photo. My loose brown waves cascade over my shoulders, and I keep my makeup natural. Since most of these pieces are raw versions of my inner thoughts, my picture should represent the same thing.

I meet Kat in the parking lot, noticing the white sedan outside of the gate. I try to pretend it's not there, but I know they want to get pictures of Evan's new flame, preferably doing something scandalous.

Kat's intuitive eyes scour the landscape, looking for the precise location best accompanied by the current lighting. She takes some pictures near the pool, which is amazingly clean, then by the freshly planted pansies, decorative cabbages, and an array of mums, a rich backdrop of fall colors. Not to mention the beautiful orange and yellows that Mother Nature provided with the changing of the seasons.

Kat brings up Evan, capturing the natural smile I make just by hearing his name.

As she snaps away, offering me direction, I feel overcome with emotion. "I just wanted to say thank you. Thank you for doing this, thank you for being one of my best friends and sticking by me through everything."

She comes to my side and embraces me. "Friends till the end, right?"

I nod, fighting back the tears, trying to shake the emotions away for now. Her words warm me from within. After she thinks she's gotten enough good shots, she comes back to my apartment and helps me finish making Timmy's lasagna.

My nerves running in nervous jolts, I'm startled by the knock on the door.

"I'll get it," Kat says, quickly wiping her hands on a towel.

We both rush to the door, wanting to be the first to greet Timmy. She pushes me out of the way and swings the door open, sticking out her tongue at me. "Timmy!" She throws her arms around him, hugging him tightly. "College does a body good." She feels his biceps, clearly noticing he's been working out. "Te ves bien, Papito."

I gag. "Gross."

They seem to find it amusing, and they play into the flirting more. I push her off my brother and wrap my arms around his waist, hugging him snuggly.

He gasps, "Can't…breathe…"

Kat retreats into the kitchen. She emerges with her purse in one hand, her camera equipment in the other. "It was good seeing you, Timmy. I've got to get home and see how these pictures came out. Call me if you need me." She gives me the biggest smooch on the cheek and closes the door behind her.

"I spoke with *your* mother yesterday. When was the last time you talked to her?" he asks, knowing how tedious that subject is. "She was hysterical."

"She tricked me into answering two days ago. Why does she only curse me out?"

He shrugs his shoulders lazily. "Don't be mad, but I kind of let it slip that you have an art show."

Timmy and I tear into the salad while the lasagna sets, talking about his school, Samantha, Evan, and my nerves about the show. He brings up Sebastian, admitting he was bummed to hear it didn't work out, since he liked seeing me visit more often. For a while, I forget why I asked him to visit in the first place. I keep pushing the conversation off, plating up the lasagna, letting him devour two plates before I can polish off a quarter of mine.

"The reason why I wanted you to come today is because I need to tell you something."

"You're pregnant." He exhales. "And you don't know if it's Evan's or Sebastian's. I'll call Maury Povich right now. He'll get to the bottom of this."

"Your imagination is colorful, but no," I say, pausing to gather my thoughts. "Do you remember when I was thirteen? When I stayed in my room and didn't come out?" It was such a long time ago, who knows if he'll remember?

"Your prolonged cootie virus. Later, I figured it was because you got your female friend." In saying the words, he shivers as if a gust of cool air hit him, still grossed out by how the female anatomy cycles.

I turn in my chair, truly facing him, and he senses the intensity of what I'm about to say. He drops his fork and turns to me, too.

"When Dana came to town that summer, she brought me to a party. Something bad happened." The look on my brother's face is unnerving. Being in college, he knows and hears about what can happen at parties. I continue, "I was alone in a room, and then this guy came in. He was drunk, and he forced himself on me." I spare the details and try to avoid using the word "rape." "I thought I'd get in trouble for going, and he threatened that if I told anyone, he'd know. I was scared."

"You were..." Timmy can barely get the words out of himself. His voice is stuck in his throat. "Raped?"

The truth feels too harsh to say aloud, so I nod. "There's a painting in the showcase, a self-portrait, of that time. I didn't want you to see it without an explanation first."

He sits speechless. The pained look on his face says everything his words cannot. His lips are white, pressed so tightly together no blood can circulate through. His shoulders are high and tense, and he's fixated on one spot of the table. He doesn't even breathe.

"Are you okay?" I ask.

His tears begin to fall, and it's at that sight that mine soon follow. His emotional display becomes a low sob, something I've never seen him do before, not when Mom thrashed at him with an extension cord, and not when Dad passed away. I get up from my chair and try to console him, letting my own tears dry on my cheeks. I need to be strong for him like when we were younger. He holds me tighter than he ever has before.

"My own sister," he sobs to himself.

"I'm okay now. Everything is okay."

He keeps holding me, and I let him. It's a big pill to swallow, and I don't expect him to be fine about it, but I'm not exactly sure what else to say other than to keep reaffirming that I'm okay.

"Do you know who it is? I'll kill him."

I shake my head, glad I don't know the name of the monster that could assault a child. For years it's been my burden to bear, becoming second nature to me, wearing it like a second skin, and now all the people who matter to me will carry a piece of it, too, because of what I mean to them.

"Does everyone know? Did Dad?"

"No one knew until recently."

Timmy and I have always been close, closer than most siblings. We were never afraid to hug each other or share our feelings. I always thought our bond was strong because we had to fend for ourselves, leaning on each other for support since Mom wasn't capable. But through the years, I've learned that while our upbringing did give us a special bond, we didn't need it. We'd have each other's back regardless. We were siblings by chance, but we've always been friends by choice.

With him knowing my darkest secret, I hope it brings our family of two that much closer.

I wave Timmy off, appreciating the brisk autumn breeze on my warmed face. Watching him sob, I realize that the sight of him so torn up is exactly the reason why I've protected him from the truth.

I wish I could take it back, erase the memory of the last hour from his brain.

I call Evan to let him know how it went, and all the emotion I kept from Timmy spills over. I break down. It's times like these that I wish Dad was alive to give me one of his hugs. Each hug was different depending on its purpose, and right now, I could go for his comforting one. But I'm grateful he never knew what happened to his little girl.

****

With the showcase a little over a week away, I organize the framed paintings, arranging them for shipment to the gallery. I call George and make arrangements to stop by and pick up the final framed pieces for the show.

In the little bit of free time I have, I drive to the mall. It isn't until that moment that I feel like I'm being followed. Evan said it could happen. Pictures of us have circulated on various websites, and on a few occasions, random people have recognized me. It's not all that it's cracked up to be. The feeling is unnerving, and I can't shake it no matter what kind of breathing I do. I look over my shoulder like some covert operative, but I see only other mall patrons. I put my earbuds in my ears, listen to one of my more calming playlists, and hope it distracts me until I return to the safety of my gated apartment complex.

I flip through racks of dresses, stopping when I find a black capped-sleeve A-line dress that falls right above the knee. Feeling triumphant that they have my size, I try to push my luck a little further and search for a statement necklace that'll accentuate the neckline. Two girls stare and whisper to one another. They either recognize me or find it odd that I left the house in paint-splattered clothes. I decide to purchase the first thing the sales girl shows me and leave. The uneasy feeling was just too overwhelming, especially being by myself.

When I get back from the mall, the white sedan that's been parked in front of my building for the past few weeks is there. I admire his dedication, but I'm still amazed that anyone cares about who I am, even if it's for the sole purpose of being Evan Saunders's girlfriend. But then again, this is Evan Saunders, actor on the rise, snagging lead roles that half of Hollywood were trying to score. To add to his list of accomplishments, he's also a dream maker. He made a dream that I never knew I wanted come true.

I hang up my new dress and feel a flutter of eagerness, realizing that before I know it, an art gallery will be showing my work for all to see, all thanks to Evan.

One Week

THE ELEVATOR DINGS, AND A delivery man peers down the hallway. I summon him in my direction.

"Elana Parks?"

I sign for the two packages, one long rectangular box and another square one. I rush into my apartment and open the long one first. The smile is instant.

The card reads:

> El,
>
> Just a little something to show you I care, now you have two pair. Haha, I rhymed. I love you.
>
> 11

I unwrap the calla lilies, careful not to harm a single petal. I've always loved the curvature of the petals, so feminine and elegant. They've always been a favorite of mine, and they have no real flowery scent.

I grab the other box and hold it to my ear like Timmy and I used to do Christmas morning. I pull on the red ribbon, releasing the bow, and tear at the matte black paper. My eyes widen as I see the magical name "Christian Louboutin" printed on the lid. My mouth drops. It's as if angels are singing above me. I slowly raise the cover off the box, peeking inside.

After removing them from the storage bag, I'm left with the most gorgeous black strappy heel. The striking red bottoms instantly make the hairs on the back of my neck stand on edge. The Christian

Louboutin Balota. The six-inch heels with two-inch platform are exquisite with their crossed, woven straps. The craftsmanship is superb, not a stitch or seam out of place compared to half of my other footwear. They are magnificent. And more importantly, they'll go perfect with my outfit on Friday.

I call Evan at once and subject his ears to my squeals of delight, as if I just saw my favorite boy band.

****

George greets me at the door. "Welcome back."

We walk to the corner of the studio, and I review the remaining pieces he had of mine, loving every single frame we designed together. They mirror what I envisioned them to look like. He's the painting whisperer, able to understand the emotion and meaning behind each work and know which frame would complement it.

Finally, I see her. The dark, tortured painting stares back at me. I gave him free range to create whatever he felt worked for her. She doesn't have an ornate or detailed frame, or even a simple one. I look at her unfinished canvas and it makes sense to me, too. My brush strokes ended before the canvas did, and in most cases the frame would fill in the gap, bringing out the center image. But with her, the unfinished edges make it more raw, more shredded and rushed, more real. At the time, it hurt too much to finish. It reflects that emotion perfectly.

"I sat with her for a while before I realized she was perfect the way she was."

"She is, isn't she?" I admit, finally seeing it, too. "Thank you so much for everything. Your work is phenomenal."

We both look at *Stolen Innocence* for a minute, really soaking her in. "My job is easier when the pieces are so lovely." "Lovely" isn't exactly the word I would use to describe her, but I know he sees something in my paintings that I don't.

He shows me one of his late wife's pieces of artwork. He was right when he said we were similar. Side by side, I can see it. She also has a self-portrait from when she was younger. She, too, is bruised and battered but also rail-thin and malnourished. I can't help but shed a tear at the sight of it, feeling the pain she must've felt.

After saying goodbye to George, I spend a few hours at the gallery, discussing lighting and placement for each piece. It's nice to have Charli there. The friendly face is appreciated, as the entire process feels so overwhelming. She and Mrs. Monarch walk through with me, trying to find the right spot for each painting, so that they are arranged in an order that provides a good flow into the gallery, telling the story of my journey.

The focal piece will have a whole wall of her own. I wanted it to be on the exposed brick wall, with just enough lighting to see her and not much else. She's been my dark secret. She still lives in the dreams that only come out at night. It's only fitting she rests in a cold, darkened corner of the gallery.

****

We both hear the knob turn. Our eyes shift to the door. I'm not sure if she knows who's going to walk through them, but I do.

"There's my girls," Evan sings sweetly.

We both rise as he walks in our direction. He drops his bag to the floor and leans in, picking Kiki up off the floor and kissing the top of her head. She closes her eyes, purring with delight.

"Seriously?" I put my hand on my hips, waiting impatiently for my kiss.

"You want one too?" Evan flashes his sexiest devilish grin.

I playfully move out of his reach. "I don't want Kiki's sloppy seconds."

He laughs and grabs me, pulling me into him. He gives me what I've been craving. She meows between us, clearly jealous, and he sets her down before wrapping me in his love again.

"You been eating?"

"Too nervous." The only thing I've been gnawing on is my nails, biting them down to stumps. And on top of that, I've lost ten pounds in a matter of three days. Most girls wouldn't complain, but I'm looking sickly, and there's nothing attractive about it.

Evan and I order food, but I'm far too anxious about tomorrow to eat. I go into the spare room to let off some steam, taking out all my worries on a clean canvas. Normally, I would curse myself about all the clutter in the studio, but with most of my work waiting for me at the gallery, the room feels naked and I miss it. I stop to think about what George said about fully going to *that* place, reaching into the heart of the darkness. It's what I need to do. I need to leave it on the canvas and not be afraid of it anymore.

I take out my headphones, grab a brush, and sink into my thoughts, letting my subconscious take control. I paint his watery lips, dimpled chin, the beauty marks on his cheek and neck, the slight bump on his nose, his large hands. I still can't remember his eyes. I know they were bloodshot, but I don't remember the shape or color, and it frustrates me. How can I not remember that? After all the nightmares he's starred in, it's the one detail I can't recall.

Before I know it, two hours fly by, and I'm looking at a finished painting. It somewhat resembles him. I know there's something else missing besides his eyes, but I can't put my finger on it.

Ever since I started painting, I've been afraid to face him head-on, but now that he's on the canvas, it's not so scary after all. George was right. I was using painting as my therapy, but I wasn't digging deep enough. Until now.

The Truth

"El, this is Samantha."

Samantha shakes my hand with determination. She's stunningly attractive—tanned skin like Sebastian, almond-shaped eyes, high cheekbones, full lips, and the most perfectly shaped brows a girl could ask for. She stands a full foot shorter than Timmy, but her smile and aura make her appear taller than she is.

Timmy introduces Evan to Samantha. She's completely starstruck, blushing as she shakes his hand. Then Timmy points it out, and she buries her head in his chest. I swat at him for making her feel uncomfortable.

"This one time, Evan and I were at a diner. It had to be like 4:00 a.m. The girl approached our table and asked for Evan's autograph." Evan starts laughing, clearly remembering this story. "She was wasted when he offered to take a pic with her. I guess between the alcohol and her excitement, she threw up on his shoes. So your reaction was actually pretty mild in comparison."

"Those were brand new Chucks too."

I can tell she's different, just by the way Timmy holds her. He looks down as she comes out of hiding, kissing her head before enveloping her in his arms. As she holds onto him tightly, I can see it in his eyes. He's in love.

We sit on the couch and kill some time getting to know Samantha before we start to get ready. It's a pleasant distraction from my nerves, but before we know it, we retreat to our spaces to get dressed for opening night.

I sit in front of my vanity, straightening my hair, when Evan walks in, already dressed—stark white shirt fitted as if it were made specifically for his body, black pants clearly tailored by a top-of-the-line seamstress, topped off with a black silk tie.

"Nervous?"

"I might throw up on your shoes."

"You can if you need to." He laughs as he gently massages my shoulders. "Everyone will be there to support you," he reminds me. "The car will be here in thirty minutes, so we can get there early. Will you be ready by then?"

I turn to him. "What if everyone hates my paintings? Or think they're weird?"

"That's not a possibility. I believe in you, and clearly Mrs. Monarch wouldn't have given you this opportunity if she didn't see something in your work." He gives me his award-winning grin and leaves me to finish getting dressed.

The longer I look in the mirror, the more nervous it makes me. The butterflies start planning a mutiny in my empty stomach, and I realize I couldn't throw up even if I wanted to.

I get off the chair and put on my dress and Evan's new gift, my new Christians.

"Babe, the car will be here in—" He stops himself. "Damn, you look...you look amazing." He stands behind me, and we look in the mirror together. We look great separately, but we look pristine together.

I take a deep breath. "I think I'm ready now."

****

My hands shake, and the butterflies are fully ready to burst. The only thing that keeps me grounded is Evan's hand in mine. We arrive to the gallery, and thankfully, it's a beautiful October night. The sky is clear, the air, crisp. We pull up to the gallery, and if it weren't for another one of Evan's quick pep talks, I might not have left the truck.

"You're here!" Charli shouts, rushing over in her own gorgeous black dress and throwing her arms around me.

I peer around like a tourist, eyes and mouth wide open, as if seeing a sight for the first time.

"It's exactly how I pictured it."

"Mrs. Monarch has been waiting for you. I'll go get her."

I walk around the large gallery, leaving everyone else behind, wanting to do a walk-through on my own. I follow the story told by my paintings, loving that every request was accommodated. And then I reach my destination, the darkened corner. It was as if I'd taken a wrong turn and found myself in an alley, with only dim lighting and cold brick to keep me company. Abandoned in that alley is *Stolen Innocence*.

Seeing her hung up there brings mixed emotions to the surface—fear, sorrow, pride, renewal. My eyes begin to well, but I don't try to fight it. I want to hug that little girl and tell her everything will be okay.

"Ms. Parks?" Mrs. Monarch says, breaking me out of my reverie.

"Everything looks amazing. Thank you so much." I gush as I blot the stray tears off my cheeks.

Mrs. Monarch gives me a side hug. The black bell-sleeves of her jacket wrap around me like a protective cape. "Don't worry, darling. This is going to be a great night for you and your work. I hope you don't mind, I've invited a few of my elite clientele. Are you ready?"

I feel ready, but before I walk away from the little girl, I blow her a kiss. This is a big night for the both of us.

As I weave my way through the gallery, I notice a few people already walking around. I spot Evan's parents immediately, needing the comfort of some familiar faces. Evan joins us, and offers me a glass of champagne, but all I can do is nurse it. I'm too nervous to drink, especially on an empty stomach.

James and Kat gather around Timmy and Samantha as others break off into little groups, staring at various works on the wall.

I'm surprised to see some of Evan's actor friends and colleagues from LA. I take a minute to myself, soaking in the gravity of the situation, one sip at a time. The elation of sharing the company of celebrities never gets old, but I try to look indifferent. I gaze around in awe, watching everyone smile and have a good time. It all feels so surreal, like a fantasy.

"Hey, good-lookin'." His smooth caramel voice, so sweet and rich, still hits the spot.

I spin around. My stomach bottoms out as Sebastian stands in front of me in his tall Roman warrior god gorgeousness. He wears his fitted navy suit and tie so well.

"You didn't think I'd miss this, did you?" He flashes me his pearly whites. "I did a walk-through already." He grabs my wrist and kisses my hand. "You're amazing at what you do."

My cheeks warm, but I can't blame the few sips of champagne for it. That's just my body's usual reaction to his words.

"So where is he? I want to meet the guy who finally came to his senses."

I look around quickly. Evan is nowhere in sight. "Um, he's around here somewhere. Thank you for coming. It wouldn't really be the same without you." I give him a huge hug and kiss on the cheek. The nerves I had moments ago vanished just like every other time I've spent with him. "There are plenty of single ladies here that would be more than willing to play nurse with you." I offer a little wink, and he rolls his eyes.

"Kat and James said they saw you. You must be Sebastian," Evan says as they size each other up. Sebastian is the first to extend his hand, and Evan takes it. I notice the power behind it, both their knuckles white, and it lasts longer than most handshakes should.

"Evan Saunders, El has told me so much about you. I'm a fan of your work."

I laugh inwardly. It seems like both are lowering the bass in their voices as they speak. Not to mention, Sebastian isn't that big of a fan. He saw one movie of his and wasn't impressed. In all fairness to Evan, he was a side character, and most of his screen time ended up on the cutting room floor. That movie bombed, but in the next one he did, he had a bigger role, and it was more successful.

Sebastian directs his attention to me again. "Congratulations, good-lookin'. I knew you were special the moment we crashed into each other, and now I realize just how right I was. You should be very proud. I know Tim is." He looks to Evan. "Evan, it was nice meeting you. She's an amazing woman. Please don't hurt her." He grabs my hand, kisses it before spotting Timmy and Samantha in the crowd, and walks away.

"Did he have to call you 'good-lookin' in front of me?" Evan finds him in the crowd and squares his shoulders. "And how tall is he anyway? Jesus."

I lace my fingers in Evan's, trying to stifle my laughter. "He calls me that all the time." It wasn't the response Evan wanted to hear. "Your jealousy is adorable, but not tonight. And I know, right, he's friggin' tall."

As I walk around, chatting with the guests, introducing myself to some of Mrs. Monarch's elite, I notice Timmy standing in front of the infamous painting, Samantha by his side. He practically runs away, leaving Samantha behind, wiping tears from his eyes. I hurry after him, following him outside of the gallery.

"Timmy, where are you going?"

"I need a minute, Els." His strides are long, too long for me in these heels, but I continue my chase.

"Timmy, talk to me."

He paces, raking his hands through his dark-blond hair. "I tried to prepare myself for what I might see, but nothing…nothing I could've imagined could come close to the reality of it." He holds out his arm, urging me to keep my distance. "I just need a minute. Please."

I hug myself as I head back into the gallery, leaving Timmy alone on the city sidewalk. I stand with Evan and some friends, trying to play the happy host as best I can when I hear the familiar voice. My insides turn to knots with each spoken word. The sound curdles my blood. My hands start to tremble. This can't be happening to me.

Unwanted Guests

ALL EYES ARE DIVERTED TOWARD the door, and that's when I see it—Timmy struggling to get a grip on our mother. She yanks her arm away from him, and he tries to wrangle her again.

"I'm her mother!" the slurred words trickle out, loudly, and aggressively.

My head falls in shame as they argue. I know I can't run away from this, so I head in their direction, offering apologetic grins to everyone's nosy gaze.

She breaks away from Timmy again, tripping over her floral frock, almost knocking over a couple standing nearby. I offer another apologetic smile.

I smell the alcohol before I'm even near her. She rushes toward me, grabbing my wrists, refusing to let go. Her hair is a matted mess on one side, and it looks like she put her makeup on with a spackle knife on a speeding subway train—her fuchsia lipstick is smeared, and her eyeliner looks like it's melting off her face. She's the epitome of hot mess.

"Here's the guest of fucking honor, everyone."

Timmy is by our side in a heartbeat, whispering in her ear, trying to pull her away from me, but she won't budge; her feet are trapped in blocks of cement. The fury in his face is evident to everyone.

"You have to leave," I demand, feeling the rage pervade every fiber of my being.

Suddenly, the room blisters like a furnace as I notice all eyes on us, and the whispers that follow.

I plead. "If you ever loved me, leave. *Please*. I'm begging you. I'll give you whatever you want, just please. Do you need money?" I start to open my clutch, rummaging for any cash I stashed inside.

She slips out of Timmy's grasp, slithering through the crowd like a drunken anaconda. Everyone escapes her path as she winds around corners, on the hunt for something.

We're right on her tail. Evan and Sebastian quickly follow us into the darkened corner where the focal piece hangs.

Her eyes grow moist, the eyeliner running down her cheeks. "You deserved this," she croaks with a scowl.

My knees weaken, and I lose all the air in my lungs. I don't know how I've managed to remain standing, until I realize Sebastian's helping me stay upright. Everyone in earshot felt my horror. Never in a million years did I expect my own blood to utter those words. My own mother.

As Timmy and Evan snatch her forcefully, she eyes me up and down with a look of sheer terror. Sebastian drags me to the back of the gallery, away from the meddling stares. My body's gone numb.

"Don't listen to her. El, look at me."

I can't move. I can't speak. I can barely fill my deflated lungs, let alone focus on anything. Then Sebastian shakes my shoulders lightly, but I remain in a fog of hurt and confusion.

Still fighting to break through the haze, I ask, "Why would she say that?"

He pulls me into his arms. Clenching him as tight as I can, I feel the warm burn of my tears, and I start bawling. The level of betrayal. I'd rather be beaten with an extension cord for the rest of my life than feel those words again. They felt like serrated daggers meant only for me. Sebastian keeps repeating that everything will be okay, rubbing between my shoulder blades. And just like on our special night, I need him now more than ever.

I hear Timmy and Evan's voices behind me. Sebastian's hand drops as Timmy tries to turn to face him, but my hold on my Roman god remains tight.

"She's gone." Timmy turns me around, determined to make things right. "I'm so sorry, Els. It's all my fault. I'm so sorry."

I pull Timmy into a hug. Blaming him had never been a thought in my mind. His hold on me tightens. "Don't blame yourself."

We both pull away, and three sets of eyes drink me in, their faces all wearing the same expression.

"I must look a mess."

"You look beautiful," Evan and Sebastian say in unison, before turning to one another. Evan bites his lip.

"Knock it off, you two." I run my finger under my eye, and it comes back with a dark stain. "Can one of you find Kat? She always has a mini Sephora in her bag."

Timmy and Sebastian do as I bid, and in no time at all she's by my side, hugging me with her bag of beauty. We quickly retreat to the bathroom, where she wipes, pats, and blots, swipes, strokes, and pokes. When I look in the mirror, the only sign of my tears are the faint remnants left in the whites of my eyes. She's a miracle worker.

I swing open the door. Evan is the only one waiting outside. He joins me at once, interlocking his fingers with mine, bringing them up to his lips.

"You okay?" he asks.

"Just don't leave my side."

"Never."

Day Off

THE LAST THING I WANT to do is traipse around the city on my day off, but here I am, hand in hand with Jessica, being dragged from one boutique to another. The only reason she brought me with her is because she wanted someone to hold her bags, like her own personal bellboy. I'm just missing the little outfit. She'd probably like dressing me up, having me play the part. Freak.

"Ooh, let's check this place out," she says, pointing to another boring ass gallery.

We need art like I need another hole in the head, but I follow her all the same. I look around, spotting the numerous guys that were also dragged in here against their will. We all wear matching looks of annoyance and defeat.

"They look so angry," Jessica comments, standing in front of one covered in red, with black lines cut through the paint. "It looks like a crime scene."

My eyes wander to the different canvases around me, each with its own distinct theme. "Well, you're the one that wanted to come here."

She takes forever looking at each painting, so I walk ahead. One abstract crapsterpiece after another, none of which anyone will ever be able to interpret but everyone will still have an opinion about all the same. There's nothing I hate more than paint splattered on a canvas, resembling the work of an infant with some ominous name like "At," and it fetches for $1.8 million with obnoxious asshats standing in front of it making comments like, "Yes, I get it, it makes total sense." Really?

164

Then I come across a painting that catches my eye. It's another blood-red painting smeared with black, but somehow, this one is different. There's something about it that hits home. I feel like a total poser, but I want it.

"Babe, come here," she beckons.

She stands in a dimly lit corner of the gallery.

"They gotta fix the light over here." I look around, noticing the intentional use of low-wattage bulbs. My interest is piqued.

I suck in a quick breath through my teeth as Jessica hooks arms with me.

"I know, how sad," she says, leaning her head on my shoulder without breaking eye contact.

My heart flutters as the image sinks in. That's my girl. That's my first. She's exactly as I remember her. Beautiful.

Jessica leaves me, finally withdrawing her eyes, but I could look at it all day. I could live here. My bite mark is right above her breast, with my handprint reddened on her cheek, and as the proud owner, I look at my hand again, trying to relive the moment my palm connected. It's perfect. Every nerve ending in my body is on high alert, like I've been struck by lightning.

I walk away from the piece with an urgency, searching for any information about the artist lying around. On a column near the purchasing desk, I see a framed photograph and summary. Elana Parks. I've always wondered what her name could be, but never would I have imagined something so beautiful, so sexy. I say her name in my head, over and over again. El-ah-na, El-ah-na.

I look at the photograph, trying to find a resemblance between the girl from that day and the one in the painting. I first see her eyes, the perfect hue of violet and blue, just like I remembered, and it freezes me where I stand. Her hair is longer and darker now, but it's definitely her. My Elana.

My palms start to sweat, and even though I quelled the urge months ago, I can feel a deep hum stirring within me, rattling my senses, gnawing at me. *I found her.* My Elana. The smile creeps up before I can stop it. I have to have her again.

"What are you looking at?" Jessica's voice rings behind me, ruining the moment.

"Uh," I stutter, "just checking out who the fucked-up artist is."

"I saw this one painting that would look amazing in the dining room," she mentions.

I think of Elana's work, hanging in my house for me to admire for years, and the thought excites me. I feel myself harden in my jeans. I try to shake it off.

"Hate to admit it, but I saw one that looked cool, too," I say. "Show me the one you were talking about, and I'll come back and put bids on them."

With my money tied up in the family business, I'll have to tap into Jessica's accounts. She'll never even notice it missing. She's got more money than a Saudi prince.

She points out the one she wants, and I spot another couple of pieces I know I must have. Elana made them for me. I can feel them in my bones, calling my name, pulling me toward them as if they were always mine.

I grab Jessica's hand and yank her into my embrace. I kiss her hard.

"What was that for?" she asks, flush with embarrassment.

"No reason." I give her another peck, secretly thanking her for bringing me here, for bringing Elana back to me.

And so it begins. Again.

New Beginnings

THE NEXT TWO WEEKS ARE a blur. Kat has kept me plenty busy, so I don't obsess over the showcase and the traffic my work has brought into the gallery.

Just as I park my truck in Lizzy's parking lot, my phone rings. Blocked number. I debate answering, but realize it could be Mrs. Monarch, confirming our meeting tomorrow.

"Hello?"

"Don't hang up," she blurts.

"What do you want?" My stomach flips hearing her voice.

"I want to apologize."

"I don't want to hear it."

"Timmy told me what I did. I don't really remember anything. I mean, I remember some things…but not everything."

At that moment I realize she's not slurring her words. She sounds completely lucid, but I'm not feeding into it, not tonight, not ever again. "Are you done?"

"I'm in rehab, Elana," she admits quickly, probably afraid I'll hang up at the drop of a dime. "I checked in the Saturday after the show. I am so sorry." She sniffles into the receiver. "I'm facing my issues head-on. I know how much pain I've caused the family. I want to make it up to you guys. I don't expect open arms, but I would like for you to give me a chance."

I remain silent. I wasted so much energy hoping for the best only to have it spit back in my face.

"I know I don't deserve anything from you after what I've said and done, but I'm working through my issues, and one day, if you're willing, I'd like to sit down with you and talk."

I press "End" as hard as I can, fearful my finger will crack the glass on my phone. I've heard this promise before. Why would this time be so different?

James sits alone at the table. It's not like Kat to be late, but she texted him, saying that she was running behind schedule.

He and I start the festivities without her. After an hour she finally shows up, smiling from ear to ear. We both notice her out-fit—tight black slacks, a low-cut camisole under a fitted blazer—not her normal Friday attire, but she looks smoking hot.

"Why are you dressed like a secretary in a porno?" James asks, checking out her goods, eyes fixed on her ample bosom.

"I have a date Sunday," she boasts.

"So you got dressed three days early?" he teases, unimpressed. "That'll save you on time."

She ignores him. "A friend of a potential client came in last week. He couldn't resist my charms. Most men can't."

James does a wicked rendition of the classic eye roll, and I'm right there with him. "I don't know. Mixing business with pleasure never ends well. You might have to wait until your boss gets his com-mission first before you ghost him," I suggest.

"Or you could avoid the date altogether since you're going to hate him in four hours anyways," James drawls, but his eyes stay on the appetizer menu. I know he's not reading it. He orders the same thing every Friday.

She shoots her infamous glare, but that doesn't stop her from gushing about her new prospect. "He's twenty-eight, smart, and so good looking, oh my God. I can't wait." She claps her hands.

"What does he do for a living?"

"Well," she draws out, but James and I can predict the next words before she says them. "He's out of work right now. You know, with the economy and all, everyone's having a challenging time finding work."

"I have a job," James points to himself, then me. "El, you have a job, right?"

"Shut up, James," Kat fires back.

"This conversation is boring me," James adds, not wanting to hear anymore of Kat's details about her new jobless boy toy. He whips out his phone and occupies his attention with a game.

After our bellies are full of wings and beer, we gather our things and call it a night. We walk Kat to her car, then James walks me to mine, noticing a flat tire.

"You have a spare?"

I pop the trunk. James goes to retrieve it while I stare at the sky, thanking my lucky stars that he's here to help.

"Um, El? You don't by any chance have two spares, do you? Your rear passenger side is flat, too."

I race to the back of the truck, peeking around the side, and see the rim touching the concrete. "How the hell does that happen?"

"Lock it up. We'll get another tire in the morning." He runs backward toward Lizzy's. "I'm gonna tell Liz so she doesn't have it towed."

No sooner than he closes the door behind him does my phone ring.

"Hello?" I ask again and again. Nothing but silence. In just a few hours, she must've had a change of heart and left rehab. I hang up, and of course it rings again.

"Hey, babe. You home yet?" Evan's voice lifts my spirits.

"I would've been, but I got two flats. James is bringing me home."

"How'd that happen?" he asks, though it must've been a hypothetical question, because he doesn't wait for an answer. "After Mr. Sam comes back, you're coming to LA, right?"

"I'm looking forward to being on your turf for once. Babe, James is coming back. I'm heading home now."

I hang up with Evan up and hop into James's car. It's a total guy's car—completely blacked-out, leather seats that looked freshly shined, and an engine with more horsepower than any human could possibly need, but somehow it still manages to purr like Kiki.

When it's just he and I, a different side comes out—a kind-hearted, gentler side. His face softens a bit as he drops that macho attitude he flosses when we hang out in a group.

All night I could sense something bothering him, but before I can ask what's wrong, I see him looking in his rear-view with a concerned look.

"What's the matter?"

"I think we're being followed by a white car." His eyes remain on the mirror. He takes a few unnecessary turns, confirming we have a tail.

"One of the fun perks of dating Evan," I say nonchalantly. "That's Peter. He works for the *Daily Social* or something. I introduced myself a couple of weeks ago. Figured if he was following me around, I should at least know his name." I shrug. "There will probably be pictures of us with a headline in bold: 'Evan Saunders's new girlfriend and her secret lover. Can't this guy ever catch a break?'"

"That's creepy as fuck."

"I look at it as my personal bodyguard, but rather than big muscles, they have a huge telescopic lens."

"Either we lost him, or he got bored catching us doing nothing scandalous, because he's gone."

"I'd be bored following me, too."

We enter the gate. I see Peter's car parked on the side of the building when James drops me off. He must've found a shortcut and beat us home.

I run upstairs, grab Jack and his leash, taking him for a quick walk before bed. I rush over to the designated doggie business area, and Jack starts barking at the fence. I see what he's looking at on the other side: Peter's parked car. His bark becomes a howl unlike any I've ever heard.

"Shhh!" I reprimand him. "You're gonna wake everyone up." I give his leash a tug, and he tries to hold his ground, but I win the war—his twenty-pound frame is no match for me. Still, his barking and growling persists. "C'mon, loud mouth."

I give a little wave to Peter, not sure if he can see me or not. Day or night, rain or shine, he's there, waiting for the perfect opportunity to present itself, and just like Jack's barking, he's incessant.

Changes for the Better

I hand James a smoking hot cup of my special blend, and he takes it gratefully.

"Thanks." His eyes are barely open as he sips away, still groggy from sleep. "Where's your photographer friend? Thought you said he sits there all the time."

I look around, and he's right, Peter's not in his usual spot, nor the spot from last night. "He's probably tired, too, wanted to sleep in."

After trying two places, we finally find a store that had the tire I needed. We head over to my truck and get to work.

"Where's your man when you need him?" James jokes, as he struggles to take the lug nuts off.

Though I laugh at his frustration, I find myself still relishing the fact that Evan is *my man*. But since he isn't here and James is my hero today, I make sure he knows I appreciate him. "Who needs Evan when I have Superman live in the flesh," I joke back. "I haven't heard you talking about any new chicks lately. Slow week?"

"Ugh, I hate it when you call me that," he whines, laboring to loosen another lug nut, but I see the smirk on his face. "Even I need a break from time to time. So what do you think of Kat's new catch of the day?"

I simply shrug. I hadn't given much thought to her latest interest. We both agree she'll probably get annoyed that he doesn't have any money to pay for their first date and end up dumping him before the entrees arrive.

By the time James finishes replacing my tires, I'm behind schedule for my meeting in the city. James sees me off, and I speed to the gallery.

I walk through the doors, and at once I see two men carefully removing my paintings. One looks at a clipboard while pointing to one of the two piles of paintings laid against the wall. The interior of the place feels so lonely with no art hung up, like a vacant building still under construction. Another painting is removed, then placed in the remarkably larger pile. The smaller one has only a handful of paintings grouped together, while the bigger one is a compilation of most of my works.

"Are you ready to hear the great news?" Mrs. Monarch asks, approaching me from behind. She offers a gentle hug and two air kisses, and her enormous glasses actually kiss the skin of my cheeks. "There's been a great flow of traffic in here, especially for an unknown artist." She grabs her tablet, swiping her slender finger across the screen. "I have a few potential clients lined up for you, big spenders, lots of homes and rooms to decorate. They asked specifically to see any new pieces you create. How do you feel about that?"

My stomach feels like a cloud at the thought of people asking to see more work. I don't know if it's validation of my talent, or the fear of not being able to create pieces they'll like. Lightning rarely strikes the same place twice.

"You don't have to look so petrified, darling. While you think about it, let's discuss the paintings that people inquired about—which was practically all of them."

She hands me a spreadsheet with the list of paintings, their dimensions, and the highest offer for each work. All but seven had an offer next to the name. My eyes feel like they're being tricked as I survey the amounts listed down the column. I swallow my gum when I see the grand total at the bottom of the grid.

"$217,551," I stammer.

As I try to register the number, I peruse the paper, spotting the largest bid. When my eyes travel to the painting's name, I can feel my heart tighten in my chest.

"Someone wants her for $150,001?"

"Mmm, yes. I was quite amazed by that as well. As powerful as that piece is, I thought it'd be the hardest sell."

Never in a million years would I have thought *Stolen Innocence* and the word "sell" would be in the same sentence, let alone it actually happening.

"You go home, review the spreadsheet, and let me know which ones you want to part with. Every bidder signed an agreement acknowledging you could deny their bid, so don't you worry about that. Think about what we've discussed and get back to me."

I drive home in a daze, not even remembering getting into my truck; somehow my brain went into autopilot and navigated me home safely.

I imagine all the places paintings can be hung—foyers, over a bed, over a fireplace, lining a hallway, but none of those would ever be right for her. The only place she belongs is with me, sitting behind my desk.

I sit on the couch in my apartment, gazing out the window. I pull a pillow up to my nose and inhale Evan's scent, which still lingers on its fabric. If he can't be here, I'll take any reminder of him I can get. I call Kat to make sure she's still taking care of Kiki when I go to LA, and her giggly tone is a sure sign she's not alone. She confirms her arrangements with me before ending the call, completely distracted by whoever she's with.

With that feeling of unease, I retreat to the only place that's provided me comfort. The studio is barren. The clutter now sits in the gallery with the fate of their residence hanging in the air. Doubt about Mrs. Monarch's proposal racks my nerves.

Since being with Evan, my nightmares haven't haunted me like in the past. They're still there, but their intensity has subsided. They've always been my unwanted muse. What if my talent only exists because of the pain and struggle my brush was able to relay? I grab a brush, and for the first time, I don't know what to do. I throw it down and leave the room, tossing myself into a steamy shower to clear my thoughts instead.

The stream of hot water is soothing, but even that pleasure soon fades away, when my phone's ringer wails. I get out and answer, still wet. No one answers, and I hear a click.

I grab my weekender bag and start filling it with things I'll need when I visit Evan, trying to occupy my thoughts with anything and everything not related to painting and Mom's obvious relapse. It's only a brief distraction, however, when I realize I'm a quicker packer than I thought.

I pull up my laptop and surf the web for anything interesting. I stumble upon a celebrity gossip site. Out of curiosity, I search Evan's name, and pictures start to load on the screen. There are pictures of me, too. And I'm not the only familiar face I see.

I break out my phone and call him.

"Dude, you need to check your email. I sent you something."

After a length of silence he says, "Holy shit, that's awesome. And I look really good, so you're welcome because it looks like you're at least cheating on him with someone good-looking, not someone ugly like Genine did." I can feel the wide grin on James's face as he talks, admiring the flattering picture of himself plastered on the website.

"They might start following you around, waiting to catch us in the act."

"Guess we really need to watch our backs, huh?"

As we look at the site together over the phone, it seems like we come across the same picture at the same time. Neither of us know what to say, so I offer my best excuse to hang up.

All the tension I had before returns, only multiplied. I feel like I need a complete cleanse, so I dial the number of the person I know can make it happen.

"Hi, this is Elana. I've thought about it, and I think I'm ready."

Eleven All This Time

HERDS OF PEOPLE RUSH THROUGH LAX, whizzing past, knocking into my bag. At one point it even slips off my shoulder, but I'm a New Yorker, and it takes a lot more than that to alter my mood, especially today.

I squeal with exhilaration once I see him parked nearby. It's like a scene out of a movie. I leap into his arms, hugging him tight until our lips meet.

"Welcome to LA." I feel him smiling against my lips.

Enveloped in his arms, I tilt my face toward the sun, feeling its warmth seep into my bones, replacing the chill that the crisp New York air embedded in me.

"You really need to get out more." He kisses the underside of my chin as I bask in the sun's glory. "Take a leave from work and come with me to London next month."

His suggestion hangs between us, and a comfortable silence ensues as he begins to drive. We pull up to a contemporary house—large, frosted-glass double doors, two-car garage, and a huge picture-framed window on the second floor.

I jump out before the car is even in park. I skip to his side, waiting for him as he grabs my bag from the backseat. The thought of seeing his space tingles my skin. The last time Kat and I visited, he was staying at some dingy apartment, but he's moved up in the movie world and the upgrade is substantial.

The front of the house pales in comparison to the inside. Furniture with clean lines, all very contemporary, fill the house. The floor-to-ceiling windows in the rear slide open, opening the whole room to the backyard. The view is breathtaking, from the infinity pool and Jacuzzi to the backdrop of the city below. It's not a large backyard, but what you lack in space, you more than make up for in view. I think of all the times he's invited me here, I gave him excuse after excuse why I couldn't. Seeing it now confirms that I've made some horrible life choices in the past.

He leads me around the house, showing me where everything is. Then he stands me in front of a closed door, and asks me to open it.

Perplexed, I look at him, but do as I'm told. The walls are glistening white, and in the corner of the room by a small terrace is a large easel with a brand-new white canvas on it.

"What's this?"

"I figured since the new house won't be done for a while, this could be your studio till then. You never know when you're going to need to paint, right? Consider this your second home...unless you've changed your mind and want to make it your only home?" His grin widens; he's clearly hopeful my mind will change sooner than later.

The terrace beckons me. The view is truly spectacular. I start imagining things I can paint, starting with a collage of beautiful blues and lush greens, scattered whimsically on a white canvas. I can't think of a particular use for the red or black colors, pigments in which I should own stock.

He shows me his bedroom, which is simple and bare. I slide out of my sneakers and jump onto his bed. He does the same. "So what do you want to do?"

"I can think of something." My eyes wander over him and my fingers soon follow. I lift the hem of his shirt, exposing his torso before getting rid of the fabric altogether.

He presses his lips hard against mine, passionately, *possessively*. His hands travel down the center of my blouse, and he rips it open, sending buttons flying across the room. I look at him in surprise, and he raises a gratified brow.

"Is this what you had in mind?"

My smile is undeniable. "It's what I *had* in mind, but I think my blouse might feel differently."

His lips find my neck. His hands run down my body, warming it further. A low moan hums in our throats. My hip begins to vibrate, and it isn't until I hear the chorus to *California* by Phantom Planet that I realize the vibration is my phone.

Evan lets out a huge sigh.

"Hello?"

"How was your flight, good-lookin'?"

I sit up in the bed, holding the phone closer to my ear, hoping Evan who's on the other end. "It was fine. Sorry I didn't text you." Evan stares at me. His good mood is fading.

"Whatcha doing?" Sebastian asks.

"Just trying to figure out what the plans are."

"Okay. Just checking in, nothing special. Call me when you get home. Have fun out there. Miss you."

I hang up the phone, and Evan's bedroom eyes have turned to jealous flames. He jumps off the bed, grabbing a shirt from the closet and tossing it in my direction.

I follow him to the kitchen, running after him like a loyal puppy. My own anger begins to simmer, so I stop in my tracks.

"You know, I never said anything about your lunch with Genine before the showcase. I saw the pics online."

He stops mid-step, frozen where he stands. Then he spins toward me. "It's not what you think."

That one sentence is infamous for always being what one thinks, but for me, I believe him when he says it. The only part that bothered me was the fact that he didn't feel the need to mention it, seeing how I've always been honest about staying in touch with Sebastian.

"I was going to tell you, but you were upset about telling Timmy, and it just didn't feel like the right time. You know I would never cheat on you or do anything to hurt—"

I hold my hand up, not wanting to hear it. "I didn't freak out because I trust you, no matter how much I hate her. Sebastian is my friend."

He rakes his hands through his hair. "I trust you. I don't trust him."

I pace slowly toward Evan. "Well, I do. He's a friend, and I need him as much as I need you, just in a different way." His body tenses at whatever thought just ran through his mind. "I don't think I need to remind you all of the ways I need you, do I?" I add.

I run the tips of my fingers along his sides, and I see his muscles clench under my delicate touch. My fingers lace around his neck, and I pull his face toward mine.

"If you need reminding, I'll show you."

****

We snuggle on the soft comforter, soaking in each other's love as I trace the lines of his tattooed chest and arms, following the line work.

"I never realized how big this has gotten. What does it mean again?"

"It doesn't look familiar?" When I don't respond, he jumps out of bed and says, "Don't move." He bolts out of the room, his footsteps fading in the distance. He releases a loud curse as something crashes to the floor down the hall. Thirty seconds later, he returns with a book in his hand and a smile on his face.

Evan flashes the cover of our yearbook. I still draw a blank, not making the connection between the two.

Frustrated by my horrible memory, he sighs loudly and starts flipping through the book, stopping on a photo Kat took of us. I wrote a long-winded paragraph to him.

> My Other 1,
>
> You know I can't just write some generic statement, so here goes. Ever since we were little, I knew you were extraordinary. You've always been a star, the brightest star in MY sky, and I know you'll be one in Cali. You deserve this more than anyone. No matter what, you'll always be my other half, and in my heart, even on the other side of the country.
>
> Always Love,
> Your best friend
> Your 11
> Your Elana

Under my lengthy sentiment, I must've gotten bored and started doodling on the entire page. I wrote the number 11 and added bold lines, both swirling and jagged around the number, almost concealing it inside an accidental heart. You wouldn't know it was even there unless you were looking for it. I look over at his bare chest and follow the pattern, and there it is, my doodle, tattooed on his skin, moving up to his shoulder and onto his arm. The concealed "11" is perfectly centered over his heart.

"So I've been on your heart this whole time?" I ask breathlessly.

"At the time I just thought it was cool. Then one night I was homesick and I saw it, a subliminal message only I understood. It sucks having to cover it up when I'm working, but it's a small price to pay for love."

I lay my head on his chest and listen to his heart, the one that beats "11."

LA

EVAN AND I START A game of grape tossing while trying to decide what to eat. He gets ready for the next grape I launch when my cell phone rings, throwing my aim off. It almost takes his eye out.

"Ugh. Hello?"

"Hey, El. How's Cali?"

"Evan might have to wear an eye patch now, but it's nice out here. You really need to come next time. Everything okay?"

Evan yells that I pelted him with a grape, but Kat doesn't seem to care. "Kiki's acting weird, meowing and hissing. I don't know what her problem is. She's never been this bratty with me before."

"I'm sure she's fine. She's just being dramatic." Kiki whines in the background while Kat tells her to put the claws away.

"Okay, just wanted you to know. Have fun, guys!"

Before she hangs up, she yells at Kiki not to attack. I assume my last position, launching grape in 3, 2, 1, and release.

"Kiki is being a total drama mama. Sounded like she was about to attack Kat before she hung up."

Evan picks up a handful of grapes, readying for his turn. Instead of tossing one, he heaves the whole bunch at my head. I stare at him slack-jawed, stunned by the disqualifying technique, while he laughs to himself.

"I'm not cleaning this up," I say through my own laughter. "You started it."

He comes around to my side of the counter and removes a grape that has somehow lodged itself in my hair. I lean into his touch, pushing my hips toward his body, leaving no space between us. I'm lost in his orbit.

"Are you trying to make moves on me, Ms. Parks?"

My smile hides nothing. I look down at his sweatpants and notice he wants what I want. His eyes are fierce with desire. He leans in and licks the tip of my lips, enjoying the sweetness of the grapes, tasting me before delving inside. I moan and sink further into his openmouthed kiss. All I can feel is my sweet spot tighten with anticipation as he liberates me of my shirt. My hands find his waistband, tugging his sweatpants down, freeing him, too.

He lifts me up, and I wrap my legs around his body as he carries me to the table, laying me on its cold surface. Caught off guard, I suck in a quick breath. Our embrace never disconnects, and the table warms as my yearning grows.

He strokes my cheek with his finger, brushing my lip and outlining my mouth. I try to bite it, but he's too quick, moving it out of reach. My brow furrows with disappointment until he finally delivers his teasing finger to my waiting mouth. I suck on it as he slides it in and out, while his other hand glides along my skin, fueled with passion. Evan reaches down, grabbing his erection, hovering the head over my wet spot, teasing and driving me wild.

I bite down on his finger with enough pressure to get his attention, and he keeps running his hard presence over my clitoris and back down to my yearning desire. He's driving me insane.

Then he touches my breast. Ardently, he caresses them, letting the tips of his fingers rub across my hardened nipples. His mouth is so close to mine, barely an inch away, till we devour each other senselessly. I let out a soft moan and sink my fingers into his hair, holding him in place.

My senses break down. My stomach quivers with a hunger I can't explain. My moan deepens as he slowly slips his warm fingers in my sensitive flesh. His kiss intensifies with the tempo of his fingers, showing me no mercy.

He moves his mouth to the sensitive spot below my ear—sucking, licking, kissing me with a burning lust. My back arches, his erection still pressed against my thigh, teasing in only the way he can. His mouth is demanding in a dominant way, one that makes my insides clench tight like a vise.

He flicks his wet tongue over my nipples, tracing them before taking them in one at a time, sucking on them with his own urgency. With every tug an intense desire, starting at the center of my legs, sends me to the ledge. He reaches for his length and again toys with me. His finger finds its way back into my mouth, tasting of me. He gives an approving smile. Every perfectly formed tattooed muscle towers over me, and I raise my hips for him, unable to wait any longer.

Our joining is grand. My body stretches, taking him in, taking him all in.

He thrusts hard, and my insides tremble. Holding me in place, he quickens his pace and I suck harder on his finger, reeling in the moment, needing him to fill me more.

The table scratches the floor as it shifts with our motion. His hips move in a way that fits me perfectly, while his tongue laps over my nipples again, gently tugging on them with his lips.

"Yes," I moan.

The warmth of his breath on my skin sends shocks down my spine. He lets out a guttural moan, nearly a feral growl, as our hips join as one.

"Open your eyes, Elana," he whispers in his raspy voice, savoring each thrust.

I open my eyes, and his mouth collides into mine. The strokes of his tongue, so primitive and raw, takes me by surprise.

My once-seductive tone can no longer be controlled. My moaning grows louder and louder until I'm screaming with pleasure. I let him have me completely, unable to control how my body reacts under him.

"Evan... Evan... Oh my god...yes...yes..." I shout louder still.

His touch is supernatural, making my body do things it's never done before. I can feel the tingling rise in me for a second time. My insides feel as if they're about to shatter into a million pieces, bringing me closer to heaven.

My body crumbles. The vibrations control me as pleasure rolls through my core, tightening every muscle in my body, consuming every part of me. I let out a low, uncontrollable groan as he holds me down, gripping my hips with no intention of letting go until he's had his fill. His hips begin to buck, and I feel that he's near the finish line. I'm still riding the high when he releases into me.

He collapses on top of me, the exhaustion taking us both as his breath inches closer to normalcy. Our hearts drum in perfect harmony.

"I'll never be able to eat breakfast at this table"—he manages, still gasping for air—"without thinking about this moment."

I smile at the thought of him eating a bowl of Fruit Loops, thinking about us. "I guess dinner with your folks here is out of the question then."

The Delivery

"Can I help you?" I say into the intercom.

"Delivery for Elana Parks."

I rush to the window, seeing the DHL truck, so I buzz him in. He slides the thin box inside of my doorway as I sign for the package.

I get my scissors and slice the tape, then start to realize that it's been shipped similar to how I packed my paintings. I open it up more, and sure enough, it's a painting, *my* painting. Someone bought it for a generous sum of money only to send it back to me. The only person insane enough to do that is Evan, so I speed dial his number.

"I can't believe you did this," I blurt without even saying hello. "I'm giving you the money back."

"Did what?"

"You know...you bought *Stolen Innocence*. I just got your delivery."

"Babe, what the heck are you talking about?" His voice remains even, and I realize he's being sincere. He didn't buy it.

"Well, if you didn't do this...who did?"

I lean the painting up against the back of my couch, trying to figure out who would do this. My mind runs wild, but I draw a complete blank.

"Since we're on the phone, I wanted to let you know I'll be in town tomorrow, but I have an interview in the city. After that, I'm all yours. Maybe we can break in your table?"

I choke on my own saliva, caught off-guard by the image flashing in my mind. "My table isn't built for that type of abuse. Kiki, no!"

184

She jumps on the back of the couch, rubbing her body against the corner of the canvas, pushing it forward. The painting falls smack dab on the floor. The sound jolts us both.

"What was that?"

"Dumb cat just knocked the—"

My chin starts to tremble, and my hand flies up to catch my gasp. I begin to hyperventilate. My pulse quickens, and my heartbeats resonate in my ears.

"El, what's wrong?"

On the back of the canvas, right under where I wrote *Stolen Innocence*, I see a message.

You were a good fuck.

It's Time

I CAN'T SLEEP. MY BODY won't allow it. The drumming of my heartbeat keeps me awake. I see the written words whether my eyes are open or closed, haunting me every time I blink, and even when I don't.

My ass grows numb as I sit in the window by my fire escape, waiting for Evan to arrive. The cold, crisp air helps me stay awake. Peter's car is parked in his usual spot, but he gets out once he sees the black town car pull through the gates. He snaps a few pictures of Evan before retreating to the warmth of his idling vehicle.

I swing the door open, hearing the ding of the elevator, and I throw myself in Evan's arms, pushing him against the hallway wall. The tears start to pour, and my body starts to shake in his embrace. He leads us back into my apartment and closes the door, but never lets me go.

Evan tries to console me, but I know it's not okay. My past has joined my present—he's back.

Evan sits me on the couch, placing my throw blanket over my shoulders, and closes the window. He removes the sheet off the painting, studying his message to me.

He calls Charli, and two minutes later, her knock startles me. She starts immediately, "A guy called in that bid. After El approved all sales, I called him back, and within a few hours, someone showed up with a money order and took the paintings."

"What did he look like?" I stammer.

"Tall, dark hair, Latino," she starts.

"It's not him." The words come out in a panic.

"We should call the police," Evan interjects.

"No!" I shout from the couch. "No, no, no, no..." I rock back and forth, blocking out everything around me.

Memories of that day start playing in my head; it feels like forever since I thought about it. Evan has been the best distraction, but all too quickly, the fear invades me all over again, crippling my senses.

"If you ever tell anybody, I'll know," repeats in my head, over and over, a broken loop.

"Elana, listen to me. We have to call the police. If he did send this, he knows where you live."

They shuffle behind me, and Charli's voice drops to a whisper. The only words I catch are "Disconnected," "Jagged Shadows," and "Twisted Dream."

I know at once she's reciting the names of my paintings. *Jagged Shadows* was a piece I did after one of my worst nightmares. Usually, only snippets of the experience invade my dream, but this specific one was the entire experience, from start to finish.

I manage to slow my racing heart, and a scary serenity sets in. I know what must be done.

Upon arrival of the officers, the questions begin, and I explain what happened all those years ago—the painting, the showcase, and the subsequent message he's sent now. The officer takes a statement from all of us, even requesting Mrs. Monarch to give all information pertaining to the purchase of the paintings. Charli tells the officers the name on the invoice is Marc Pullman. Somehow, it doesn't feel right to me, but my feeling isn't based off anything but gut instinct.

Even though Charli made me a cup of tea, my insides remain cold and numb. The officers leave, taking the painting away, packaging it carefully to check for prints. I sit with my hot cup of tea, remembering my biggest fear was him finding me, hurting me again. I can't let it come true.

Evan hustles into the bedroom, causing a commotion.

"What are you doing?"

"I'm taking you to a hotel."

Too physically and emotionally drained, I don't argue. Evan drops Kiki off at Mr. Sam's, and we head into the city. The shadows of the tall, concrete buildings make me feel colder on the inside. As we drive in, Evan calls Timmy and fills him in, trying to convince my brother I'm okay.

I don't even register the beauty of the hotel. I move like a zombie, devoid of life. All I want to do is pass out but I'm scared that once I do, I'll have an unwelcomed visitor in my dreams. With no verbal request, Evan lies beside me, cradling me in his arms. I close my eyes, nuzzling my cheek on his chest, taking in his scent. His embrace is exactly what I need to relax.

When I open my eyes again, Evan is no longer beside me, let alone in the bed. The fear of being alone surfaces, and I jump up and replace my sweat-soaked clothes with a robe.

"Are you okay?" He rises from the chair, but I wave him to sit back down. "I didn't want to wake you."

"You look exhausted, too."

"Can't sleep," he admits, his voice heavy with strain. He's probably worried I'll lock myself in a room for two weeks again like when I was younger.

My stomach claws at me from the inside, demanding something to eat. "Can we order food?"

We both order a turkey sandwich, and I devour all of mine while Evan picks at his. He doesn't say much, so I toss a couple of my cucumbers at him to get him to smile. He doesn't.

"Thanks for being here with me."

"You're thanking me. This is all my fault."

"It's not." My tone *feels* strong, but it doesn't sound it.

I get off my chair and straddle his lap. I press my lips softly to his. He doesn't kiss me back, so I pull away.

"Listen to me, Evan William Saunders. If it weren't for you, I probably would have ended things years ago, but I didn't because of you. I know I'll be fine as long as you're by my side." I know the words I say are true as I feel them in my heart.

"I can't always be around," he insists. "I'm traveling back and forth, and I can't leave you by yourself at that apartment, not anymore."

I know he's right, but I've been thinking about his offer ever since I left California. "Maybe it's time I try painting on that terrace of yours."

A hint of a smile appears on his face, and his eyes find mine. "I don't want you moving in with me because you're afraid, but I'll take it under the circumstances."

"That's not the reason. I mean, it's one of them, but I realized I'm not really happy unless you're around, and if you're in LA, I want to be in LA, too. I'm sure I can find a job out there, or just leech off you for a while," I joke, trying to rouse a smile out of him.

He kisses me gently as his hands stroke my dampened hair. I try to increase the intensity of our touch, but he doesn't allow it, keeping his kisses soft and tender. I can feel the love he has for me in each one of them.

After the last forty-eight hours, I would've thought the last thing I wanted or needed was to be intimate, but I need to feel loved and not scared. I need Evan.

I can feel it in his body—the wanting matches my own. He confesses his love for me over and over as our hands and mouth explore one another. The connection we have is unlike anything ever written in a book or filmed in a movie.

We remove each other's clothes and make love, forgetting about the nightmare that came into both of our lives again, only living for the moment.

His lips graze along my jaw, moving down my neck, leaving the hairs on end. Our eyes meet again, and we share another kiss. We taste one another as he pushes his pelvis, entering me deeply and slowly, with purpose.

"I love you so much, Elana."

"I love you, Evan."

He holds my face and kisses me with unparalleled love and affection. I know this will be the start of something new.

Waking Nightmare

AFTER QUITTING MY JOB WITH little to no regrets the day before, I spend my Friday packing up my apartment. No one likes the idea of me being alone but having a babysitter feels foolish too. I have plenty of knives handy and my trusty bodyguard, Kiki, to protect me in case anything happens. As I sift through my belongings, it's hard not to get sentimental, saying goodbye to a place I've called home for the last three years.

What will be harder is saying goodbye to Timmy, Kat, James, and Sebastian. I know they are only a plane ticket away but having them close was comforting for so long. The fear of being alone in California, with no friends, starts to make me uneasy, but I try to push that worry aside, as I'm too busy dealing with every other fear that circulates through my body.

Until they find Marc Pullman, I know I'll be safer somewhere else.

"Babe, my flight is delayed three hours, and it might change again. There's a storm out here," Evan says into the receiver.

"No," I whine. "This is one of the last times we're going to be out here for a while."

He lets out a long, frustrated groan. "Just be careful. Hopefully, I'll be at the apartment by the time you get home. If I get there sooner, I'll meet you at Lizzy's."

I wash away the disappointed feeling and get ready for Lizzy's, excited to take a break from packing, and thrilled to meet Kat's new boy toy. Surprisingly, she hasn't discarded him as quickly as James and I thought.

When I arrive, James is waiting by himself, running a finger along the rim of his glass, still filled with bourbon. Every facial feature looks turned-down, muting all his normal upbeat expressions. He barely lifts his head to receive my kiss hello, but before I can get into what's wrong, Kat and Andrew walk in, hand in hand. Her face is lit up like the Rockefeller Christmas tree. James gulps down his drink, slamming it back to the table.

"Bad day?" I utter before they reach us.

"You can say that."

Andrew introduces himself to us, and we all extend our hands to him, although James looks a bit reluctant. His smile is bright and he's quite good looking—dark brown eyes, close-cut brown hair, tall, muscular. Per usual, James doesn't seem all that impressed.

Overall, he seems nice, but more importantly, he puts a smile on my friend's face.

I keep nudging James to cheer him up, but nothing seems to work. I cling to him, trying to absorb as much of him as I can, and he clings to me, too, something he doesn't normally do. It's hard to figure out why he's so moody. It could be all the changes taking place around him, the thought that my past is rearing its ugly head. Or it could be both.

James walks me to my truck, giving me the biggest hug imaginable. I built a wall, trying to keep the tears at bay, but with the strength of his embrace, it collapses in a heartbeat.

He wipes away my tears. "I'm gonna miss you, Els, but this isn't goodbye forever." I'm gonna miss my Superman more than he knows, but my emotions won't let me say the words. "They'll find him, and when they do, you'll feel safe here again."

Disappointment registers as I walk into my empty apartment, not only because my belongings are tucked away in boxes, but because there is no Evan greeting me at the door. A bitter silence fills the apartment, leaving a bad taste in my mouth.

I shoot him a text as I trudge into the bedroom, change into a nightgown, and collapse onto the bed. The gravity of the evening took its toll on me. My eyelids are heavy, and it isn't long before I drift off, and Evan responds to my text.

****

Evan's touch is sensational—his hands are soft and warm, caressing my body with care. I've missed him, and my face shows it as my lips curl at the sight of him. I'm enjoying his wandering hands. They travel down, exploring my body, rubbing his finger over his favorite spot, yet they continue to wander. I frown, wishing he would concentrate on pleasing me. I spread my legs for him, and he moves my panties to the side. His fingers circle my clitoris. He enters me, in and out as my body pushes onto him. I want him deeper.

It feels so real. It feels so good, but it's hard to tell if I'm awake or trapped in a dream.

"Mmmm," I moan.

He continues, increasing his speed, pleasing me with his fingers. His movement is fluid and tender, and then his fingers quicken. At first it's nice, but then it starts to hurt. Sensing me tense up, he slows down again, returning to the pace I like. His thumb circles over my clitoris, working his magic on me while his other hand grazes my inner thigh, squeezing firmly before traveling under my nightgown to touch my breasts. He cups one in his hand but it's different this time.

Kiki meows incessantly, that pesky cat. Now I know I'm not dreaming. I inhale deeply with longing, and my eyes fly open, smelling him. Only it's not Evan.

He quickly pins me down with his body. His knees hold down my shoulders and arms and covers my mouth with his palm. I can taste myself on his fingers.

He leans forward, his knees crushing my shoulders, but my screams are muffled.

"Shhhh," he says calmly. "Someone was enjoying herself." He switches hands, bringing the one that smells like me to his nose and mouth.

Tears blur my vision as I blink frantically, trying to clear my sight, but his weight only causes more tears.

"You've been thinking about me," he says, nodding his head to the left. I look over hesitantly. I see my painting, the one that looks like him. "Why didn't you paint my eyes?"

Kiki is now wailing and hissing from the doorway. Her body appears arched, her tail stiff.

"You're so wet right now. I was enjoying myself, too." He gives a twisted smile.

His knees continue to dig into my shoulders, and I struggle to catch my breath through the pain. I feel dizzy from the lack of oxygen. He must see how disoriented I look. He licks his lips with satisfaction, putting more pressure on his knees. I'm able to take a breath when one knee slips off, but his hand quickly shifts over my mouth. I bite his finger and unleash a blood-curdling scream, as loud as my lungs will allow.

His arm whips across his body, striking me in the face. The sharp sting rings through my cheek and lip as he cups my mouth with his hand again, careful not to let me bite him a second time. The salty, metallic blood hits my taste buds. I'm forced to swallow it, but I choke instead, coughing onto his hand, gagging on the taste.

"You wanna play dirty?"

I hear pounding. I swear my heart is trying to push its way through my rib cage and out my chest. I start hyperventilating as his knees dig into me again. Quickly, we both realize the pounding isn't coming from me. It's my door.

I see his eyes now—the palest hue of blue, with specks of brown and amber—and my brain rewinds to the first time I met him, placing the missing puzzle piece back into the picture.

"I'll be seeing you." He leans down, inhales deeply, and kisses my forehead before throwing himself off me, digging his kneecaps into my shoulders a final time.

He jets out to the living room. I hear his hurried steps down the fire escape, the rails creak from the metal grinding on metal under his feet.

I jump out of bed and race to the door, practically swinging it off it's hinges.

"He was in my apartment."

****

"Ma'am, you said you had an intruder?"

I hear all the police radios going off, chatter in the hallway, chatter all around, but all I can think about is his fingers inside me, burning everywhere he touched.

"He climbed down the fire escape when he heard Mr. Sam banging on the door." My voice has a void to it, missing the hysteria I had minutes ago.

A couple of officers leave the apartment, some stay behind. I try to collect my thoughts, but all I hear is his voice in my head—his deep growl as I bit his finger, and the raspy tone of his own pleasure at the thought I was enjoying myself. The bile rises slowly in my throat.

"Ms. Parks, can you please tell me what happened? There's blood on you. Is it his or yours?"

"Both, maybe. Everything happened so fast."

He pulls the radio from his shoulder and gives the call to send an ambulance. The metallic taste hits my tongue again, and the thought that it could be him nauseates me.

Even though I'm not cold, the pain in my shoulder causes me to shiver. I rock in place, holding the blanket Mr. Sam put over my shoulders for comfort.

"We need to know what happened while it's still fresh in your mind."

I keep rocking where I sit while I recount what took place—the history I had with him, the dream, thinking it was Evan, his fingers, being pinned down, biting, the slap. Even though the tears filled my eyes, it was still crystal clear in my thoughts.

"He heard the pounding on the door, got spooked, and went down the fire escape."

The officer calls the detective investigating the painting incident, and I continue my rocking chair motion.

"What the fuck happened? I'm her boyfriend!" His voice booms in the hallway. "Is she okay? Elana!" he yells, his voice snapping me back to reality.

When they finally let him into the apartment, he stands terrified in the doorway. He drops his bag to the floor and races over.

Right before he reaches me, an officer steps between us. "You can't touch her, sir," he warns. "We don't want any evidence to be contaminated."

"Evidence? What happened to you? Your lip? Whose blood is that?" Evan grows breathless, shouting one question after another as he stands there, panting, waiting for someone to answer him.

"Ms. Parks had an intruder in her apartment this evening."

My tears well as I look to Evan.

"How the hell did he get into the building, let alone the fucking apartment?" Evan shouts at the officer as he makes his way toward me, more carefully this time. He takes a seat on the couch, close, but still keeping a fair amount of space between us.

"We are trying to find all of this out, sir."

Chaos surrounds me, but all I see is Evan and the look in his eyes, and all I hear is *his* voice, trapped in my head. I hold my ears with my palms, trying to block out the noise, but it only makes his voice louder.

"Ms. Parks, the ambulance is here. They'll take you to the hospital, treat you for your injuries, run a full rape kit."

"Rape kit?" Evan asks in pure horror, all the wind sucked out of him.

Before I can speak, the officer answers, "Yes. She was sexually assaulted."

The Beginning of Her End

THE RAPE KIT IS INTRUSIVE. I'm swabbed, scraped, photographed, and my clothes are bagged for evidence. I feel completely humiliated again—broken, tired, and unbelievably distraught. I internalize everything. I feel empty inside, and I want everyone and everything to go away.

"El, I brought you some tea," Evan says, trying to help. "Please take a sip." I stare at the cup, but I don't speak or reach for it. I look at him and turn away, hearing him let out a deep breath. "Please say something," Evan begs. "You haven't said anything in four hours."

I remain silent, crippled by my thoughts, burying my face in the sheets, wanting to unleash a furious scream. When the doctors or officers come into the room, I see their mouths move, but the only voice I hear is *his*. And all I smell is him, forever trapped in my nostrils. It's embedded so far in my own nose I can taste it. Even the spots where he touched me burns, as if he's still touching me.

"The psychologist said this is normal behavior," Timmy whispers to Evan, as if I weren't even in the room. Physically, I'm in a hospital bed, surrounded by people I know, but mentally, I'm gone, trapped in a waking nightmare, paralyzed. It's like the world continues to spin, but I'm the only one frozen at a standstill.

"Can you please excuse me and Ms. Parks for a moment?" the doctor asks Evan and Timmy. "Elana, my name is Dr. Rachel Harris. How are you feeling?"

I shrug one of my better shoulders.

"Here's a prescription for the pain. I'm also giving you one for Valium. You don't have to take it, but if you need it, it'll be available to you. And if you need someone to talk to, I've written down a phone number you can call that helps women who've been raped. I urge you to contact them. You don't have to go through this alone. I know your boyfriend and family are all here for you, but if you want to hear from people who've been through this, it might help the healing process."

"I'm scared."

"That's completely understandable, given everything you've been through."

"That's not what I mean." I turn to face her. The doctor's bright white coat blinds me. "I'm scared I'll never be normal again," I confess. I try to explain how hard it was to be with Evan the first time, how the thought of anyone ever touching me again repulses every fiber of my being, but my tears muffle every word, and I sound like a gargled mess. The sadness and fear turn into blistering rage. "How the fuck am I supposed to recover from this?"

"Everything you're feeling is normal, Elana. I recommend calling the number I gave you. It's not going to be easy, but life after a trauma like this is possible. Do you have any other questions I can help you with?"

"Questions?" My heart races again, and my fists clench and unclench while my extremities shake. "I have questions, but you don't have any fucking answers. All you have is a fucking prescription pad. Unless you can prescribe a pill that erases the memory of me getting raped two times by the same sick son of a bitch, you can't help me with shit. Just get out." I stare at her as she says nothing. "GET OUT!"

****

I remain silent while Evan drives us to a place to spend the night. He tries asking me questions, keeping the conversation light, trying to offer words that will help, but nothing will work, not now. I stare out the window, seeing nothing as the tears fall where they may. I stopped trying to wipe them away hours ago.

I head straight into the bathroom and jump in the shower, scrubbing him off me, leaving tender red welts on my skin. But no matter how hard I scrub, I can still feel him on me, his fingers inside of me, and the worst part, me getting pleasure from it. I start dry-heaving at the thought. Then I fall to the shower floor, sobbing uncontrollably under the scolding hot water.

Evan knocks on the door as my cries louden.

"El?" He pushes open the shower door and tries to pull me up, but I flinch at his touch and cower to the corner. He pulls his arms back, as if he could also feel the burning sensation on my skin. "Let me help you."

"Just leave me alone," I manage. I throw my head in my hands, covering myself with shame. "Please," I beg in a whisper. Like a wounded dog, he backs out of the bathroom, defeated.

****

I throw on more layers of clothes than I need and look for Evan. I find him on the couch, face buried in his palm; his shoulders move up and down, and I hear him crying. He quickly tries to pull himself together, trying to be strong for me, but as much as I don't want him upset, I also don't even care.

"Are you hungry? Can I get you anything?" He wipes away his tears with the back of his hand.

"Do you have the Valium?"

He shuffles through the different bottles, hands me a pill, and I swallow it without water. "Did you want me to lie down next to you?" he asks, but he already knows the answer.

****

I wake up in the middle of the night, sweating and out of breath. I know I had a dream, but luckily, I can't remember it. Quietly, I walk into the living room, where Evan is sprawled out on the couch, looking uncomfortable, but beautiful still.

Tears pool in my eyes. Part of me—a small part—wishes he would hold me and never let go. I know he'd do it. He'd do anything I asked. But a larger part never wants to be touched by anyone ever again.

I go into the bedroom and drag the comforter back into the living room. I drape it over him, and curl myself up in the chair near the couch, wanting to be close, just not close enough to touch.

****

When I wake up, the room is empty. I'm glad. I'll feel better knowing I can't push him away further if he's not here.

Dozens of texts from Timmy, Kat, James, and Sebastian flood my phone. I have no desire to talk to my brother. He'll just insist on hovering constantly while Kat will think I need a babysitter. James might not be so bad, probably because he'll have no idea what to say. But then there's Sebastian.

I don't think I'd mind hearing his voice. I always found it relaxing. I know he's worried. Besides his texts, he's called me seven times since Timmy told him. I wish he can heal me with his hands, like he did that night, feeding his energy to me, relaxing every nerve and bone in my body. The more I think of him, the more I think I need him, now more than ever.

I dial his number, and it barely rings once before he picks up. The moment I hear his voice, a stream trickles down my cheeks, and I can't even get the words out. But he knows I'm listening, he knows I'm here.

"You don't have to say anything if you don't want to. Just tap on the phone to let me know you're okay."

I tap once. My silent sobbing continues.

"You don't have to do this alone. I know it took a lot for you to call, and I don't know why you chose me or what it all means, but I'm here for you. Timmy is here for you, Evan is there for you, and we all can help get you through this."

He keeps saying everything I'd expect of him, things I already know, but somehow, hearing it from him helps. I listen to his words as they encapsulate me, tapping on the phone when he needs confirmation. I may be alone in the suite, but I feel like Sebastian is with me in my time of need. Again.

I hear the card key unlock the door, and I disconnect the call without warning and rush into the bedroom, slamming the door behind me before he can see my face.

I take out a pill and swallow it down, summoning my sleep-induced coma.

Gone

Instead of going to LA, I choose to stay at my old house, the one Dad left Timmy and me, mainly because I want to be alone. If I went to LA, Evan would try every three seconds to get me to talk or eat.

I stare out the picture window in the front, watching Mrs. Wrona's house. It's exactly the same as it was when I was growing up, and her routine hasn't changed either. She gets the paper at 8:00 a.m., then opens the blinds with her pug mug in hand. She reads for about twenty minutes on the recliner, then heads to the bedroom or bathroom to get ready for work. Her husband kisses her goodbye.

When I'm done staring out the window, I grab a handful of whatever dry cereal Evan bought, shove it in my mouth, drink water, and take a pill. Then I lock myself in my room, even though there isn't anyone else here to keep out.

My cell phone hasn't been turned on in days, and I haven't spoken to Sebastian since I hung up on him. I'm in a proverbial tunnel, trapped in the darkness with no glimmer of light at the end, and it feels remarkably the same as when I was thirteen years old.

Timmy tried coming over one weekend. All I did was ignore him, slamming doors just to feel the satisfaction of taking my anger out on something. I will give him credit though. He tried to break the door down after I slammed it in his face, yelling at me to just talk to him, telling me how he can help, but I tuned him out and propped myself against the door so he couldn't bust it down. Eventually, he tired out and gave up.

James and Kat take turns coming over, making sure I haven't swallowed the whole bottle of pills. Even when I'm not left alone, I'm still all by myself. No one understands what I'm going through.

I wake up from one of my ten-hour naps and decide to check my voicemail. Messages from everyone fill my mailbox, but there's only one person I listen for—my only exception.

He's dealt with loss before, and I've lost a part of me I won't ever see again—the Elana who loved and cared, the one who smiled and talked. What's the point of living if you stop caring? Maybe he can show me how to find that part of me again. He can tell me how to move forward.

I call his phone and get his voicemail. I'm okay with that.

"I don't know what to do. I don't want to talk to anyone but you. How were you able to move on after your sister passed?" My voice starts to shake, and the tears begin to fall. I try to swallow down the sobs that inch their way up. "You must think I'm pathetic. Your sister died. That's real loss. But I feel dead inside, Sebastian, like he stole the best parts of me again. I can still feel him. I can still feel him touching me, taking everything I love. I wish I was dead," I confess. "I just want the pain to go away." The sobs pick up steam until I can't control them, and I begin to hyperventilate. I drop the phone before I disconnect the call and continue to cry hysterically, gasping for air. "Why me?" I cry over and over again.

I drag myself to the desk and take another pill. I just want it all to end—the heartache, his voice in my head, the touch of his hands on my body. I want it all gone, wiped away, a clean slate. The only way I know how to achieve that is to take another pill. I don't even bother crawling into bed. My back presses into the hard floor as my sobbing dies down from the heaviness of my swollen, bloodshot eyes.

Eat. Stare out the window. Watch Mrs. Wrona. Take a pill. Sleep.

Eat. Stare out the window. Watch Mrs. Wrona. Take a pill. Sleep.

Eat. Stare out the window. Watch Mrs. Wrona. Take a pill. Sleep.

I've managed to shut mostly everyone out. I fire up my phone, revealing another full mailbox. Evan's voice makes me sad, because I do miss him when he's away for work. Certain things just couldn't be canceled, not without certain backlash. Like before, there are voicemails from everyone, but there's only one I'm hoping for. Sebastian's.

"Elana, I've been thinking about you nonstop. If it's okay, I wanna come see you. Please call me back. God, I wish you'd answer your phone." I feel the heaviness of his sigh. "You asked how I got through my sister's passing, and it's simple. I surrounded myself with the people I loved, I didn't shut them out. You must try, Elana. Don't shut us out. Evan is losing his mind. We all are. We just want you to talk to us. Please call me back, I want to talk to you, I want to hear your voice."

Toward the end of his voicemail he starts crying. I take a pill out of the bottle and swallow, crying into my hands, too.

Eat. Stare out the window, watch Mrs. Wrona, take a pill. Sleep.

Eat. Stare out the window, watch Mrs. Wrona, take a pill. Sleep.

Eat. Stare out the window, watch Mrs. Wrona, take a pill. Sleep.

The days mesh into nights and vice versa. Evan jumps through hoops for me, flying to his different jobs only to come back to this house to be with a person who barely acknowledges his presence. He returns from one of his trips, and I'm still where he left me two days later, staring out the window. I've lost more weight, and my pants are in danger of falling off my hips as I wither away day by day.

On one of the rare occasions I look in the mirror, my complexion surprises me. I'm paler than normal, almost gray, and my hair looks lifeless and dull, pulled back in a matted mess.

"Elana, you need to speak to someone. Everyone is really worried about you. *I'm* really worried about you," he says angrily, but I know it's just his frustration.

I remain motionless and silent, gazing into the fast-paced world that is Mrs. Wrona's living room window.

"This is what I'm talking about. If you aren't staring out of the window, you're sleeping." His tone grows more aggressive and worrisome.

He places his hand on my shoulder, and I jump from my seat. I cower into the corner, sinking to the floor with my arms wrapped around my knees, like a child. He, too, drops to the floor, throwing his head in his hands, defeated again.

I'm a lost cause, broken for eternity, but the sight of the man before me hurts deep within my soul. It's the first time I've felt anything. I think of what Sebastian said: "Surround yourself with people you love."

My once tall and muscular man has become small, frail, and tortured, like me, and it's my fault. He and I are the same, hurt to the depths of our core, except I'm the one who hurt him.

I get up slowly and move toward Evan, afraid, but I make myself do it. I sit down beside the man whom I know, in my heart, I still love. He doesn't react when he feels my presence. He remains still, crying into his palms.

I try to remove one of his hands from his face. Doubtfully, I inhale deeply, and make him touch me. I place his hand on my cheek, and he allows me to control the movement. His hand is soft and warm. Little by little, I remember his touch, and how I used to love it once.

I inhale the scent of his skin, its familiarity slowly bringing me back to him. He lifts his head, blinking away the tears as I study his hand, reprogramming myself with it.

Gradually, I move his hand from my cheek and make him touch my lips, moving his fingers around and down to my neck. I close my eyes, recalling a time when this felt amazing. For a moment, I feel it. It's there, very faintly, but there all the same, hidden behind the dark shadows that have taken up residency in my mind. I inhale once more, soaking in his woodsy aroma. I make his hands travel downward, though I can feel him hesitate.

"I want you to," I say softly, almost whispering the words, keeping my eyes closed.

His large hands glide carefully down my face, then over my shoulders. His warmth permeates through the thick robe. My breathing quickens again. The nerves start to manifest in my trembling hands, and he stops.

"It's okay," I assure him, though I'm not too sure of it myself. I move his hand down, opening my robe and placing his hand over my heart. Even though I'm clothed underneath, I can feel his warmth and love through the fabric, and it feels like he's touching my bare skin. My eyes flutter open. I look at him.

"Kiss me...please," I beg.

"I don't think that's—" but I cut him off and press my lips to his. Too scared to startle me, he doesn't kiss me back.

His lips are flush against mine, frozen and unmoving, but I hold his face in my hands, forcing him to maintain contact, to keep kissing me, to keep him close. It's nice and familiar even though he's holding back.

Then, eyes shut once more, I push him away slowly, reveling in his warm touch, allowing myself to feel the emotions running through me. I'm allowing myself to feel.

I remember the kiss at the baseball game, our hug at the park when he was drunk, his confession of love in my living room. A faint smile shines through, and I open my eyes. His beautiful blue-green eyes are looking for any sign of life. Until now, I've been an empty shell. I see all the pain I've caused—the lines of stress are written all over his face.

I give him a half-smile, letting him know a part of me is back and here with him.

"I promise I'll get help."

California Girl

THE SUNNY LA SKY IS hard to get used to, especially in the winter, but I must admit, I don't miss the snowy, dreary New York days—the snow plows or the crappy parking due to the dirty snow mountains piled on the streets.

While Evan is filming in the UK, I've been busy painting to sate Mrs. Monarch's elite clients' appetites for artwork. Kiki doesn't mind her new digs either, as she's now fully engulfed in her new lazy lifestyle.

Like I'd promised, I see a therapist and attend meetings for women who've been abused and assaulted. Speaking about my experience to others who've been through similar situations helps me realize how normal my feelings are. The anxiety, heightened alertness, numbness, and severe mood swings are all common reactions, and for once, being common feels pretty good.

There isn't a day I don't speak with Sebastian. He's the light to my darkness, reviving a part of me that was once comatose. Even Evan is grateful to him. Under different circumstances, Evan might've been jealous or angry that I turned to another man for support, but he's just glad I'm getting back to some form of normalcy, no matter who was the catalyst for my return.

The sound of the doorbell startles me, but I know my package has finally arrived. I silently curse Kat and James for making it so heavy, but I'm grateful to them for shipping me some of my things. It smells as if someone threw fifty satchels of strong, rapist-scented potpourri inside the box. It reeks of him, and my body reacts before my brain can.

I close the lid. The label was definitely written by James, so I know the box didn't come from *him*. In therapy, I've learned so much about how I react to certain triggers, and I know my brain is playing tricks on me, correlating my apartment with him.

I open up the flaps again, careful not to breathe too deep. It's like Christmas came early, as I pull out odds and ends from the apartment and a whole slew of clothes, which is great because the supply I had when we escaped New York was slim. It's nice to have *my* stuff again.

James packed some of my brushes and painting knives, and I know Kat had a say in what went into the box, too, sending the camera she bought me a year ago, along with a bunch of pictures.

I take the clothes out of the box and bring them to the laundry room, knowing a good wash and soak will remove the nonexistent smell from my clothes.

****

"So how's your mother doing?" my therapist Emma asks.

"She's been clean for months now, still doing the steps. She'll be in sober living soon," I add. I can't help but notice a sense of pride when I talk about her progress.

We discuss the call I received prior to my appointment about the ongoing investigation. Nothing came back with the blood DNA, and no prints matched anything in their records. Everything is at a standstill. My frustration is evident when I talk about it. I know I won't feel fully safe until he's behind bars.

"I loved that apartment. I miss my neighbors, I miss my friends. I miss New York. But I know I can't go back until they find him, not yet. I just want to hit someone."

"Is that why you took all those self-defense classes?"

"I felt empowered taking them. I hated feeling helpless all the time. Since Evan isn't always going to be around, I wanted to know how to defend myself. For my own security. And sanity."

"Right now, you're in the hyper-vigilance stage, always on high alert for sounds, smells, people, behaviors, anything reminiscent of your trauma. You have this heightened sense that when you are placed in a situation where your safety is at stake, you will be able to properly defend yourself, but you have to be careful. I'm not saying you aren't capable, but you cannot rely on this feeling, that you can overtake someone trying to harm you. Being extra cautious is one thing, but you must remember, you aren't Superman either."

"I experienced the heightened senses. James and Kat sent me some of my things, and they smelled like him."

"Your brain correlates your apartment and possessions with him because he invaded your space, your comfort zone, your safe haven. It'll fade in time. He could end up dead tomorrow but you could still have these reactions. It's how your brain copes. You just have to remind yourself that it may be a ruse," she explains.

We finish our session talking about Evan and Sebastian and their constant support, the continuous dreams, and the feeling of being homesick on top of everything else.

****

I find myself wandering aimlessly around the house, bored out of my mind. I've finished another painting this morning, leaving me drained of my creative juices for the time being.

I troll Facebook and waste time looking at Kat's updated pictures of her and Andrew. Seeing my friend happy and in love makes me smile, but at the same time, it makes me miss home and my friends even more. I miss going to Lizzy's, teasing James about his chauvinistic ways, and having Kat give me a hard time about nothing in particular.

I notice a new email hit my mailbox.

> Elana,
>
> I am extremely grateful you've been giving me a chance, even after I've let you down for so long. In order to build some sort of relationship, I need to be completely honest with you.

Ever since I stopped drinking, little memories pop up here and there, and I've heard it's a gradual process. In time, more memories will surface. I have to admit, I'm not looking forward to them, but I will not go back to the way I was either.

His name was Harold. He was a family friend, whom your grandparents trusted. He and his wife would watch me on occasion. He used to kiss me, and he once told me, "This is what you do to people you love, like your family." I was very young, and it became normal behavior to me, until I went up to your grandmother and tried to kiss her. She slapped my arm for being fresh and told me kids didn't do that.

I was confused, but the next time I went to his house, I told him what Mom said, but he waved her comments away, telling me I misunderstood, that it was something only boys and girls did together, not two girls.

Your grandpa and grandma weren't very vocal about feelings in our house, so it felt nice— different but nice. Eventually, he got comfortable and pushed the limits further. I started to feel uncomfortable going there.

I remember one time, I intentionally got in trouble on the way to his house, hoping they'd turn the car around, but they didn't. When your grandfather dropped me off, he told Harold I was on punishment. When I was left alone with him, he went into his closet for his belt, pulled my pants down, and whipped me. When he was done, I was told to sit on the bed as he undressed in front of me. He explained this was how bad girls were punished.

He coached me on what to do. I just remember the pain and tears. I was afraid he'd tell my dad I was bad, so I fought through the pain, but not without scratching Harold first. When it was over, he said, "You probably deserved this."

I broke down in front of our house, screaming how I never wanted to go back there, how sorry I was, because I didn't want to be punished like that again. When your grandpa called me a brat for thinking "no TV" was such a horrible punishment, I told him everything Harold did. After that night, your grandfather vowed to keep me safe, safe from him.

I never lost the feeling of being vulnerable and unsafe, except when your grandfather was around, but when he passed, I lost it. He was my support, and poof, it all disappeared. The nightmares started coming back, and the only way to stop them was drinking myself into oblivion.

I know this doesn't give you or Timmy any of those years back, but I hope it'll help all of us move forward. I know this is a lot to digest, and I don't mean to upset you, but maybe we can help each other heal. This time of the year is always hard for me because of what happened, and it's going to be the first year I'll be going through it sober. It'd be nice to know I have you on my side.

Mom

I let out a deep breath, leaning back on the couch, my body completely stiff. My eyes are far from dry as I try to digest everything she's written.

Finding out she and I shared a similar experience, a similar identity, I'd be inhuman if I didn't feel for her. I think about all the times I wanted to drown my past but stopped myself because I didn't want to end up like her. She drank while I painted. I feel a sudden desire to extend an olive branch, to make amends.

Mom,

I know it must be difficult to talk about, as it was for me. Thank you for sharing. As long as you and I continue our therapy and find healthy ways to cope, I'll be by your side. I'm not going to lie and say I'm not apprehensive, but I'm hopeful.

Timmy has been begging me to come home for Christmas. How would you feel about spending it with us at the house? Think about it and let me know.

Elana

Family First

As I step out of JFK, the sharp chill of the air stings my tanned cheeks, reminding me of the way winter should feel.

New York has already had their share of winter weather. Mounds of dirty white snow are piled along a distant curb, and I can't help but smile, missing not only the feeling of snow crunching under my boots, but the way the snowflakes land on my face. The simple things I took for granted when I was here are now things I wish for in LA.

"Where are you?" I ask into the phone, rather impatiently.

"Turn to your left and you'll see me. It's fuckin' freezing out. Doesn't the air hurt your gums? Stop smiling like that."

I hang up on him and do as I'm told. James steps out of the car, and my feet move faster while my breaths leave a trail behind me. Then, the passenger door opens, and my mother steps out.

"Did we surprise you?" Mom asks.

I nod fervently, overcome with emotions I didn't think I'd have. I pull them both into a hug. "This is going to be the best Christmas ever."

The drivers behind us lean on their horns, waiting to get a closer spot, but I ignore them and flash them the finger for good measure. I missed New York.

Any anxiety I had about returning has faded as I gush about my new LA life, while they fill me in about what's been going on here. But the moment we pull up to the house I barricaded myself into, I can't help but feel a certain way.

"Are you okay?" James asks.

"I will be."

Having gone to tons of therapy sessions, I know I can overcome anything thrown at me as long as I surround myself with the people I hold close. Practically everyone I care about will be here, in this house, with me. If I can't feel safe under these circumstances, I've got deeper problems than I thought.

The three of us unload the bags out of the car, and James goes back, lugging out a large box.

"James and I got a tree and some decorations." Mom's eyes light up, clearly proud of her part in the surprise. "This should be a Christmas to remember. But we can't decorate, not yet," she adds, and a devilish grin spreads, one I vaguely remember seeing before it all fell apart. It definitely feels like good days are ahead.

I look over to James. He's hiding something, too, as they glance sneakily at each other.

"What did you guys do?"

Neither responds. They only unload the groceries and place them in the fridge for our feast in two days when someone knocks. I look nervously at my mother. Her eyes fly open as she rushes to the door.

"Who's here?" I ask.

James returns a pleasant smile, grabbing my arm and pulling me to the living room near the front door. I link my arm in his and lean on his shoulder as she swings open the door in one grand gesture, welcoming whoever is behind it.

Timmy, Samantha, and Kat stand in the doorway, bundled up in their finest winter apparel. I knew they were coming, I just didn't expect them for another day. The squeal passes my lips before I even know it. I rush toward everyone.

"Hold the door," he shouts, and the silky-smooth voice registers instantly. Sebastian walks in, holding even more groceries.

"Now we can decorate," Mom enthuses, grabbing the bags from him and shuffling into the kitchen.

Everyone I'd ever want to spend the holidays with is here, except for Evan, but I'm not given too much time to dwell. I'm thrown into my decorating duties straight away. Surrounded by friends and family, and the jolly holiday tunes blasting through the speakers, we hang the shimmering garlands, twinkling lights, and red bows.

"LA looks good on you, El," Sebastian whispers in my ear as I hand Timmy the star to place on top of the tree.

I wrap my arm around his waist, watching Timmy try to straighten it. "How long are you staying?"

"I'll be heading home later tonight, sadly. But I heard you wanted me lying under your tree with only a red bow covering my unmentionables." He shakes with a bit of disapproval. "I didn't think it was very appropriate with your brother here, but I'll do it if that's what you want." He grins with lazy satisfaction.

I roll my eyes per usual though I smile like the Cheshire cat and kiss his cheek. "Your presence is present enough."

Once the decorations are hung with care, we each take a seat, admiring our work. The house looks like Christmas threw up in it, and it's just what we needed.

Sebastian sits in my father's old chair, listening to James and me on the floor, arguing over the rules to our gift-exchanging game, when I notice Kat checking her watch every thirty seconds. James sees it, too, and relays his disgust audibly.

"Expecting someone?" I ask.

"Andrew is on his way. I'm gonna wait outside."

"If he can't follow simple directions," James says, "he's got a bigger problem than just being unemployed."

She throws on her coat, ignoring him as best as she can. She retreats outside, letting in a blast of freezing air. Sebastian and Timmy wait until she leaves to laugh at James's comment.

"If you like her, just tell her," Sebastian announces.

"Seriously. You've liked Kat since what, high school?" Timmy adds.

James says nothing.

"I knew it," I boast.

"Slow much?" Timmy mocks. "Girls are oblivious."

Samantha slaps his stomach playfully, and I shoot her a thankful wink.

"I knew the first time I met him." Sebastian throws in for good measure.

"Can you all stop fucking talking about me like I'm not here? She's with him now. It doesn't matter." James eyes the door.

I throw my arm around him, knowing how he must feel. Then the door opens and in walks Andrew, hand in hand with Kat. If I had no clue how he felt, after going through the same thing with Evan, it's written all over his face now. He lets out a faint sigh, leaning his head on my shoulder. Everyone greets Andrew, but I just wave, feeling the need to be less enthusiastic about his presence for James's sake.

"Dinner's officially ready!" Mom shouts from the kitchen.

Our dining table has never seen so many plates before, squeezing all the place settings together, all of us sitting elbow to elbow. The food looks mouth-watering. Mom's hard work has paid off. She couldn't look happier to put this meal together for her kids and all our friends. She's really done it, really become the mom I didn't think she could be. Shows what I know.

We all dig in, filling ourselves to the max with lasagna, chicken parm, spinach, and garlic bread, a home-cooked meal we've all been without for quite some time. Any weight I still had to put on was accomplished at this dinner.

We all help with the dishes, and Mom retreats to the bedroom for the night, leaving the rest of us alone.

I notice Sebastian putting on his coat with his keys in his hand. "Walk me to my car?"

He hands me my coat and a scarf. The cool air fills our lungs, leaving a cloud of mist with every breath. "I wanted to give you this." He hands me a small wrapped box. "I saw it and thought of you."

I unwrap the velvet jewelry box and raise the lid. Inside is a beautiful white-gold paintbrush pendant. I gush over it. I immediately unwrap my scarf and add the new pendant to the one Evan gave me. I pull Sebastian into my arms, resting my cheek on his chest.

"This really is turning into the best Christmas. Thank you."

"It'll get better," he adds. "Trust me." I've never not trusted him, and I refuse to start now. "Love you, Els."

"I love you, too, Sebastian."

I run back into the house, noticing James trying to keep himself entertained with his phone while Kat plays kissy face with Andrew. I plop myself next to James, and he leans into me, whispering, "He texts a lot. Remind you of anybody?"

Casually, I glance up casually. Andrew is typing away on his phone. I observe it throughout the night, little texts here and there, even during our heated game of charades. Kat says nothing, so she's either oblivious or superb at keeping her thoughts to herself, which is out of character for her.

Eventually, the yawns grow more frequent, and everyone calls it a night. Andrew and Kat leave, Timmy and Sam retreat into his old room, and James and I fall asleep on the couch, watching old Christmas movies. Not a single worried thought crosses my mind, especially when I have Superman by my side.

A Very Merry Christmas

THE HOUSE IS ADORNED WITH more decorations than I can count. It's as if someone took a Christmas bazooka and blasted tinsel, and garland, and bows and lights everywhere. There isn't a single fucking surface that doesn't ooze holiday cheer. It's obscene and nauseating, but I keep my mouth shut, not wanting to disrupt the Christmas cheer overflowing from Jessica's loins, even though I'm going to be sneezing glitter until Spring.

She's outdone herself on the cooking front, hosting Christmas dinner—a large turkey, ham, string beans, mashed and au gratin potatoes, and more sides than I know what to do with. It's a feast for a king. I stand proudly, smiling at the head of our table with a large carving knife in hand, ready to feed the family.

But the smile on my lips isn't for them nor the holiday. It's because I know Elana will have gotten her present today.

"Son, are you going to carve it or smile at it?" my father asks impatiently, and I feel the waiting stares on me.

I tend to the bird, carving the juicy white meat while eyeing her painting on the opposite wall, thinking about her as my mouth salivates, not from the food, but from the thought of another imminent fest, in which she's the main course. I can't wait to fill her again—great, now *my* Christmas balls ache.

"So, Luke, are we ever going to meet your new girlfriend?"

He laughs. "I don't think that's a smart idea." He takes a large gulp of his cocktail, giving me a sidelong glance.

"Anyone that'll put up with you as long as she has is worth marrying," Dad starts. "You aren't getting any younger. When I was your age, I was already married with a child."

"And what a great specimen he's turned out to be," Luke mocks, but I try to brush off his comments. Now is not the time to have a "which son is the biggest disappointment" contest.

My leg bounces under the table, bobbing up and down nervously as I wait for Kat to call Luke about Elana. I know she will. Kat always does when her friend is upset, needing some form of comfort for herself.

"I have to admit, Jess," my mom says, "I wasn't sure about this painting, but it really complements the room."

We all take a moment to view the framed masterpiece. The dull yet satisfying throb commences as I feel the emotion she put into it.

"I love it," Jessica starts. "She had this one piece I couldn't even look at. It was horrible. There was this little girl, beaten. Ugh," she dry-retches and nods towards me. "He had to walk away from it, too."

"I'm sure he didn't *have* to walk away," Luke contests, shoving a forkful of food into his mouth. "He loves shit like that."

"Can't we have one family dinner without all the profanity?" Dad scolds us. "It's the holidays for goodness' sake."

The wailing of Luke's obnoxious ringer breaks the newfound silence. This has got to be Kat.

He stands up from the table. "I'll be right back. I've gotta take this."

"Anyone want a refill?" I ask, dumping the remainder of the decanter in my glass, quickly making my way into the kitchen, trailing Luke's footsteps before anyone has a chance to answer.

"Babe, slow down." He holds the phone away from his ear with a smile. He's starting to get a knack for this, too. It's unnerving.

I lean my head into his conversation. Kat's hysterics are loud enough that he doesn't need to put it on speaker phone.

"There was a present under the tree for her. How the hell did he find her again?" Kat sobs. It seems quiet behind her cries, and I wonder where all the chaos is.

"Just breathe," he says calmly, looking in my direction. "Everything will be fine. Just tell me what happened."

She takes a deep breath. "We were all opening presents, and when she got to her last one, no one knew where it came from, so Evan told her to go into the kitchen. Next thing we know, Evan's cursing and Timmy's calling the police."

My veins twitch, and I grind my teeth, seething with fury. That was a gift for *her*. *She* was supposed to open it and see what I gave her, not Evan. Fuck. He ruins everything.

"Evan?" Luke asks. "When did *he* show up?" He doesn't quite hide the disgust in his voice when he refers to Evan.

"He surprised all of us this morning."

When Luke told me he'd be eating dinner at her old house, the plan wrote itself. I pulled the old tin out of the vent in my basement wall, the tin I've held onto for years because it was the only thing I had to remind me of her. The emotions I felt every time I lifted the lid cannot compare to the real thing, but it was satisfying enough. It would evoke enough gratification to sustain the urge—not for long, but just enough. I wanted her to have it now. I wanted her to feel the emotions of that day again—the fear, the pain, the connection that was so perfect.

Kat continues, "El rushed out of the kitchen and saw what he left for her, some piece of clothing."

It wasn't just some irrelevant piece of clothing, like ashes are to a cigarette. It was the ripped pink tank top that she left in the room, stained with our union.

"I thought she was going to pass out. All the color drained from her face, and she couldn't breathe. She disappeared into the laundry room, spoke with Timmy, and I think Sebastian. We all thought she was gonna have a heart attack; her breathing was so erratic." Kat allows another sob. "Then all of a sudden she grew calm, a scary calm, as if it didn't bother her anymore. They're taking the first flight out of here." She breathes heavily into the receiver, finally catching her breath. "I wish you were here."

"I wish you were there, too," I whisper to Luke. He punches my arm.

While Luke tells Kat that Elana will be okay, I shake my head, dismissing that. She won't be. Until I have her again, this isn't over.

Kat continues to sniffle as I try to make out the voices in the background. My mind starts wandering, trying to recreate the chain of events. I try to imagine the face she made when she saw her shirt, and the ragged breaths that must've followed. I think of her beneath me, her gasping, her eyes wide and wet, the pain mapped out on her face. She's so beautiful when she looks tortured and broken.

"What are you doing?" Luke whispers, breaking me out of my thoughts. "You're a sick fuck," he adds, probably realizing what I was daydreaming about.

With all of this excitement, I just want to lock myself in the basement and enjoy my thoughts of her, alone. I could use the release, but there are too many people in the dining room waiting on us.

"I'm sorry for calling. I wanted to hear your voice," Kat says, still worked up. "I love you."

"Love you, too, babe. Call me later."

He hangs up the phone, and I look at him, shaking my head. "Love you, too, babe?"

He punches my arm again, hurting me this time. "Tell her what she wants to hear. Isn't that what you said?"

I give him another glance as I try to figure out whom he's actually lying to, but just like me, he's good at disguising things.

I throw my hands up in defeat—defeated that Evan stole my moment, defeated that she seemed to recover so quickly, defeated that my brother is a huge fucking disappointment.

New Year, New Roots

ONCE MY FEET HIT THE LA sidewalk I feel my heart rate return to normal. It's odd how it can go from one extreme to the next just from crossing state lines. The tranquility LA gives me is a blessing.

Maybe it's the sun, the way it glistens gold sparkles down on everything, giving the world below a divine radiance. Or maybe it's the high-tech security system, and the camera surveillance that makes me feel cozier. No matter what the reason is, this is my new home, and this is where I want to be.

On our way back, Evan tried to understand how I was able to calm myself after what happened on Christmas day, but I don't think I can fully explain it to him. I realized the fear I have doesn't matter anymore. Waking up early Christmas morning to the cries of my mother—seeing her thrash out of her nightmares—pierced something inside of me. I'm sick of living in fear. I don't want to carry this around like she has anymore. I want to be strong and live life unencumbered.

"What are we eating?"

"There's really not much in here," I say, opening the fridge. "What do you want?"

Evan stands behind me, lays a kiss on my shoulder. "You."

Behind me, he can't see the smile drop, but I know he can feel it. It feels like years since we've been intimate, limiting our affection to hugs and pecks. I've made a tremendous amount of progress since my apartment was broken into, but I still have a few mental hurdles I have to clear.

"Then what am I gonna eat?" I joke.

I turn to him and give him a loving kiss, running my fingers underneath his shirt. My mouth opens, giving him access, venturing my tongue along his lip, tasting his sweet love for me. His tongue brushes against mine, stirring long-dormant nerve endings.

He swiftly lifts me up, placing me onto the cold granite countertop, standing between my legs, gripping my outer thighs firmly. I can tell he wants this, and in my heart, I do, too. With my eyes closed, I kiss him deeper, reminding myself who's touching me. His hands glide smoothly over my jeans, along the top of my thighs, closer to my waist. I want to forget about everything. I lock my feet around him while his hands travel up my back, and our lips continue their play. He breaks away, running his tongue along my neck. My breath hitches away in uneven gasps.

"I'm sorry," he says, raking both hands through his hair, escaping my locked legs. "I shouldn't have pushed it, not after everything that's happened the past week."

I hop off the counter, mostly frustrated, though a bit grateful. My eyes run counter to my wishes, and start to burn. The sting of my past still bleeds into Evan's world, saturating his thoughts. I let out a groan. "Ugh!"

He chases after me. "I'm sorry, I didn't mean to upset you." His steps quicken, hot on my trail. "I don't want to rush you into anything."

I stop abruptly, turning on my heel. "Evan, you don't under—"

"I've waited God only knows how many years to be with you." He strides over to me, holding me in his arms again, and kisses my forehead. "It's going to take a lot more than this to get rid of me. No one said relationships are easy."

The frustration is suffocating. "Yeah, but—"

"No buts. Come on, let's go get something to eat. You're withering away on me."

Evan and I sit in the living room, bellies full of sushi, cuddled next to one another, watching all of the New Year's Eve events on TV. Neither of us are in the mood to be out celebrating, and we both know he'll have to travel back to the UK in a few days to finish filming, so we make sure we soak in our time together.

Our phones buzz when midnight reaches everyone in New York. Then we wait our turn, bringing in the stroke of midnight just as we both wanted—lips locked.

I silently vow to make this new year the best year, not letting anyone or anything come between me and my happiness, no matter what. I fall into Evan's eyes, willing to turn my resolution into a reality.

****

I wake up from a restful night's sleep, with my head on Evan's chest and only a minimal amount of drool. This time tomorrow, he'll be headed back to London to finish filming. The thought sends a prickle to my eyes. I trace my fingers over his smooth skin. I'm still amazed at how awestruck I am when he's lying beside me, knowing he's mine and I'm his.

The chilly shower water washes the impure thoughts away, along with any tears that try to escape. If I know Evan, I know what'll put an everlasting smile on his face. Breakfast.

I head down to the kitchen and make some pancakes, eggs, and bacon, hoping to surprise him with breakfast in bed. As careful as I can be, I head up the stairs with the tray of food, spilling only half the orange juice.

"Wakey, wakey, eggs and—" I sing. I exhale sharply when I notice the empty bed. I lay the tray on the mattress and start hunting for him.

When I find him in my studio, I say, "Ya know, breakfast in bed only works when the person is *in* the bed when I arrive with the breakfast."

I walk to his side, and he kisses my temple. "Thought you'd be in here after last night."

I think about last night, our bodies touching one another, and the sudden apprehension as I neared closing the deal. He stopped it before I could work through my feelings, ignoring my whines.

He views my most recent painting on the easel—another red one, raised paint in the corner, ripping down the piece. "This looks bad...another nightmare?"

"Was actually thinking about Mom's experience for this one."

He shakes his head, probably thinking about all the terrible things that have happened to my family. "Remind me to call the detective later."

"Why bother?"

Evan turns to me in disbelief.

"I'm dead serious. I'm over this whole thing," I say, waving it off. "Mom is still in fear of her attacker, and he's probably dead by now. I can't let him have that much power over me. The best revenge is to move on and go about my day. Now come on," I tug at his arm, dragging him back to the bedroom. "Your breakfast is getting cold."

He follows begrudgingly. Evan squints with caution at my lackadaisical approach. "Just because you say otherwise doesn't mean you can act as if everything is fine." He sits on the edge of the bed, eyes worn and hollow.

"Wanna make a bet?" I push him down, straddling his body with mine.

"I don't have to bet. What are you doing?"

I lean over him, determined to prove I'm over it. Before my thoughts can betray what my body wants, I move quickly. My tongue enters his mouth, his hands grip my hips, the tips of his fingers dig into me, and I can feel how much we both want this.

I kiss and lick his neck, moving down quicker than my brain can process. My tongue travels over his warm skin, and I feel his erection underneath me. The thought of him entering me makes me tremble, but I move my body to disguise the uncontrollable shudders. I keep caressing his skin with my mouth, moving further down, when he sits up on the bed and pushes me off him.

"What's the matter?" My pulse races, and all of a sudden I'm out of breath, hiding my shaking hands from his view.

"You're only doing this to prove a point," he adds. "I can't do this."

"Can't?" I playfully eye the bulge under the fabric of his pajama pants.

"It's been months, El, of course I want this...but I know you aren't ready. I felt you shaking."

He jumps out of the bed, kisses me on my forehead, and I lie there alone, defeated once again. I don't want to admit that he's right, and I hate it when he's right. I wish I were ready and I could put everything behind me, living as if nothing happened. I cover my face with his pillow and scream, as all my pain and frustration swell within me. But Evan isn't *entirely* right. I know how I feel. Being afraid of *him* has turned into my own personal race, and only I can see the finish line. The fear of him isn't gone completely, but the end of his rule over me is nigh. It's only the intimacy that's lagging behind, needing only a few laps to catch up.

****

As we near the house, Evan shows no remnants of the morning's events, already discarded as a distant memory. All I can do is dwell on it, however.

Evan punches in our access code, and the dark cherry gate swings open. We drive up the long, circular driveway, me glancing at him, waiting to see the look on his face, but he doesn't give anything away.

The last time he saw the house, they had just started reconstruction—the inside was gutted, and the outside was just as barren. But now it looks as if it's almost complete, the lush landscaping and beautiful Sycamore trees filling in all the empty space surrounding Evan's dream house. It's beautiful during the day, but the magic truly shines at night, with the soft lighting that lines the slate steps. All the landscape looks freshly manicured, framing the house like a well-trimmed beard.

I skip to the front door, waiting for him. We exchange smirks as he slides the key into the lock and opens the door slowly, unsure what he'll see next.

He peeks his head in before opening it all the way. I follow behind, smiling, knowing how anxious he must feel. Still he doesn't show it.

Though still not completely finished, the house looks amazing. The grand entrance boasts soaring coffered ceilings and a custom chandelier, all his mother's doing. To the left is the great room, which connects the foyer to the formal living room, where the first of three fireplaces rests.

The main floor hosts one of the many rooms that have their own connected bathrooms and walk-in closets. I'm not sure if the two of us have enough things to fill one closet, let alone all of them.

Unlike his current house, the furniture in this one will be cozier, the kind you want to sink into on a rainy day, with only a blanket and a book.

I grab his hand and lead him to the kitchen, where his eyes show the first signs of life. The lighting and the bright white cabinets pleasantly surprise him. He runs his hand over the gray countertop, inspecting the specks of silver and black in the slab, complementing the black cabinets below. The room is packed with high-end appliances and a large center island. But my favorite part is the breakfast nook, right in front of a large window facing the backyard.

I imagine us sitting here in comfortable silence while the sun dances off the pool, eating Grape Nuts in our old age.

He opens the French doors that lead to the backyard, and I trail behind quietly. As Evan leans down to feel the pool's temperature I fantasize about pushing him in—but I wouldn't dare, at least not until we've moved in.

He chuckles to himself. I assume he's having similar thoughts as I lean down to feel the water as well.

"Don't even think about it," I warn him.

"Why not? You were."

The backyard is a dream, just enough lawn-to-pool ratio. There's a built-in BBQ, sound system, and fire pit, and the lights at night look like fireflies.

While he's inspecting the other parts of the house, I go to our bedroom, taking the stairs two at a time. It's the very picture of serenity, with lofty exposed beam ceilings, a Romeo-and-Juliet balcony overlooking the backyard, the biggest walk-in closet, and the most luxurious master bath, packed with a steam shower and jetted tub.

With all the white walls, I'm still unsure if we should add any color. There is at least one main decoration; a giant canvas, the biggest I've ever painted. Blues and greens like Evan's eyes, and subtle violets like mine, scattered about, fading in and out, distorting the line between where one color ends and the next one begins. Splashes of white fade into grays, with only a little black used for contrast. This piece undeniably embodies Evan and me.

The raised black platform bed is already made up with a black-and-white bedspread. It's a simple pattern, but to me it resembles dusky tree limbs, similar to George's statue, branching out across the fabric with the root pattern twisting on the bottom. It made me think of Evan and his remark about planting roots with this house. It all just seemed so fitting. I found beautiful decorative pillows with colors that accentuate the cool-hued tones in the painting.

I open the white drapes, letting the sunlight fill the room. He calls my name as he walks up the stairs.

When he walks in, his head is down, looking at his phone. I wait—rather impatiently—for him to look up and see what I made for us. He finally raises his head, mesmerized by the canvas.

"I know we were going to go with something more neutral, browns and beiges, but I just started painting this and I thought—"

He holds up his hand to stop me from talking. Another minute passes before he speaks. "I'm going to say something that sounds really stupid in my head, so I'm sure it'll sound stupid out loud, but I don't care." His face lightens, as his thought materializes into words. "I see us in that painting."

I hold out my hand for him, lacing our fingers into one another. We both look at it together. "That's what I see, too."

He's getting lost in it just as I did when I created it.

"When I bought this place," he starts, "I knew it needed work, but I envisioned it as a place I would feel at peace in when I wasn't working. But a part of me knew it was missing something." He pulls me in front of him and hugs me from behind. "It was missing you. This is our home now."

Mantras

With Evan set up in an apartment in New York for another movie filming, I decide to stay with him. The apartment has security in the lobby, and no one can gain access without the guard inserting his card in the elevator. Kiki and I adjust to our temporary surroundings; although this place is far more secure than my old apartment or childhood home, we both feel a bit tense.

While he's on set, I keep myself busy. I visit Mrs. Monarch and deliver another painting for one of her clients. She proposes another offer, begging me to produce a few more pieces for a charity event she's hosting with her most valued artists donating artwork. As if raising money for charity wasn't enough of a sell, she mentions her biggest spenders will be present, and a few have insisted on my attendance and participation.

After the journey I've experienced, all of the ups and downs I've put on the canvas, I can finally hold my chin high. I gladly accept the prospect, excited to help raise money. It isn't long before I send out my own invites via text.

I head back to the apartment, thrilled to share the news with Evan when he gets home for the day. When I swing the door open, there he is, napping on the couch with Kiki. She lifts her head up and offers me a hello.

He slowly wakes and meets me in the kitchen, grabbing a water from the fridge.

"So guess what happened to me today?"

"You're doing another showcase?"

"What? How'd you know? I purposefully didn't text you because I wanted to tell you in person." I start scrolling through my phone to see if I added him to the group text in a Freudian slip.

His smile is wide and full of secrets. "A little birdie told me." The smile drops a touch. "Well, he kinda spilled the beans for you. I figured you didn't tell me on purpose."

He reaches to give me a congratulatory hug when the phone rings. Evan takes the call.

"Okay, bring it up." he says into the phone.

"Bring what up?" I ask.

"I'm waiting on a revised script. This should be it."

He opens the door, and the guard brings up the delivery.

The scent invades the apartment without even being able to see the actual delivery. Flowers. He's found me again.

Evan immediately sends them away and shuts the door, but I've already retreated to the floor. My eyes turn dark. The stars start twinkling behind my lids, and the air grows thicker. I know I'm headed for a full-blown panic attack. The deeper I breathe in, the less air I consume, spiraling the cycle faster and faster until I'm caught in a tornado of panic.

I draw my knees to my chest, trying to focus on getting my breathing under control, rocking back and forth, humming to myself to tune out the sound of his voice that starts resonating in my head.

My breathing exercises help, but I hold my chest, trying to calm my heart rate as his voice gets louder, taunting me with each passing second. I will not succumb to this fear. I mustn't.

"Shut up, shut up, shut up, shut up," I say to *him*, but I can still hear it. *See you soon.* His guttural voice spins like a record on constant loop. "Shut up, shut up," I repeat until it becomes my mantra.

Even with my closed eyes, I see the darkness looming over me, but I know it's Evan nearby. Slowly, my chanting ceases, and my breathing normalizes. My shaking begins to dwindle, and I know the attack is coming to an end. I stretch my legs in front of me, no longer needing them pressed against my chest.

I open my eyes. Evan's face is long. He eyes me cautiously, as if staring in one place too long will burn his retinas.

"They aren't as bad as they used to be." My voice is low. I'm still coming out of the fog, a bit scared to talk.

"Who were you telling to shut up?"

"Sometimes," I say, leaning my head back closing my eyes again, "all I hear is his voice in my head." I shake the memory to the back of my thoughts and I look to Evan. "The only way to get rid of it is to look insane and talk to myself. It's actually less crazy when I'm alone," I joke.

"This is what you go through when I'm away?"

I nod and take in a few deep breaths, fighting off the final shrouds of panic. Evan helps me off the floor. "I've gotten it down to a couple of minutes, and now it's even shorter. Was there a note or anything? We should call the police," I say dusting myself off.

"It wasn't from him," he confirms, internalizing what I told him.

Guilt overwhelms me. All of that panic and terror was for naught. I don't have it all figured out, and the finish line isn't as close as I had hoped. I'm still laps behind.

****

While I keep myself holed up in the apartment, I do what comes naturally. I paint. Having to create a few new paintings for the art event, I choose to create three focal pieces, each representing my past, present, and future. All are larger than my normal works. They're meant to be kept together, but would look nice separately, too.

All of the fear I grew up with is thrown onto the canvas with precise strokes. It represents my first piece, my past. The dark reds and blacks slashes signify all that's happened, all the pain I've been through. The second piece will show the struggle I face each day, trying to break away from the sharp, jagged strokes into something more fluid and controlled. The colors will bleed from the first onto the second, but as your eyes travel to the third painting, only faint remnants linger in a more whimsical approach. The colors are lighter and brighter, full of hope and promise of better days ahead. Hidden inside the paintings are two solid vertical strokes, the number 11, which only Evan and I can see.

It's the best therapy session I've had, pouring my soul into my art. But it's not without its downside. I look in the mirror. My hair is pulled up in a messy bun, paint streaks my chin and cheeks, a speck or three dot on my nose and forehead, and I can see it written all over my face. Exhaustion. To constantly feel all the time, always having your emotions front and center, clawing its way to escape to the surface…it drains you. A part of me wishes to never see another paintbrush, while another part wishes to keep going until I've let it all out.

For now, I can't give anymore of myself to the canvas, and for once this large apartment feels tiny and suffocating. I clean up the mess I've created in my painting nook, requiring some fresh air and some space between me and these walls.

I roam the streets, hitting the pavement hard, walking in no particular direction with no particular destination. I look in the windows of the shops I pass, and stumble upon a small boutique. The dress in the window stops me in my tracks; the color summoned me before my brain even registered what I was looking at. The bright cobalt blue—one of my favorite colors—catches my sights, as if I were seeing color for the first time.

"We just got that one in," the salesgirl mentions, noticing the obvious look on my face. "You should try it on."

I know I'm in trouble once I spot my size. I bring the dress into the fitting room, realizing the color looks great against my skin tone. Most bondage dresses look like they're for a fun girl's night out, but this one's different. The material is so flattering, and clearly tailored to a woman's body. The seamless, form-fitting dress hugs all of my curves, the few I have left. It has a dramatic scooped neck, daringly low cut, leaving my scar completely exposed.

The salesgirl zips up the back for me, and I pose in front of the mirror, unraveling my hair and letting it cascade down my back. The irregular waves gained from being tucked up all day gives me volume for days, and for once the scar isn't the first thing I see when I look at my reflection. The dress was made for me. I don't have a tremendous amount of cleavage, but what I do have looks very revealing.

The hem skims my knee, and I turn to the side, watching it hug the curve of my rear. I've never been one to admire myself, as I've always been self-conscious but finally *I'm* wearing this dress. It isn't wearing me.

A Cause to Celebrate

GEORGE GREETS ME AT THE door in the same overalls he had on the first time we met, except there's a few extra paint splatters on them this time around.

Being in George's studio grounds me, offering the same catharsis my laundry room gives me, the art comforting me like a warm cup of cocoa on a freezing day. I envy him and the space he's acquired over the years. This is only a taste of what it must feel like to have a wide, open space, with only the limits of your imagination to inhibit you.

Before taking care of business, we fall into a conversation about his wife, art, Evan, the show, and before I know it, I'm behind schedule. He helps load a few of my pieces before sending me off.

"See you soon." He waves from the sidewalk before rushing back inside.

I'm left to think on my way to the gallery, one of my least favorite things to do these days. The thought of my apartment comes to mind. I know I can't go in by myself, but I know I want to see it before I leave, clean it out for good, and put that part of my life behind me.

I drop off the final pieces, arranging with Charli and the staff the order I want them to hang, before heading home to change. It feels like centuries since I've hung out with the gang, so a night at Lizzy's is on the top of my list. Knowing everyone expects me to be late anyways, I decide to make a pit stop. I turn the ignition off and sit there, staring at what used to be my home. Taking the keys out of the ignition, I slowly get out of the car and look up to my window. Remembering all of the nights I would sit with Kiki on the couch, staring out the glass, watching the sky change before our eyes. The bright yellows would fade into rich orange and fuchsias that slowly receded into purples and indigo blues as the night crept in. I was safe here once.

I pull out my ringing phone, and Kat says, "Where are you?"

"I'm on my way." I hang up before she can say anything else. I sit for a minute to watch the sky change above me, missing the New York night. But I know this isn't my home anymore. This is my past, and I need to let it go.

I'll be back, I know I will, and it'll be soon. I can feel it. I hop off the hood of the car and drive to my all-time favorite place.

****

I pull up to Lizzy's, barely able to snag a spot—the lot is filled to capacity. Kat is outside pacing on her phone, so I refrain from running to her, screaming with excitement.

"What are you doing?"

She hangs up whatever call she was on and gives me a big hug. "It's loud in there, and I couldn't hear."

"Andrew coming?"

"We're done. Again. C'mon."

We walk up to the doors, which I promptly swing them open, ready to down a martini or two and soak in the life I once had here for what feels like a final time.

"SURPRISE!" the room erupts.

"What the fuck?" My hands fly up to my mouth. Everyone laughs, applauds, and cheers. All I see are familiar faces—Mom, Timmy, Samantha, Sebastian, all my friends, George, Charli, Mrs. Monarch, Mrs. and Mr. Saunders, many of Evan's friends from LA, including his manager and agent, and Evan himself. Anyone I could have possibly wanted to have at a party, plus some.

The party starts, the music kicking on as I make my way through the carousel of hugs, wondering what the event is even about.

Evan finally gets his turn and spins me. "We're all so proud of you. One showcase down, another one to go."

Lizzy's is decorated with "Congratulations" signs and balloons scattered everywhere. I've never seen it more festive than tonight. The drinks flow freely as people laugh, mingle, dance, eat.

"Hey, good-lookin'." He stands by the bar, waiting for his order.

Unable to keep a secret, Sebastian spills the beans about the party's planning and how everyone played a part, including him.

"Are you guys gonna have a bromance or something?"

He clutches his heart and bats his eyes. "Why? Do you think I'm his type?"

I take a sip of my drink. "You're all insane. You know that, right?"

Without a word, Sebastian gets his drinks, kisses the top of my head, and brings them to a table with a bunch of guys I don't recognize.

I walk over to our usual table and climb into my preferred seat. Everyone is in their usual spots, and it's as if I never left.

"So I guess this means you won't be bringing Andrew on Friday," I ask Kat.

"Nope."

James's expression lightens, but keeps whatever smartass comment he has to himself—his most intelligent move to date.

Spotting Mom at a table away from the bar, I approach her, realizing how hard it must be for her to be here.

"You okay?" I rest my hand on her shoulder. Her hand finds mine, and neither of us hurry to move it.

"Yup, I have my soda. You don't have to babysit me."

Timmy sees the two of us and joins our table. "Ya know, I never thought I'd see this, the two of you getting along. That says a lot about how far we've all come. I'm proud of both of you."

My mom's eyes begin to well, and mine also start to sting. When did he get so mature? She hops off her stool and beckons us to come closer, pulling us into a group hug. This is the mom I want to remember, the one who smells like sweet almond milk and not the bottom of a bottle, one who is lucid and not whipping us with some sort of device. A mother who is loving and caring, the mom who's hugging us right now.

Evan's voice rings through the speakers. "Can you come here, El, just for a moment? I want to make a speech, and the guest of honor has to be front and center." Evan's grin is huge as I walk slowly toward the front of the room, petrified that all eyes are on me. I don't need a speech. I didn't invent gravity; I just threw paint on a canvas, but I play along.

"I just want to thank everyone for coming tonight. It took some clever planning to get all of you guys here, especially without El finding out.

"Elana has always been artistic, doodling over any surface—books, walls, napkins, even my mom's coffee table," he says with a smile, and I look at his mother, mouthing, "sorry." "You name it, she found a way to leave her mark on it." He looks to me and grabs my hand. "But I lied to you and everyone here." I look at him suspiciously, as does everyone else. Groups of people chatter amongst themselves, wondering what lie Evan has told them.

"I told you and everyone that this was a party to celebrate your newest success, but that's not entirely true." His eyes find mine. "You've been the most important person in my life for longer than I can remember. You've always been my best friend, and my strongest supporter through everything."

Evan pulls me closer to him, placing my hand over his heart. He doesn't once break eye contact. The room feels warmer, but it could just be the feeling I get when he looks at me like this, our bodies close to one another, feeling the love that keeps our souls tethered together.

Speaking as if I'm the only person in the room, only with the help of a microphone, he goes on. "You've managed to leave your mark on my heart. I simply cannot imagine my life without you in it." The confidence in his voice disappears as I stare at him, at a loss for words. "Elana Parks, would you do me the extraordinary honor of being my wife from now until eternity, and maybe even after that?" He bends down on one knee and pulls a box out of his pocket, opening it, waiting for my answer.

My hands fly up to my mouth, I look at Evan, then the ring, sparkling bright in the dimly lit bar. Completely in shock, I shoot my eyes back to Evan.

"Forever and then even after that? I dunno," I deadpan, "that's a long time."

His head drops, his shoulders shaking as he laughs to himself. The crowd offers their own bout of laughter. Someone, I think his mom, starts chanting "yes," and everyone else starts shouting it, too, until it's all that can be heard.

He eyes our friends and family, and then me, waiting. "So what do you think? Can we do this forever?"

I nod fervently. "Forever!"

His smile grows bigger than I've ever seen. Then he jumps up and crashes his lips into mine.

"It's about time!" James shouts.

Before I can inspect the ring or enjoy the moment with my new fiancé, I'm being pulled left and right for hugs and kisses. Evan doesn't escape any easier, receiving his share of congratulations in the form of man hugs, handshakes, and high fives. Lizzy rings the bell over and over again. There's not a single person in the bar who doesn't have a smile tattooed on their face.

The rest of the night flies by, and before I know it, Evan and I see everyone to their cars, thanking them for coming.

He hugs me from behind as the final cars pull out of the lot, their tail-lights fading in the distance. "So were you surprised?"

"Understatement of the year." I hold my hand to my face. "I can't believe this is actually happening." I squeal with delight, skipping all the way to the car. Even gravity can't weigh me down.

"Just don't go all Bridezilla on me."

I get to the car before him, and out of the corner of my eye I notice a white sedan pull away from the sidewalk. Must be Peter, the photographer. I wonder if he got any pictures of me holding my hand up—surely that'll get him in good graces with his boss.

Evan starts the car. "The night's not over yet. Just one more place we need to go."

Once he starts driving, I know the destination instantly. The park.

My face can't manage any more strain—there's a permanent cramp in my smiling cheeks.

When we get there, I jump out of the car and frolic to the swing set like a child. The cool air gives me a second wind as I hop on and kick my legs out, inching higher and higher, but I'm already on cloud nine.

"You look happy, Els."

"I am," I cheer, blissfully. I start my descent. "I mean, I miss New York. It's where we came from." I hop off my swing and sit on his lap. "The second I landed back here, there's been a chill in my bones I can't shake. I miss LA—I miss the sun. I miss the life we have there. I miss our home." I plant a kiss on his supple lips. The warmth of his mouth smothers any and every chill inside me.

"You do know I just wanted to come here and sit in the warm car," he jokes. "But this isn't so bad." He lifts his feet off the ground and swings us together while I hold on for dear life, giggling. "Damn, I've missed that laugh," he says.

The Blue Dress

JUST LIKE WITH THE FIRST showcase, my appetite is a ghost.

I'm drying my hair as Evan speeds through the door and starts racing to get ready.

"So," I yell to him in the shower, "I was thinking about going to the apartment before I head back to LA. Would be nice to get the last of my things."

"You ready to go back?"

I've been asking myself the same question for over a week. "I think so."

"Maybe we can get the gang to help."

Evan gets dressed while I'm still fixing my makeup, and as soon as I'm done, I kick him out of the room. I want to give him the big reveal, especially since I've never worn a dress this daring before, showing more chest than I've ever done, with also allowing the scar to be dangerously visible.

I step into the body-hugging, silk-lined dress, sliding it over my hips and placing my arms into the dainty capped sleeves. I thank myself for not eating because even an ice cube would have given me a distended stomach.

I put on the necklace Evan gave me with the diamond encrusted "1," slip into a pair of plain black pumps and call Evan to the bedroom door.

With the door only wide enough for him to reach inside, I ask, "Can you zip me up?" His fingers graze along my bare back as he pulls on the zipper. I let my hair drop, slowly turn, and open the door all the way.

"So…how do I look?" I ask timidly, hoping his face will do the answering. He takes a deep breath and swallows hard. "Do you like it?" I ask more nervously now—his expression wasn't exactly the answer I was hoping for.

"Um…"

"Is it because you can see the scar? I just fell in love with it and—"

"Shut up for a second." He swallows again. "I don't know," he says oddly, "turn around." I spin for him, fearing he hates it. When I face him again, his eyes are wide open, and he's grinning from ear to ear. "I think we need to get you that dress in every color."

He walks over and bends down, whispering in my ear while his hands glide sensually down the smooth fabric over my hips. "It fits you perfectly," he says, pulling me closer. "Mmmm." I start to blush, and he kisses my neck.

"I just feel a little naked with my scar showing. I mean, it's usually covered." I start second-guessing myself, trying to think of another dress that'll be better for tonight. "Maybe I should wear a sweater with it."

He stands there in his fitted suit, looking as dapper as ever, staring at me like I've spoken German, shaking his head, not acknowledging a single thing I've said. "Damn, you look good." He licks his lips. "Don't mind me if you catch me staring all night. I'll be thinking inappropriate thoughts." He heads into the kitchen to grab a water, only then shouting, "No sweater!"

He always knows how to make me believe in myself. "In that case, I think I'm ready!"

****

We arrive at the gallery ahead of schedule, where we're immediately greeted by a mass of photographers, as if they had their own invite. Evan and I push through them as they blind us with their flashes. The gallery is still relatively empty, with only a handful of people circulating.

Mrs. Monarch greets Evan and I before leading us to the area designated to my works. Like before, they're placed how I want them, showcasing the journey I painted. It's the first time Evan has seen the three focal pieces side by side, kissing my temple with approval. It's the perfect blend of my heaven and hell.

I think about the last show and how Marc Pullman came here and saw all of my paintings, catching a glimpse into my head, how that one day in our history impacted my whole life. Now if he comes, he'll see the transition I've made. I hope it angers him beyond belief, so he knows he doesn't haunt me every day anymore. His grip on me is loosening, and there's nothing he can do about it.

The gallery begins to fill, the champagne flows, and familiar faces gather all around, along with a whole lot of new ones.

"If I didn't think Kat would hit me, I'd say something completely sexist."

I turn on my heel and see James with Kat draped on his arm. Both of them wear matching smiles, positively beaming.

"What is this?" I ask, even though the sight of them says it all.

"We had a talk."

He watches her, adoring her, fingers intertwined. I hug the two of them, and that infamous scent hits my nose. My lungs go on strike, refusing to let anymore air in, but I'm clearly the only one who can smell it.

"You okay?"

I wave off James's concern. "So I was wondering which one of my bestest friends wants to help me move the rest of my stuff?" I raise a brow, hoping all my friends will take the bait. "I'm thinking Sunday. Any takers?" Still no one answers, so I sweeten the pot. "I'll reward you with food and beer."

They both nod in unison, and Kat says, "I'll help, but I won't like it. It'll mean that it's final. You're really not coming back."

Across the room I spot Sebastian, towering over everyone, looking dapper. He approaches.

"Elana Parks, you've outdone yourself this time."

I reach up and take his temperature with my wrist. "Using my government name and not 'good-lookin'—what's gotten into you?" I kiss him on the cheek.

"Just because I didn't say it doesn't mean I wasn't thinking it. Mainly it's because my parents are here," he admits, pointing over his shoulder.

I slap his arm, laughing. "Are these lovely people your parents? It's a pleasure to meet you both. I've heard so many wonderful things." I extend my hand, but they give me a hug, making me feel as comfortable as their son did.

As with the Friday before, the night goes off without a hitch. Charli introduces me to some of the clients who've purchased past pieces of mine. I end up talking to a couple who shows interest in commissioning me to do a custom piece for them. The husband seems very eager to work with me, and he says as much when he hands me his business card, offering to compensate me handsomely for my services.

Every now and again, I notice Evan's stares from across the room. I remember what he said earlier, and images of the night we got engaged flash in my mind, like a montage of bare body parts, freckled with beads of sweat, lust, and love, tangled around one another. I finally crossed my finish line; no trembles of fear surfaced, only shivers of ecstasy.

Kat scurries to me, looking over her shoulder. "I need to talk to you about Andrew before James comes back."

"What's the matter?"

"Before your party last week, Andrew and I got together, but I ended it because he was acting weird. Tonight, he came to my apartment before James picked me up, begging me to get back with him. Like serious groveling." Before I can voice my displeasure, she waves me off. "Don't worry, I'm totally over him. I want to see what happens with James. Do you think I should tell him about Andrew?"

"Well, you weren't with James at the time, so I don't think so."

"I just didn't want to ruin it before it even starts, ya know?" She looks relieved, as if I've lifted the burden off her shoulders.

After a long night of schmoozing, Mrs. Monarch thanks all of her artists and clients for making the evening a success. It was nice to meet other artists and hear their motivations. Little by little, people call it a night, and Evan and I follow, heading back to our apartment.

We step foot in the elevator, put our card in the slot, and press our floor. The moment the doors close, his hands find my hips, and presses his body against mine. I feel his every muscle harden against me.

He moves the hair away from my ear, sending chills down my spine. My insides clench with arousal. His voice is soft and breathless with only a hint of hunger. "I've been thinking about this moment all night long."

Face the Music

IT'S A BEAUTIFUL MORNING. THE sun is strong, the air is cool, the sky is blue—but the main reason why it's a great morning is because I woke up in his arms, smiling from ear to ear. I sit up, careful not to disturb him, and watch him sleep.

My nerves jitter because of where I'm going today, but watching him sleep puts me at ease, at least for now. Knowing he and James will be joining us when they're done with their errands is comforting, too. Having everyone I care about helping with this process means more to me than they'll ever understand.

I shoot Kat a text, telling her when to be ready, and she responds with, "LATE NIGHT W/ JAMES, HUNGOVER, BUT WILL BE READY."

Evan leaves for his radio interview, and I head to the Island to pick up Kat. My anxiety is at an all-time high when I remember the last time I was in that apartment.

"We need to talk," Kat says the moment she gets into the car.

Just as I'm about to pull away, I know my mind is playing tricks on me. The floral aroma that I can't stand penetrates my nose again. I roll down the window to let out the corrupted air.

"You hot?" she asks but goes on anyway, "Andrew came by this morning. He won't take no for an answer. Then he got totally pissed off when I told him he had to leave because I was helping you pack up the rest of your stuff." She speaks so fast, trying to spit it out, and loses her breath. "I think he's crazy."

"You might be right." I fan my face, trying to move the smell around, breaking up the concentrated scent that lingers near my nose. My heart begins to quicken, and the panic starts to take over. "Can you drive?" My breaths grow erratic. "I think I'm freaking out a bit." I jump out of the car and suck in the biggest gulps of air as I pace.

"We don't have to do this. James and I can go there and take care of things for you."

"No," I insist, getting back in the car. "I need to do this." I lower the window and crank up the heat. "I just need to keep calm and remind myself that it's just an apartment, and everything will be fine." I do my breathing exercises, trying to clear my head of the panic. Then my wailing phone startles me.

"Hello?" I ask, seeing a number I don't recognize. No answer. "Hello?" I say again.

"El? Can you hear me?" Evan asks, his voice breaking up horribly on the other end.

"Barely, where are you?"

"I'm...ay...ere...ut—"

"What? You keep breaking," I say, before the call drops.

Kat enters my gate code, and we park in my old spot. This is it.

Once the car is in park, I'm overcome with sadness. This place has been my home for years. I've grown to love my neighbors, especially, Mr. Sam, who's always treated me like a granddaughter, giving me sound advice when I needed it most. I know if I dwell on it for too long, it'll start a domino effect on all the other emotions I'm trying to suppress.

Peter's white car is on the other side of the fence. He waves to me. How the hell did he know we'd come here?

The two of us head up to my apartment, Kat's steady arm linked with my shaking one. My steps slow as I near the door. "Go ahead, I'm going to talk to Mr. Sam. Put on the radio, it'll help my mood. I'll be there in a minute."

I stop in front of Mr. Sam's door, and it's as if he was expecting me, as the door swings open before I get a chance to knock.

"I heard movement in your apartment. I was just going to investigate," he says with a tired voice.

I hug him hello. "It's just Kat. We're moving the rest of my things. I wanted to see you before I got started." I hear the radio kick on. "Is the music too loud?"

"No, dear, it's fine. Stop by before you leave. I have something for you."

Before I get emotional, I give him another hug and head into my apartment. The light floral scent lingers in the air, but I block out the smell. It's all in my head. The radio plays through the speakers, and I walk a little easier, moving with the beat.

The apartment looks relatively unchanged, the boxes Kat brought up are still flattened, and I notice the bathroom door is closed. She must be in there, trying to recover from her late night with James.

I head into the kitchen and put my kettle on the stove, hoping some tea will soothe my nerves. I tread into my bedroom, expecting to see it exactly how I left it, unmade and stained from the last time I saw *him*, but it's bare, stripped of its sheets.

"Kat, are you okay in there?" I shout from the bedroom.

The tea kettle starts to whistle. I can't wait for the warmth to settle my nerves and take the chill out of my core. I bring my mug with me, sipping slowly, burning the roof of my mouth.

"Kat?" I walk into the studio, humming the song on the radio as the bass vibrates the walls. The painting I made of him is on the easel—his eyes are unfinished, but the rest of his face stares back. Kat is on the futon. Tears stream down her face. Her mouth is gagged, and her hands and feet are bound with tape.

He's here.

Cat and Mouse

My mug crashes to the ground. The scorching liquid splashes over my feet, singeing my legs through my jeans. The bathroom door flies open, and he hurls himself in my direction.

My instincts kick in as I swing the studio door close as fast as I can, but he's faster, wedging his foot in the doorway. His arm reaches through, searching for me like the antenna of an insect.

"C'mon, Elana, don't make this harder than it has to be!" He's as calm and controlled as I remember.

"Help!" My throat hurts from screaming, and my lungs burn from breathing. Tears of terror begin to pour down my cheeks, blurring my vision. The radio in the living room drowns out my voice. No one can hear me over the loud, thumping music.

I try to keep all of my weight pressed against the door, staying low to the ground, even though I know it'll never close. His arm stops searching. For a quick second, I think he might flee down the fire escape and we'll be safe. The music stops, and my sob break through the silence.

Hearing my cry, he lowers his arm and grabs a chunk of my hair, yanking violently. I lose my footing, and he's able to push open the door.

"This cat-and-mouse game ends today."

His grip tightens as he pulls my flailing body toward him. He rips out my hair in clumps, and I feel every follicle tear away from my scalp. I claw my nails at his hand, tearing at his skin, but it only makes him yank harder. He grunts his guttural hunger as his free arm wraps around my neck, lifting me off the ground, cutting off my air supply.

"Relax, Elana," he whispers close, his tongue grazing my ear. I struggle to pry his arms away, scratching at him, but he seems impervious to pain. "Look at your friend. She's behaving."

I summon all the strength left in my body and fling myself back onto him, sending the two of us crashing to the hardwood floor. His arm loosens around my neck, just enough for me to escape. I scramble to my feet and rush the door, but he grabs ahold of my ankle, pulling me back down toward him.

His elbow crashes into my stomach, knocking all the air out of my body, deflating me like a balloon. He straddles me as the music continues to blare, thumping its bass against the floor. I cough in the vain hope of air, but it doesn't come freely. His body is a tractor on top of mine. There's no need for him to cover my mouth, because I don't have enough air to scream, let alone breathe.

"Are you ready to behave?" he asks, barely winded. His face is so close. The crystal-clear blue eyes are shards of glass plunging through my soul. "I told you you'd see me soon." My lungs start to recover, and my legs start to move, kicking underneath him, trying to buck him off me. "Stop fighting." He grits his teeth at my disobedience. His hand whips across my face, and the sting is instant. My eyes whirl, disorienting me as the weight of his body disappears. I roll to my side, cupping my cheek with one hand, my stomach with the other. I try to cough, but it hurts too much. He walks to the door and bolts the locks. *Click. Click.*

I put up little fight as he wraps tape around my ankles, binding them like a mermaid's tail, then tying my wrists in front of me.

He lifts me up over his shoulder. The pain shoots through my stomach again, further weakening my breaths. Then I remember something from class, and I find the strength to lift my body up. I raise my arms above my head and slam my elbow down on the base of his neck.

He crumbles underneath me, and I fall backward off his shoulder, slamming my head on the floor. So many shades of brilliant white lights flash before my eyes until they turn pitch black. The pain rings like a high-pitched siren two inches from my ear, and I gasp for air. The back of my head grows warm and wet as I writhe, moaning in pain.

"Fucking bitch!" he curses, but my eyes won't focus. All I see is stars and static. I blink furiously. As my sight returns bit by bit, I watch him rub his neck furiously.

I reach my bound hands to the back of my head. They come back wet and scarlet red. I roll from side to side, with each cough, the pain from my head vibrates to the tips of my toes. He looms over me, infuriated. He swings back his leg, readying for a kick, but he stops himself.

"This was so much easier when you were little, but I'm kind of enjoying this. Aren't you?"

Instead of picking me up again, he drags me to the couch.

"You were my first, Elana," he admits, dropping my legs back to the floor with a thud. "And I could tell I was your first, too, so tight and sweet. I can't wait to take you again." I let out a muffled sob as he sits me up against the end of the couch. Blood drips down my neck, soaking into my shirt. My eyes dance in a frenzy.

He gently moves the hair out of my face, tucking it behind my ear before he places tape over my mouth and disappears from sight. I hear him carrying Kat over his shoulder and tossing her onto the couch. She bounces once, then falls onto the hardwood floor, right on her shoulder. Her eyes are bloodshot, full of tears and fear.

I have to make sure nothing happens to Kat. It's me he wants.

He stares at the two of us and smiles. "Katarina, Katarina, Katarina." She and I look at one another, not knowing how he could know her name. "I've heard so much about you."

Somehow, I manage to get my breathing under control. Thinking clearly is the only way I'll be able to get us out of here. He crouches over me. His scent fills my lungs, along with the smell of blood.

"Do you know what I went through for you? Do you know how special you are to me?" He eyes me closely, searching my face, looking down at me with an adoring gaze, so sick and twisted it makes my bile rise. "This is the most effort I've ever put into someone." The same calm rage that fueled him then still fuels him now, but with a vengeance. His eyes are soulless, with not a hint of life. "Your Kat was so forthcoming with information, whether she knows it or not. It's interesting what you women share in the bedroom."

My eyes bulge out of their sockets, and I've never felt more frustrated than I am now, unable to spit in his face.

"No need to be jealous, Elana. I never fucked her."

I stare at him while he talks, contemplating my next move. I lean forward, putting my head between my legs, willing him to come to me, knowing how much he loves to see my face when he talks. He does just what I thought he would and leans over.

"What's the matter, sweetheart?"

His breath grazes the top of my head as he inhales deeply, savoring my scent. I know he's close. I fling my head as hard as I can. The pain is excruciating.

It feels like someone drilled a hole in the back of my head as I slam it into him. My bound hands fly up to hold my skull, hoping to dull the sharp sting. Hearing him howl in pain is gratifying, but watching the blood pool out of his chin satisfies me even more.

"You like to play dirty? I like that." His smirk reappears. "I'm hard right now just thinking about what I'm going to do to you." His chest rises and falls faster, his breaths deeper. I can see the fire in his eyes, the lust on his lips. He crouches in front of me, holding my head still, pressing his hot, moist lips against the tape. I try to jerk my head back, but he already got what he wanted. As the music blares in the background, he bobs his head slowly to the beat.

"You know, I saw you later that summer, and I wanted to have you again." He grabs me by my chin, but I don't pull away, afraid the jerking motion will hurt me even more. His raunchy breath slams into my face, no longer reeking of alcohol, but it's still just as foul. "You were so tender. I couldn't get you out of my mind. But your friend would never leave your fucking side!" His mask crumbles at the thought of Evan. "Then all of a sudden my prayers were answered. I found you again, slashed your tires, followed you home. You even waved at me," he gloats. "We were going to be reunited that night, but that fucking dog wouldn't shut up."

My body shudders at the thought.

"You have no idea how much it hurts when I don't get what I want." He massages his crotch, reliving the pain, before planting another kiss on my lips again. "But I won't hurt much longer. I've been saving it all for you."

He looks at Kat, struggling and screaming through her tape, with a film of sweat lining her hairline.

"Don't worry—I made a promise I wouldn't harm a single hair on your head. This is just for Elana and I." He's as sweet as the devil was to Eve, drawing out my name on his tongue. Every time he says my name, my blood turns to ice. He looks to me again. "I want you to feel what you are doing to me."

He shoves his pelvis toward my hand, but I curl my wrists under, denying him the pleasure.

"Elana, you disappoint me…tsk tsk tsk."

He stands up and kicks my side. I collapse to the floor, doubled over in pain. It was just enough to throw my senses for a loop, but not enough for me to submit.

Out of the corner of my eye I see something under the couch, but before I can figure out what it is, he sits me back up. I try to inhale through my nose, but I can't get enough air in. Panic consumes me as my nostrils can't meet the demands of my lungs. I'm suffocating. He notices at once.

"I don't want you to pass out, baby. At least not until *after* we have our fun." He pulls the corner of my tape off, just enough for me to take a few quick breaths. "Why do you make this harder on yourself?" He brushes aside the hair in front of my face, stroking my cheek with his thumb. "This can be enjoyable for us both if you just give me a chance."

I nod.

"You want this, don't you?" he asks seductively, placing my hands on him. Every fiber of my being shudders, but I nod again.

He puts his short flesh by my hand. Kat turns her head, inching herself away from us. If I keep him occupied long enough, she may be able to crawl to safety. He doesn't even seem to remember she's in the room by the look on his face. He only has eyes for me.

"You want me in your mouth, don't you?"

I nod.

He rips the tape all the way off, freeing my mouth. I fight the urge to scream, but I know it'll be useless against the speakers. I wait for a break in the music, put his shortcomings in my hand, twist and yank as hard as I can. "HELP!" I cry out.

He barely registers the pain, and recovers quickly. Now he's seething, foaming at the mouth, his face a furnace from hell. He closes his fist and connects to my cheek, sending me crashing to the floor. My eyes spin in a daze, but I see the blood spray the wood beneath me. Kat screams again, to no avail.

I roll onto my knees and shoot my arms under the couch. With my face pressed against the floor, blood dripping from my mouth, I feel it in my fingertips, just what I was hoping for.

He yanks my pants down, pulling me toward him. I dig my nails into the wood, bending them back as I try to crawl away from his grasp. His hands dig into my hips, yanking me once more toward his pelvis. His erection is pressed against my bare skin as he fumbles to gain access. My throat constricts, and the blood fills my mouth with every beat of my racing heart.

"Why do you make me hurt you?" he asks, distraught. "You never learn," he grumbles through gritted teeth, a madman again in the blink of an eye.

The salty, warm metallic taste fills my mouth, spilling down my throat. I keep trying to drag myself away, spitting blood onto the floor and slipping on it. I start laughing, a delusional laughter that catches even me by surprise. He flips me back over, setting me back down on my bare ass, staring at me, confused.

"Something funny?" Sweat drips off his forehead, and his eyes say it all. He's not used to someone putting up a fight like this.

"You. Are. So. Pathetic." I enunciate each word slowly and carefully. My whole face is swollen and bloodied. I spit, spraying him. Red specks cover his pale, astonished face. He looks at me as if *I* were the certifiably insane one. He may be right. He wipes his skin with the crook of his elbow, smearing my blood everywhere.

He swings at me again, and I crash to the floor, landing on my shoulder.

He kneels close to my face. "You still think I'm pathetic, Elana?" He grips my neck and squeezes.

"Yes," I mouth, before he crushes my windpipe in his bloodied hands.

Everything fades—the music in the background, Kat's muffled cries for help, my vision, even the sound of my own heartbeat. He releases me and stands up, pacing as I gasp. I try to push myself up, but I slip on the little pools of blood. I try again with what little strength I have left, lifting myself off the floor. The pain in my stomach sears, but I can't get enough air to cry out as I start to choke on blood. I lean my back against the couch as he nears thrusting his face in front of mine. His eyes have somehow grown colder. He opens his mouth to say something, but I quickly raise my arms and plunge the pen into the crook of his neck.

He falls back, crashing into the glass coffee table almost comically, as if someone swept the rug from under his feet. The glass shatters into a million pieces as he howls and gurgles. Only a quarter of the pen is visible, the rest lodged deep within his flesh. The blood, sweat, and tears loosen my restraints, but not nearly enough to free my hands. And then I hear it—a *bang*. He looks toward the door, and I try to do the same, but the motion sends a shooting pain through my insides, briefly blinding my vision.

"Help..." The word barely registers out of my throat.

I fall back to the floor in the hope of dragging myself to the door, but he pulls me toward him, wrapping his hand around my throat. "This isn't over."

He stumbles to his feet, the glass crunching under his boots as the banging grows more frantic. He tosses the window open and flees down the fire escape. I cough, spraying the floor with more blood, gasping for air, choking on the hot liquid essence that keeps filling my mouth.

Kat inches her way toward me, crawling through glass. The banging gets louder, sounding as if someone's throwing their body against the thick wood, trying to bust the door off its hinges.

It finally bursts open, splintering under the pressure. Footsteps approach us.

"Oh my God!" Evan shouts, his voice laced with terror.

"Window," I mutter and point. Without a moment's thought Evan rushes down the fire escape after him.

I blink. Only one eye opens as I feel Kat's hands on me, unraveling the tape on my wrists and ankles. I struggle to help with hers. Every movement, even the minor ones, cripples me with pain. My back feels soaked and warm.

"What's going—" James starts, then sinks to the floor beside us. "What the fuck happened? Who did this?"

Unable to hold myself up, I collapse to the side, body splayed on the floor, the sharp stings prickling my skin. I open my eyes wide, seeing only red stains in my blurred, darkened vision.

"Elana, talk to me." James's voice is rushed and quivering. "Elana."

Darkness creeps over me.

"Kat, call 911. Elana, can you hear me?"

I moan. The pain pulsates louder. Whatever adrenaline I had coursing through my veins is slipping through my fingers, leaving only sharp pangs of agony in its wake. The real pain is starting to rear itself—the throbbing in my head and face, the bruising of my throat, the lightning bolt shooting through my gut every time I move or breathe. I lay writhing in pain.

New footsteps approach, but I can't see who it is, until I hear his voice. "Oh God," Evan cries, out of breath. I feel the comfort of his hands. "Help is on the way, don't move," he adds with urgency.

"I fought back," I whisper, but I can't tell if anyone can hear.

"Don't talk, baby. Everything is going to be okay."

A chill settles over me, spreading like wildfire. I feel soaked all over. Only my blood-filled throat is warm. Kat cries over me. Sirens wail in the distance, but I know there isn't much time left. It's harder to focus now, and even harder to stay awake.

I whisper, trying to force the name out of my throat.

"What'd you say?" Evan asks, leaning in closer.

My breaths become shallow. I just want to sleep. Even with my eyes closed, I feel dizzy, like I was tied to a spinning wheel. I open my good eye and notice Evan looking down at me. The veil of darkness is lifted in that brief moment.

The Caribbean Sea in his eyes brings little warmth to me now—the frost is too far set in. His teary eyes are streaked with fear, and his cheeks are smeared with blood. I don't know if it's his or mine.

Still, his face is beautiful, even now. I want to touch him, but he's so far away and I can't fight against gravity. I have no strength left; I'm barely able to squeeze Kat's hand, letting her know I feel her beside me.

As my eyes roll back, I remember Evan's face. I'll never forget the happiness he's given me. His love is the only thing that buries the pain, dulling it ever so briefly.

James and Kat both call my name, but they sound miles away.

"Elana, don't close your eyes," Evan cries. "Baby, I need you to stay with me."

But I can't.

There Will Be Light

BEEP. BEEP. BEEP.

I slowly peel open my eyes, squinting from the bright fluorescent lights overhead. The machine beeps behind me. I look down, seeing the intravenous line attached to the back of my hand. The smell of bleach and disinfectant overwhelms me. The last thing I remember is being in my apartment, surrounded by Evan, James and Kat—and then nothing, only darkness. I try to sit up, but a shooting pain stops me, hitching my breath.

"Oh my God." Kat rushes over to the bed. "You're awake."

She grabs my hand gently, and I give it a squeeze back. I don't know how long I've been here, but Kat doesn't look all that different since I last saw her.

I try to reach up to my face, but Kat stops me. "Don't."

"How long have I been here?" I ask.

"Let me get the doctor." She starts toward the door.

"Wait," I insist, as she hurries out of the room.

The door closes, and I'm alone again. I test the limits of my body—moving my legs slowly, trying to shuffle my middle—but I realize the less I move, the better. My arms are sore and heavy as I reach up to touch my face, feeling the swollen skin on my cheek. My left eye is closed shut, and my lip is split down the center.

Even though I'm riddled with aches and pains, I feel okay, considering.

A doctor and nurse enter the room, checking my vitals, asking how I'm feeling before rambling off a laundry list of ailments. I stop listening after a while, because it doesn't matter. The feeling I have inside is all I need to know.

Once they leave the room, Evan pushes through the doors. His breaths are rushed, his eyes, wet. I reach out for his hands, which he provides. They feel cold against mine. Collapsing into the chair, he starts crying, leaning his head on the bed for support. I squeeze his hand, but he doesn't move.

"Did they find him?" I whisper, preparing myself for an answer I'm not sure I'll be ready to hear.

He lifts his head slowly. His tear-streaked cheeks make my heart break. "Yeah."

Relief floods through my every vein. I don't ask any more questions—just knowing that much is good enough for me.

One by one my friends and family come in to visit. They all wear the same expression, and are too afraid to touch me. Considering I feel like I went through a meat grinder, it might not be such a bad thing.

I send everyone away, ordering them to get some rest. I lie, telling them I need rest, too, but I couldn't be more awake, more alert. Every inch of me feels different. All my fears have been exorcised.

I lie in the quiet room, collecting my thoughts. I know Evan only left to take a shower, he'll be back without getting any sleep, so I soak in the silence, trying to work through my emotions.

My eyes open to find someone in the doorway. Sebastian.

He looks as bad as everyone else who's graced me with their presence today. Hesitantly, he walks over to my bed.

"Hey, good-lookin'," he says with the same conviction as always. I ignore the fact that his demeanor says otherwise.

"I knew you wouldn't disappoint me."

A smile reaches his face, but it quickly disappears as he approaches.

"Damn, El." He sits on the edge of my bed. I catch my breath as I press the button to raise the hospital bed. "Are you okay?"

"Just sore. So," I drawl, "tell me what everyone else is refusing to say."

He looks down at his hands. "What makes you think they're hiding something?" I simply stare at him with my half-swollen eye, burning a hole in his head. "Okay, okay, just stop looking at me like that. Evan warned me about that look, ya know."

My stare persists until he spills the beans.

"Okay. First of all, you look horrible. Have they given you a mirror?" I shake my head. "Good, because you don't want to see yourself. What else do you want to know?"

"Does everyone know what happened?"

"Kat told us and the police what she saw, but she said she was stuck in the room by herself for a while, and didn't see everything. From the looks of it, you put up one hell of a fight."

"You should see the other guy." I chuckle lightly, scared if I give it my all, I'll pop a stitch.

"Cut it out, Elana," Sebastian barks. "You keep joking with everyone. There's nothing funny about it. You almost died." Sebastian's eyes fill with tears as the words spill out, catching me off guard. That's what everyone's been hiding. No one mentioned that fact. "Everyone was worried they were going to lose you, and you wake up joking like it's nothing. I started thinking the worst, and I—" Sebastian stops, breaking down in front of me. He cries in his hands, covering his face.

He's always been so strong and supportive, comforting me when I needed him, but now he's the one who needs soothing. But it doesn't change anything for me. Physically, I'm a mess, but mentally, I feel reborn. *Strong.*

"Look, I understand this is serious. Sebastian, look at me." He lifts his head, and his eyes bore into mine, leaking down his face. "I get it. I can't explain why it's different this time, but isn't it better than being hysterical, locking myself in a room?" I reach out my hand, and he takes it.

"I already lost my sister. I can't lose anyone else I love." I don't say anything, but I don't plan on going anywhere. I feel more alive than ever before.

He wipes away his tears. "Please tell me you're done playing vigilante." I nod reluctantly. "So you stabbed him with a pen?"

I nod again, beaming with pride.

"Nice." Sebastian offers me a half-smile, wiping his nose and cheeks with a tissue.

He and I talk a little while longer before Evan returns, as I suspected he would. The three of us discuss what the plan is when I'm discharged, and who's going to watch over me while he's working, knowing he won't leave me alone anytime soon.

Evan and Sebastian exchange silent looks. I catch Evan shaking his head. It's so subtle I almost miss it.

"What?" I look at Sebastian, the easier nut to crack. "Sebastian, what's going on?" He avoids my eyes, directing them toward Evan.

"Don't," Evan says with purpose.

"What the hell is going on?" The heart rate monitor beeps faster. "Tell me. Now."

Sebastian caves. "They can't—" but he's cut off by Evan again. "Nothing."

"Really? I'm going to find out anyway. Either tell me now while I'm under the care of a physician, or tell me later when there's no one to monitor my reaction."

Evan stares at his nails, plucking imaginary dirt out from under them. His shoulders are tense, and his jaw looks tight. I turn back to Sebastian.

"Don't you think I should know what I'm up against? I know you're trying to protect me, but I've been stuck in the dark because of this person. I don't want to live like that anymore." I try to hide the desperation, but I don't do a decent job.

"They're still looking for Kat's ex-boyfriend," Evan finally says. "He was the factor that linked you to him. His real name is Luke Jacobs. His brother, the one who hurt you," he goes on with a softened voice, "is Benjamin Jacobs. They arrested him, but no one knows where Luke is."

I lean back, closing my eyes. The darkness helps me think. I knew his name wasn't Marc Pullman. They explain to me who the Jacobs brothers are, how Benjamin used Luke to get to Kat, how Luke used Kat to get to me. A tidy circle.

"We need to make sure Kat is taken care of, in case he tries to get to her," I say, overcome with fear for her safety.

I wish I had known this earlier when she was here, so I could have held her and told her she'd be okay. She must be so afraid.

"One step ahead of you, Columbo." Sebastian slumps back in the chair, drained. They both know the nightmare is far from over. The three of us sit in silence for a while longer, the sound of the heart monitor gives a melodic backdrop.

After visiting hours are over, the nurse kicks out Sebastian. He leans in, kisses my forehead, and squeezes my hand. As he walks past Evan, he grips his shoulder. They exchange a silent nod.

****

Detective Malone sits in my hospital room, explaining how they caught Benjamin Jacobs. I'm relieved he's off the streets, but I know we can't celebrate yet.

"You can thank the photographer who aided in his arrest." He flips through a pad the size of his hand. "Mr. Peter Wells provided us with a license plate and an image of the suspect. The plates are registered to a woman in New Jersey, Jessica Jacobs. While we questioned her, we noticed a painting similar to your work. She admitted to purchasing it from a gallery in October. Then an officer noticed a wedding photo, matching the photo we had, and the description Ms. Katarina Lopez gave."

Evan strokes my hand in his, rubbing his thumb over my knuckles as my mom sits beside the bed, fidgeting her own hands. Timmy stands in the corner, staring out the window, clenching his jaw with every detail.

The detective continues, "We also noticed the man fitting the description of Ms. Lopez's ex-boyfriend in the picture. Mrs. Jacobs advised us that he was her husband's brother, Luke Jacobs. We went to their place of business and arrested Benjamin on the spot. The brother's still missing. We've got eyes on a few locations, and we're tracking his credit card usage. He'll turn up." He sounds so sure of his words, but I'm not. "The apartment Ms. Lopez visited was emptied. All we found inside was the phone he used to contact Ms. Lopez and his brother."

"How did he get into the apartment?" Evan asks.

"The suspect lawyered up immediately, but we gather it was through his brother's interactions with Ms. Lopez. She admitted to bringing him to the apartment once to feed a cat, and another time to pack some things for Ms. Parks. We think he made a copy of the key. There was no sign of forced entry."

Memories from the past replay in my head, images of Kat calling me when I was visiting Evan in California, with Kiki in the background hissing and wailing. All the times I smelled that hideous scent when I was with Kat right after she'd just seen Andrew, or should I say Luke. They're brothers, working at the same job, reeking that same putrid odor. There is a modicum of relief knowing I'm not insane. That smell was real.

I can see the fear in everyone's faces, but I have none, not for myself at least. I fear for Kat. I know how she feels. It's too familiar, knowing there's someone out there, someone from your past who could potentially show up at any moment, invading your future. Will he track her down like Benjamin Jacobs did to me, or was she just a pawn in the game?

The detective leaves after a few more minutes, and the room goes silent. The tension is so thick, it almost becomes a game to see who'll breathe first. Timmy comes to my bedside, kisses my forehead, and leaves without saying a word. My mother and I share a knowing glance, and she goes after him.

"Evan," I say. He looks up at me, brow furrowed, shoulders hunched. The light inside of him is fading, like a dying candle. I reach for his hand, and he obliges, bringing my knuckles to his lips. It's a figment of a kiss, barely registering on my skin.

I tug on his hand, wanting him beside me no matter how much discomfort it causes me. I'll welcome the pain as long as his body is touching mine, but he refuses.

"No. I don't want to hurt you."

I beg, not only with my words, but with my eyes, heart, and soul. He gives in reluctantly, lying carefully next to me. I try to kiss him, knowing it'll make me feel better, but he doesn't reciprocate like

I need him to. He hesitates. The worry reeks off him like a horrible stench, and I see it clearly then.

All the vulnerabilities I had before—the quick inhalations, the shaky hands, the timid touch—stare back at me as if through a mirror, except it's not my face in the reflection. It's Evan's.

He's the one who's scared to be touched. Maybe all the evidence from the attack is still too much to bear, or maybe it's something else. But I do know that we are eleven, we are light, we are forever. He waited for me to be comfortable, so I'll wait, too.

I'll give him eleven days.

Epilogue

KAT AND I SIT IN her living room, playing a quiet game of Scrabble, avoiding turning on the television. Neither of us wants to hear any mention of the case or the trial, and chances are, if we turn it on, we'll see something.

I think about when I went into the courtroom for an impromptu hearing a few months ago, seeing him for the first time since the attack. His smiles and stares sent shivers down to my core, like jagged shards of ice coursing through my veins. Everyone noticed them— Evan, Timmy, Sebastian—their eyes were fixed on him the entire time. They surrounded me like a protective membrane. At one point I thought Timmy would charge him, but I kept my arm linked in his, making sure he stayed seated. Sebastian lent him a menacing smile. After that he stopped looking in my direction for a while.

Benjamin Jacobs looked the same, save for a busted lip and a swollen eye. I remember thinking I could've kissed the person that dealt him those blows. His wife sat on the other side of the room, dressed like the perfect Stepford wife, remaining loyal to her husband, showing not an inkling of emotion when the prosecutor reminded the judge why his bail should be revoked after being caught outside the range his ankle monitor allowed.

As we walked back from the courthouse to our cars, I noticed Evan and Sebastian shared a grin. The judge had just ruled in the prosecutor's favor and remanded Benjamin in custody, but this wasn't the source of their joy.

"Make her stop looking at me," Sebastian complained to Evan.

"Sebastian just so happened to be at the right place at the right time. But according to his phone records, he was nowhere near the scene of the crime, but talking on the phone with me all night," Evan gloats.

I shot both of them a death glare as they walked with their shoulders back, and their chins held high.

"Are you both fucking nuts?"

"Listen," Sebastian said, placing his hand on my shoulder, "it was bullshit that he got bail in the first place. Now he's not free." He said it as if it were a simple fact I should've accepted. "Tim would have killed him, and your boy over there is too recognizable."

"Did he get a good look at you?" I asked.

"How many six-foot-six Roman warrior gods do you see standing around? He recognized me, all right." Sebastian paused. He grinded his jaw, and his eyes darkened. "He even started talking shit while I was pummeling his face," he finished through gritted teeth. Whatever Benjamin Jacobs said to him still hit a nerve.

As much as I wanted to be angry at them for conspiring, it felt nice to have them work together in a makeshift crime-fighting crew, all in my honor. I stopped in the middle of the sidewalk, and they followed suit. I moved to Sebastian, cupped his cheeks and raised my lips to meet his, catching him off guard, much like our first kiss, but this time I gave him a grateful smooch.

Evan coughed. "I helped, too."

I walked beside Evan, wrapped my arms around his neck. "Thank you." His lips met mine in the gentlest yet most powerful way.

I backhanded both of their stomachs. "That's for doing something so incredibly insane."

Kat didn't go to that court hearing, or any hearing thereafter. She knows she'll have to testify eventually, but until then, she's remained secluded from everything, not ready to face it yet. She might never be ready. I don't blame her though—she's got a lot going on right now. She's lucky she has James as I have Evan. He's been so supportive every step of the way and I think he's the reason why she's managed so well. Even if they weren't together, I know he'd be by her side. We're a loyal group, always having each other's back.

While the others are in court today, serving as our eyes and ears, she and I act as if it's just another day. We try to gain some sense of normalcy while our fate rests in the judicial system. Neither of us is hopeful. Just when you think you have a slam dunk, in comes a loophole and something gets rejected.

We break from our game and make lunch together. Thankfully, she's gotten her appetite back. She fixes herself a sky-high sandwich while I make us both a salad, adding a hard-boiled egg to hers; it's her current obsession.

I tread lightly with my questions, trying not to stress her too much, but I know she needs to talk about it. Since she and I were involved with this whole ordeal together, she confides in me more than anyone.

"Have you decided yet?"

"No, but James will stand by me regardless. He's so amazing. Sometimes I think we could, and then I remember the truth of it all, and—" she breaks off, staring at nothing in particular. "The whole situation sucks, especially when I think of the future and all the questions we'd have to answer."

My phone interrupts us. Nothing special is supposed to happen today, but the guys wanted to make sure Benjamin didn't forget they were there. If he was relaying anything to Luke, hopefully their presence showed the Jacobs brothers they'll have to get through them first.

"Hey."

"He changed his plea," Timmy announces. "He's pleading guilty, hoping it'll reduce his sentence. He won't be getting out for a while, Els," he cheers. I hear the chaotic elation in the background.

Kat watches my jaw drop. "He's pleading guilty," I say with a smile.

Shrugging her shoulders, she continues to mutilate her sandwich as if she couldn't care less. I know a part of her does, but he wasn't her threat—Luke was, and he's still missing. He hasn't contacted Kat or anyone we know of, and he might never, but he's still out there somewhere.

"Els, how do you feel?" Evan asks through the receiver.

"It's great news," I admit rather calmly, even though I'm ecstatic on the inside.

I glance at Kat, and she's wearing a different face altogether. She's stopped eating, and her eyes have drifted down. She grimaces in pain.

"What's the matter, Kat?"

"What's wrong with Kat?" Evan asks. I hear James questioning him before stealing the phone.

"El? What's going on?" James asks, rushed. "Is she okay?"

Holding her stomach, Kat stands up from her chair, still looking down. My incredulous eyes follow hers as James shouts through the phone, demanding an answer.

"Um…I think her water just broke."

She looks at me again—her beautiful brown eyes have turned dark, tortured, horror-struck. A tear escapes each. "Take me to the hospital. I have to get that monster's baby out of me."

About the Author

STEFANIE STRATTON WAS BORN AND raised on Long Island, New York. In high school, she loved to write, and as she got older, her dreams fueled weird ideas that would eventually become stories. Not only did writing become a hobby, but it was often her form of therapy too, helping her escape into the worlds she would create. With other ideas in the works, she hopes to share more of these worlds with others.

Follow her on Instagram at StefanieStratton and StefanieStratt2 on Twitter.

CPSIA information can be obtained
at www.ICGtesting.com
Printed in the USA
LVHW041110290420
654636LV00004B/300